Some Like Murder Hot

Jacqueline Vick

Cover Art by GoOnWrite

ISBN Print 978-1-945403-52-1

ISBN eBook 978-1-945403-53-8

To the ones who make me laugh the most. You know who you are.

And to Winston, late of the San Diego Zoo. You'll be missed.

The Cast of Characters

Frankie Chandler Bowers - pet psychic on her honeymoon
Detective Martin Bowers - her new husband
Edward Harlow - ghost writer of the Aunt Civility etiquette books
Nicholas Harlow - Edward's brother and secretary
Harry Reed - San Diego Zoo veterinarian
Susan Sweeney - President of the *Some Like It Hot* fan club
Rhonda and Willie Fisher - happiest couple on earth and convention fans
Jimmy Bianchi - member of a Southern California "family"
Julian "Scar" Fabrezio - Jimmy's right hand man
Dot - convention fan
Polka - Dot's sister
Ellie Tartwell - convention fan with a service animal
Tanner - Ellie's chihuahua and comfort animal
Cynthia Ferrara - Ellie's beautiful niece and companion

Osgood Fielding the Third - convention fan who dresses like Osgood Fielding the Third (surprise!)
Dr. Sylvia Yang - San Diego Zoo veterinarian

Some Like Murder Hot

Chapter One

Frankie: The Honeymoon Begins

The Hotel del Coronado. Home to history, ghosts, and celebrities. The location used in *Some Like It Hot*, a movie made famous by Marilyn Monroe's sexy outfits. At least that's what I'd read.

Yesterday afternoon, Bowers and I stepped off a plane at the San Diego airport and kicked off our honeymoon at the iconic hotel. Finally.

I'd recovered from my sprained ankle before Bowers recuperated from his broken collarbone, a broken tibia, cracked ribs, and lots of bruises. We're not into extreme sports. A nefarious killer inflicted these injuries when he pushed us both—at separate times—over the steep edge of a hillside littered with cacti and rocks. Big rocks. Possibly boulders.

At one point, I thought Bowers might not recover, but that was because the police wouldn't allow me access to him in the hospital. I'd gotten over my fit of pique once I learned their ruling was for his safety from the guy who pushed him off that hillside. The same guy hadn't pushed me yet, so I wasn't aware he existed. Make sense?

Once we caught Dale Bennett (Pierre the goat knocked him down the same hill, which I thought was fair) we decided life was too short, and we married as soon as possible after getting a dispensation from the local bishop.

It took a while to—you know—consummate our relationship. One flesh, as the Bible puts it, which sounds creepy, like the name of a horror movie. One Flesh: The Beast from Outer Space.

Anyway, I was terrified I'd re-injure his leg. So, I tiptoed around him, coming to bed after he was asleep, slipping away when he reached for me, until that morning I overslept. Bowers pulled me to him and growled, "I didn't marry you so we could be pals." And it turned out fine. More than fine.

And now, I was a Wife. Such a big title. A bit overwhelming when you've lived most of your adult life alone. As a confirmed slob. My cat, Emily, didn't care if a pile of laundry didn't make it to the bedroom hamper. Or if it took me two days to wash the dishes. Really, she enjoyed sleeping in the laundry and licking the dishes. So, I wasn't a slob but a generous cat parent.

During our recovery, we'd had meals delivered and lounged around, mostly because walking was painful.

But now, I had to throw off the blanket of laziness and hop into my role. I just wasn't sure what that role included. According to the book my mother had given me as a wedding present, a good wife kept her husband in a perpetual state of suspense with random surprises. I took the advice seriously and had a whopper of a surprise waiting for Bowers this weekend.

When we arrived at the hotel and I followed my husband, Detective Martin Bowers, through the front doors—or just Martin Bowers, now that we were married—my breath caught in my throat. The place was enormous. Majestic. Historic. Intimidating. And this was just the lobby. Rich, warm wood stretched from a patterned floor and up the walls and pillars to the second-floor railings, where it swept across the high ceiling. I felt as if I'd entered a hotel in a Western.

Except the casts in Westerns had dusty, unwashed men spitting into spittoons and women whom I suspected were just as dirty under their garters and fancy dresses. Except the hero and heroine. They knew where the bathing water was and used it.

As I scanned my fellow guests, I might have preferred the dirty, spitting men and women. This place boasted society's elite. Designer clothing. Leather luggage. Perfectly coiffed hair, and that included the men. Even the two children with the wholesome-looking family. I imagined their weekly allowances were double what I made in a year.

An enormous chandelier hovered over a round, plush, three-section couch in lime green. A strange place for a chandelier. I mean, it was directly over the chair. As in one good earthquake and the people sitting in the pretty chair would be goners. Nothing could make me sit in that chair. But it looked nice. Too nice for me to sit on in my old jeans.

Stop it, I told myself. Just enjoy the elegant and slightly intimidating surroundings. I'd been to nice places before. Like La Hacienda Chop House, the restaurant of my dreams with their blue-cheese and mushroom smothered filet. I wondered if the hotel had blue-cheese and mushroom smothered filet on the menu? Though I'd been to La Hacienda twice, I'd never been able to claim my steak for various reasons. Last time, I'd fed it to the dog who'd saved our lives.

I nudged my mind to focus on the point. Our honeymoon.

While my husband—husband!—stood in line, I wandered casually to a table near the entrance. Piles of Some Like It Hot 2023 Convention shirts called to me. T-shirts mingled with sweatshirts and polo shirts. With the title over the pocket and a large pair of hot pink lips on the back, I couldn't resist purchasing one for Bowers. He'd balk least over a polo shirt, and it would be a gentle way to tell him I'd bought tickets for the convention. That was my big surprise.

Stuffing his gift into my purse, I hurried back to him as he stepped up to the front desk. "You have a reservation for Mr. And Mrs. Martin Bowers." He winked at me, and I grinned.

That was another problem. My name. I'd always called Bowers by his last name. Now I was Frankie Bowers. It was like two first names. Should I now call him Marty like his sisters did? Or Martin? Good grief. The latter sounded so formal. It wasn't in me to make up a name like Huggabear or Snookums.

My gaze drifted around the room, taking in the other guests. They still reeked of class. And money. I tugged at my denim jacket, wrinkled from the plane ride, ran my fingers through my ponytail of auburn hair, and wished I'd used a brush this morning. A touch of makeup wouldn't have hurt.

I brushed a hand over my derriere and wondered if any of the women slinking through the lobby wore sizes over a six. You'd think with all that money they could afford some binge eating.

Next to these people, I looked like the scullery maid, whatever a scullery was. Would one of the staff, that harried man who darted around the lobby and chatted up guests like a church greeter, would he spot me and direct me to the servant's entrance? They probably called it the employee entrance these days.

My eyes back on Bowers, I noticed I wasn't the only one admiring my husband. A stunning brunette in a silk blouse over tight, black pants, her hair twisted into a French knot, stood unreasonably close to my man. She leaned in front of him, brushing against him like my cat Emily does when she wants a scratch behind her ears. I'd be happy to scratch her if that's what she wanted. He smiled and stepped out of the way.

I couldn't blame her. During his recovery, my husband's hair had grown out and curled around his collar. His daily shave had turned into a weekly trim, and he now had one of those stubbly beards. At six-feet tall, with dark brown hair, dark-blue eyes that crinkled around the edges when he smiled, and the signs of someone who'd been through an ordeal—something that looks good on men, darn them—my husband was a looker. But he was my husband. I changed my mind. I could blame her. Couldn't she see his wedding ring?

She was reaching for a pen. Allegedly. One sat on the counter two feet from her right side.

I snatched a ballpoint out of the container and handed it to her. "Don't strain yourself."

She eyed me as if reevaluating the competition coming from the scullery maid. I took Bowers' hand in mine and squeezed. "How much longer, darling?"

His eyebrows went up. Darling. I'd overdone it.

He kissed the top of my head and murmured in my ear. "Are you eager to get to our room?"

My face got warm. He laughed, delighted, signed the credit card receipt, and accepted the keys. He did an immediate U-turn and returned to the counter.

"I'm afraid you've given me the wrong keys. I booked a room in The Victorian."

The clerk's barely controlled grin grew. "You, sir, are in The Cabanas. An upgrade, courtesy of the Wolfe Creek Police Department. And they asked me to give you this note."

Stunned, Bowers set down our luggage and unfolded the sheet of paper. Every member had signed it, even Juanita Gutierrez, his sometime partner, sometime competition.

The largest signature belonged to Smitty: It has taken so long for you to get here; I hope you haven't forgotten how 'it' works. HA!

Tears made me blink, and for a moment, I thought Bowers might cry, too. This was an incredible start to our honeymoon. A sign from Heaven that our union had His blessings, and He'd watch over us this weekend.

Just in case He was busy, I vowed nothing would interfere with our first vacation as a married couple. But then, I've always been a worrier. What could happen at a beach resort crowded with snooty people and those who celebrated old movies?

"Thank you," Bowers said sincerely, and we headed in a different direction than planned. A dazzling woman in a dress as white as her hair impeded our progress. She parted her full, red lips and whispered, "Take a flyer, handsome."

Bowers let go of my hand long enough to accept her gift. She ran her gaze over him and gave him an extra bright smile.

"That's funny."

I leaned in and read the headline. Some Like It Hot Fan Convention. A Sizzling Good Time. "What's funny?"

He waved the flyer at the bombshell, who had moved her attention to a young couple. "The convention is for *Some Like It Hot*, but her outfit is from *Seven Year Itch*."

I shook my head. "Who says detectives aren't smart?" While I wondered what recess of his brain he'd pulled that information from, he led us out of The Victorian and to The Views.

"It's a bit of a hike. Are you up for it?"

I raised one foot and wiggled it. "I'm armed with tennis shoes." The toe of my shoe had a muddy paw print on it, a hazard of my job working with animals. "Dang it." Using the heel of my other shoe, I rubbed at the spot. The mud seemed dry, but I hadn't counted on the gum stuck to the bottom of my top shoe. As I lifted it to look at the paw print, strings of gum stretched between my sneakers.

A woman with more folds than a Shar Pei huffed as she passed, showing her opinion of my scuffed, gummy, tennies.

We finally arrived at our room, which was in a separate building past a swimming pool. Bowers set down the luggage, unlocked the door, swept me off my feet, and carried me inside.

"What are you doing?"

"I never had the chance to carry you over the threshold."

"Your leg," I shrieked.

He set me down and frowned. "Stop thinking of me as an invalid."

"I'm a worrier."

"I love that you care about me, but worrying is a waste of time."

"Oh, Bowers," I whispered, and he joined me in examining our room.

A king-sized bed covered most of a blue carpet with an off-white striped pattern. The rest of the floor was white tile. There was a desk, should we get the urge to write someone a note, and a couch, should we decide to have company.

Glass sliding doors opened onto a patio with furniture surrounding a fire pit. Blue-and-white striped cloth formed a canopy that draped down the sides in a privacy curtain to block the wind and prying eyes. Beyond a strip of grass and a small mound, ocean waves lapped against the shore.

"It's perfect."

He moved behind me and wrapped his arms around my middle, resting his chin on my head. "I'm glad you like it."

When I turned and kissed him, he kissed me back. After a few moments, he raised his head.

"I don't know about you, but I could use a shower after all that travel."

"Good idea," I said, crossing the room and flipping on the bathroom light. Once I stepped inside, I turned. "You could always supervise."

He grinned and followed me in. "Yes, ma'am."

And that was the first night of our honeymoon. Not bad.

But it was the last peaceful night we would have.

Chapter Two

Nicholas: The Unhappy Arrival

"This is your idea of a hideout?" I spared a glance at the Victorian hotel with a Queen Anne layout, its steeply pitched roofs and dominant central turret. The subject of many postcards.

A silver Mercedes pulled under the porte-cochère, and several valets swarmed the car. "Seriously, Edward. I cross the bridge and I'm back in San Diego."

After I'd given testimony against a crooked cop who I'd witnessed doing something naughty, a San Diego Sheriff's investigator and sometimes friend strongly suggested I disappear for a few days while they rounded up the woman's associates, the idea being they might not be happy with me. Maybe because Officer Sherry Hermes' final words to me were, "I hope they get you!"

"There is little chance anyone associated with Officer Hermes will spend the weekend at the Hotel del Coronado. Especially at a *Some Like It Hot* convention."

"And why do *you* need to be here?" I asked.

My idea of traveling incognito did not include having my brother at my side. At six-foot-two with dark hair that tended to curl, trim whiskers around his mouth and firm chin, and gray eyes that rarely twinkled with delight, fans of the Aunt Civility etiquette series regularly recognized him as the author's alleged nephew.

He authored the books, but Edward's physique didn't match the publisher's idea of what Auntie should look like. So, they told her public she suffered from agoraphobia, and my brother made appearances on her behalf, which pleased his female fans. Most of his readers were female.

He'd also released his own book last year under his own name. The subject was former Chicago Cub's center fielder Rick Monday. So, another segment of readers might recognize him, and, therefore, me, since as his assistant, secretary, and gopher, I was never far from him.

But he'd insisted on coming along, even though the Hotel del Coronado was only a forty-minute drive from our house. I told him I would reach out daily, but he said he felt responsible for me.

A woman in a white dress stood in the lobby and shoved a flyer at me. My brother's not the only good looker in the family. I have the same dark hair and gray eyes, though I'm a few inches shorter, skipped the facial hair, and am built like a running back instead of a linebacker, which are the positions we played in college.

We get a pass from women when we make silly moves, something I take advantage of often. Since both hands were busy with our bags, I took the paper in my teeth. Instead of repulsing the woman, she giggled.

Edward took a seat on the tufted circular sofa in the center of the room. The one under the crystal chandelier. He spread his arms along the back and absorbed the atmosphere like a man admiring his new home.

When it was my turn for service, I set the luggage down by the front counter and rattled off my reservation number to a guy who looked like he'd been waiting all day just for me. That's what seven hundred bucks a night will buy you.

"Edward and Nicholas Harlow." I'd refused to use an alias.

The front desk clerk didn't recognize his name, and I took that as a good omen, but then he slipped a glance at my ring finger.

"We're brothers, brother, so don't send us any champaign or flowers."

Most of the guests arriving had the air of *Some Like It Hot* Convention attendees. Too much enthusiasm. As far as I was concerned, they were a bunch of nuts who liked an old movie enough to gather at the hotel where they filmed the exterior shots.

A guy in his late forties with short, blond hair dressed in khakis, a blue-and-red plaid shirt, and leather sandals tried to muscle in on me. With my nerves on edge because of the threat, I pulled back a fist in case this was it, but it turned out he was only rude.

He slung his backpack over one shoulder, leaned one elbow against the counter, and waved a hand to catch the clerk's attention. "My name is Harry Reed. I'd like to leave a message for a guest, but I don't know the room number."

"One moment please."

"This is important."

The clerk raised one eyebrow in an imperious manner. "I'll be with you as soon as I'm finished with *this* guest."

This guest being me. I turned sideways to give the guy

my full glare, and damned if he didn't open his eyes wide and skitter away, his backpack flapping against his hip as he hurried out the front entrance. I'd have to repeat that look in the mirror. I didn't consider it my most ferocious glare, but I'd have to reevaluate.

Once I returned the company credit card to my wallet and accepted two room keys, I picked up the luggage and found my brother engaged in conversation with a woman in one of those fifties' dresses with the tight waist.

Edward, oblivious to the rules of hiding out, introduced us. "This is Susan Sweeney. She's the president of the *Some Like It Hot* fan club."

Susan reached for my hand, but when I didn't drop the luggage to accommodate her, she retracted her offer of a handshake and smiled instead. "We are so thrilled to have *the* Edward Harlow attending our conference. Thrilled."

I glared at Edward. "Did you announce our arrival? I could get you a bullhorn if you want to make sure everyone hears."

My brother ignored me and absorbed the adulation as if it were his due, which I suppose it was. He worked hard. So did I, but I didn't plan to spend the day in the lobby talking to a nut who would head up a fan club for an old movie. Besides. Now that he'd been recognized, I felt exposed.

As I turned toward the elevator, Edward said, "Hold it. I want a picture with that delightful Marilyn Monroe."

"You do realize that's not the real actress."

He gave me a sour look and charged ahead. The actress—not the dead one but the impersonator—was delighted. She was an Aunt Civility fan, and from the way she snuggled with my brother, an Edward Harlow fan, too.

After setting down the luggage and pulling my phone from my suit jacket pocket, I pretended to snap a few photos while my brother grinned like a big ape.

"Make sure to send me one for my social media." The actress rattled off her email. That gave me a twinge of guilt.

"Let's get one more pose." When Edward narrowed his eyes at me, I shrugged. "She had her eyes closed in the last one."

"Ooh. You better get a good one." This time, she ignored my brother and worked on her expression. She threw back her head, parted her full lips to show her white teeth, and dropped one shoulder forward, holding it until I gave a thumbs up.

"Funny thing, Edward. You said we had a suite on the first floor, but the room number starts with a five. In my experience, that means fifth floor."

"Yes. Er. About that. There's been a change. I'm sure this room will be just as nice."

I followed him to an old-fashioned elevator in a gold cage manned by an operator.

"Line starts back there."

I followed the pointing finger of a tubby guy with his wife and children. The people waiting to enjoy the unique experience stretched down the hallway.

"We'll walk," Edward said, veering to the stairway alongside the elevator. "It will do us good."

Easy for him to say. He wasn't carrying the luggage.

On the way to the second floor, I admired the colorful beach umbrellas painted on the wall. By the fourth floor, I hated the sight of those sickly sweet images. By the time we made it to floor five, I could smell my own sweat. It didn't help that I was wearing a suit jacket over my dress shirt. My tie was strangling me.

Our room was at the bend in the hallway. Once I unlocked the door, Edward preceded me into a small square crammed with a queen-sized bed, a desk, and a chair.

"What happened to your suite?"

"I had to pay for the room myself. Since we're staying a few nights, I kept the cost down."

"Where am I supposed to sleep?"

"Order a cot from room service."

"And put it where?" I dropped the luggage with a thud and had to block it with my foot when it rolled on the warped floor. "I've got a better idea. Why don't I go home and sleep in my own bed?"

"That could be dangerous. Besides. A cot will do you fine. You're too used to luxuries."

An unwillingness to drape my six-foot, two-hundred-pound frame onto a cot without falling out or hanging over the edges hardly fell under snobbery. Before you think I'm a slob, the weight is all muscle.

"I'd be more comfortable in my own bed. You wanted to get me out of town. Okay. I concede that Coronado is not San Diego and is officially out of town. But I'm the one who's hiding out. Not you. Now that I'm here safe and sound, why don't you go home and leave me the bed?"

"Nicholas, Nicholas, Nicholas."

He repeated my name in that condescending way that makes me want to punch him.

"I gave Mrs. Abernathy the week off and came with

you so there would be no one at home. Would you like it if someone kidnapped me to get to you?"

"Try me."

"And since I own the car you drive and the house you live in, well, I have a right to protect my property."

I hadn't thought about anyone burning down Edward's house. Chills skipped down my spine.

"Besides. I told mother I would look after you—"

"When I was five. That excuse wore thin years ago." I loosened my tie. "I'm not wearing a suit all weekend. I'll stand out like a sore thumb."

"At this conference, you'll stand out if you *don't* wear a suit. Unless you prefer to put on a dress."

I didn't bother responding to the dress suggestion. "That's too bad." I snapped open the locks on my luggage and raised the lid. "I packed casual clothes—what the hell?"

"I had Mrs. Abernathy repack your suitcase."

I considered the wisdom of running home to grab jeans.

"Tonight is the first dinner of the convention, followed by the mixer."

"If I'm avoiding people, is a mixer the best place for me to be? Why don't I stay in and order room service?"

"Nonsense. I tell you there is nothing to worry about. This convention attracts people of good taste."

"How would you know? It's their first one."

"The movie. *Some Like It Hot.* It brings out the best in people."

"So that's it. Your romantic side has staged a coup and taken over your senses. You want to flirt with Marilyn Monroe lookalikes. You want to wear a gangster outfit. You want to ditch the twenty-first century and pretend people have manners and women don't stage protests when you call them the gentler sex."

"Smell that ocean air." Edward fiddled with the blinds. The window, which looked out over the parking lot, didn't open. The only thing coming through the glass was bright sunlight.

I put my hands on my hips and nodded. "While I'm running for my life, you're on vacation." I made a noise of disgust. "We live in San Diego County. We smell the ocean every day."

I swung Edward's luggage onto the bed and stepped over to a thin, white door and opened it. The closet. I'd be lucky to fit his suitcase in here, let alone the contents of both our suitcases.

With a little maneuvering, I got everything crammed into the small space. He looked up from perusing the room service menu. "You'd better see about that cot."

Preferring to do it in person, which would give me a break from my brother, I went to the front desk. Before I returned to our room, I dropped by the table by the door and bought a polo shirt bearing the convention's logo. I planned to wear it every day, just to show Edward.

Chapter Three

Frankie: Meeting Suri

The next morning, as we were dressing, I handed Bowers his first honeymoon surprise.

"What's this?" He shook out the polo shirt, held it up, and turned it around so he could see the lips on the back. "Thank you. It's . . . cute. I'll put it on first thing when we get home."

My smile tightened. Breaking the news of the convention might be more difficult than I'd thought. "I have a better idea. Put in on now and show some Marilyn Monroe spirit. For goodness' sakes. You recognized her in the lobby right away. You must be a fan."

"I'll feel like a walking advertisement."

"Who are you advertising to? The guests already know about the convention."

We were headed for an argument, our first as a married couple. I planned on saving that experience for something less petty, so I pulled my checklist from my purse.

"What's on the agenda for today? Do you want to hit

the world-famous San Diego Zoo? I thought we could go to Old Town tomorrow. See the statue of the nurse and soldier kissing."

As he refolded the shirt, he said, "They took it down."

"The kissing couple is gone?" Panic welled in my chest. "They still have that statue of Bob Hope and the soldiers, don't they? And we can still tour the military ship? Or did they take that down, too? What's the world coming to?"

"You didn't let me finish. They replaced it a year later. The USS Midway is still in port, as is Unconditional Surrender. The kissing statue."

"And Bob Hope?"

"Still making them laugh."

I released my breath. "We'll need to plan to make sure we cover everything. The zoo it is."

"Frankie," Bowers began, hesitating as he chose his words. Finally, he came out with it. "Is the zoo a good idea?" He ran his fingers through his hair and his left eye twitched. I recognized the signs.

"You have nothing to worry about. I've shut the door, locked it, and thrown away the key."

When I began hearing from people's pets, I had to come up with a way to retain my sanity. I had to block their voices—as far as they had voices—and, more often, the constant images and feelings they sent.

The door I referred to was an imaginary wooden door —a technique I'd developed to keep out the thoughts of animals. It sounds silly, but it works. Usually. Sometimes.

"You're sure?"

"As sure as I can be about something I have little control over." He blanched. "I'm kidding." No, I wasn't.

"You and I are on vacation. We've left our day jobs behind. You don't tackle any criminals while we're here, and I promise not to communicate with any animals."

With that, I made an excuse, told him I'd meet him in the lobby, and left him to finish dressing while I made some final arrangements.

Once I talked to the wardrobe woman in charge of *Some-Like-It-Hot*-themed costumes and came to an understanding, I returned to the lobby where I spotted Bowers leaning over the check-in counter. I could see the pair of lips on the back of the shirt from here. What a lucky girl I am, I thought. Bowers was strong, kind, funny, patient, brave . . . and he had a great butt. I could say that, now that we were married.

I tiptoed up behind him, pinched his bottom, and when he jerked straight, I threw my arms around his middle and squeezed, resting my head against his back. He'd worn the shirt!

Bowers muscles seemed . . . different. Harder. Bulkier. And he didn't smell like Bowers. But I hardly had time to consider before he spun and sent me flying with an upper arm block.

I landed on my butt and slid a few feet. When I looked up, dazed, the face belonged to a man I'd never seen before.

Running footsteps ended with Bowers standing between me and the guy, who looked as surprised as I did.

"Oh no," he said. "I am so sorry." Bowers met his step forward, responding in kind, so he leaned against the counter and ran his fingers through his short, dark hair. "It was an accident. Well, not an accident, but I didn't realize

. . . I reacted before I saw . . . after the butt pinch, I should have known."

Bowers, still facing him, held out his hand to me. "You pinched his butt?"

"It was the shirt. I thought it was you." My face burned at the thought of pinching a strange man. "I'm so sorry." I took Bowers' proffered hand and let him pull me to my feet. "I thought you were my husband."

"Lucky man." His baritone was slightly lower than Bowers' voice.

Bowers gestured. "You mistook him for me?"

While I rubbed my collarbone, I studied the stranger. The man's hair was darker than my husband's, almost black. Seen from the front, his hair was also shorter than my husband's. Neater. When he crossed his arms over his chest and leaned back against the counter, his muscles showed the definition of an athlete or one of those crazy people who works out every day. The two men were the same height, or close enough, and though Bowers was more handsome, the guy had the face of a movie star. It might have been the intense, gray eyes.

"Not now that I can see his face," I said with a dismissive snort. "He wasn't facing me when I saw him. From behind . . . I'll prove it. Why don't I close my eyes and you both turn around and lean over the counter? Mix it up so I don't know which is which."

"I'll pass." With a nod, Bowers steered me away to the sound of the other man's laughter.

We spent most of the drive to the zoo debating how I could mistake another man for Bowers.

"I knew it wasn't you as soon as I hugged him. His muscles felt different, and he didn't smell like you."

"I smell?"

"Everybody smells. It was the shirt. I thought you had worn the shirt."

"You wear a shirt like that once you return home from vacation. It's a reminder. It seems silly to wear it while we're at the hotel. People might mistake us for members of that crazy convention."

"We wouldn't want that." Inside, my stomach squeezed, threatening to set off hiccups. I shouldn't have planned my surprise for Bowers without first consulting him. But that would have ruined the surprise. Which I was thinking might be for the best.

Bowers pulled into a parking lot half-filled with cars and found us a spot close to the entrance. I'd brought my cell phone along to take pictures. At least I assumed it took pictures. Me and my phone aren't on intimate terms.

We passed a humongous statue of a lion caught in mid leap. A desire to capture memories of my marriage starting from ground zero emboldened me to call out to a passing couple. They declined to take our picture. I thought it was a custom that you had to take someone's photo when they asked.

Fortunately, a mother herding three young children heard my plea.

"I'll do it."

She deftly hoisted the youngest onto her hip and, with him balanced there, took several pictures, even angling the phone to get the lion into the shot. She managed this while her toddler yanked her long, brown hair and played peekaboo with her unoccupied eye.

After I delivered my thanks, she gathered up her rugrats and moved to a special line for people with passes.

To my surprise, the pictures were perfect. Never underestimate a mom. Once Bowers handed over our tickets and we passed through the turnstile, he opened the complimentary map. "Where to first?"

I hooked my arm through his. "Let's just wander."

"We could see more if we planned a route."

My husband has an ordered mind. The thought of wandering aimlessly through the park could drive him mad. He would want to strategize a route to ensure we visited every enclosure.

I decided on a compromise. After glancing at the map, I pointed straight ahead, the key word being straight. Direct. Uncluttered.

"Let's take a stroll down Treetops Lane and decide then."

It was a partial plan, and it satisfied us both.

First up on the left were the flamingos. Pretty but boring. We made a side loop to see the orangutans. Always in motion, their heavy, ginger bodies swung from their man-made jungle gym for some afternoon exercise. The one exception sat atop the structure and stared at us like a king overlooking his subjects.

"Reminds me of Smitty," Bowers said referring to another detective who had been promoted to sergeant.

I snorted. "You're so bad. Smitty's a nice guy."

"That may be a nice monkey. I make no judgment."

"Come on." I pulled him across the lane to the baboons. "I never thought I'd say this about a non-human primate, but they're beautiful. At least that one is." I pointed to one with a silver mane. His face had a snout like a dog's. A hairless dog. Long fur flowed over his shoulders. "He looks like he's wearing a cape."

"It says here he's the male." Bowers informed me

these were hamadryas baboons and continued to read aloud from the plaque. When two of the females approached the male and began grooming his hair, he added, "Maybe I need a harem to wait on me."

"Are you telling me you want me to check your hair for bugs?"

He grinned. "I deserved that."

When the male yawned, he had the fangs of a lion. "Yikes."

Speaking of big teeth, we backtracked and got on Tiger Trail.

"Look at that big guy." Bowers gestured behind me. I turned my head toward the tiger display and froze. Peering out from a temporary den that didn't quite fit the rest of the enclosure, a white tiger rose to her feet and stepped forward. She was just as large and beautiful as a regular tiger but white where she should have been orange.

Flashes came of the first time I'd seen one—not on purpose—in circumstances I'd rather forget, but that had more to do with the bad man who'd kidnapped me to read the big cat's mind than the animal itself.

The only thing separating visitors from certain death was a chain link fence and some grass.

The tiger held her head high with a regal majesty that caught my breath. If she intended to intimidate passers-by, it worked. Almost. A tiny cub attacked her right foot, dissolving the awe into an, "Aw, how cute," from the woman next to me.

"You should take a picture of her for Emily." Bowers snickered at the thought of my pet's reaction to meeting her larger kin. Not my cat. Our cat. I wondered if Emily suspected she now had two full-time servants.

"She'll probably shred it, but why not give her that pleasure?" I held my phone up and squinted through the camera hole thingy. "Where's the focus button?"

"Unless you want a picture of your eyeball, you need to turn it around." Bowers sighed and took the phone from me, rearranged it, and handed it back. "Just point and hit that white circle."

As I held the phone and swiped at the screen with my pointer finger and thumb to make the image a closeup, the screen blurred and then snapped into focus. The tiger's crystal-blue eyes filled my vision. And then the wave crashed into me.

My breathing stopped. It hurt to expand my chest. Tears threatened to stream down my face. So much sorrow I couldn't bear it. I drew in a ragged breath, lowered the phone, and whispered, "What is it, baby girl?"

"What is what?"

Bowers' voice snapped me out of my trance.

"I'm talking to myself. To my phone."

"Did you get the shot?"

My voice caught. "It—it's not nice to tease Emily."

I don't think his concerned look had anything to do with my cat's feelings. He was right to be worried.

Whenever I connected to an animal, whether willingly or through no fault of my own—I thought of it as a mental mugging—I occasionally felt as if I were the animal. It's hard to explain. I once ate a client's raw steak and the joy that ran through me tanked only when I looked at my bloody fingers.

Another surge of sadness came with the image of a small ball of fur, and it seemed to relate to . . .

Resting against the fence on the public's side, a

stuffed bunny who'd seen better days waited for a rescue. Chewing had removed one eye, and a tear stretched across its belly, revealing stuffing.

Before I could tell them no, my muscles tensed. I crouched and leaned back, prepared to pounce. And then I did.

"Frankie! Get back here!"

With the rabbit in my mouth, I climbed the links, grabbing with my fingers and the toes of my tennis shoes. The tiger trotted forward, tense, and ready to defend its young.

"What's that woman doing?" a female voice cried.

Two hands grabbed my waist and yanked me down. It took three tries to shake me loose from the fence. The rabbit fell from my mouth, and I stretched my arms and wiggled my fingers to reach it even as Bowers carried me back to the pavement.

By the time he set me down, the skin on his face had flushed red. His lips pressed together so tightly it looked like he didn't have lips. Just like a Muppet.

"I didn't try to listen. Honest. She misses her bunny and . . ."

Bowers snatched the toy from the ground and lobbed it over the fence, where it landed within three feet of the tiger. She looked bigger up close.

"There. All better now." He glanced over my shoulder. "Or maybe not."

Three men approached us, two of them in tan shirts. They weren't smiling.

"If you could please come with us," the man in a suit said. We had no choice but to go with them.

Once we were seated in an office that I assume most guests never saw, the older man, who introduced himself as Antonio Sabato, curator of mammals, took a seat behind the desk. The other two remained standing.

"You climbed the fence next to the tiger enclosure."

"Um, yes."

"Why?"

I blurted out the first thing that came to mind. "Rudolph. Um, I love Rudolph. You know, the television special? The island of misfit toys made me sad. Ever since, I can't stand to see an abandoned toy. And—I saw a stuffed bunny." I brushed my hand through the air. "Naturally, there being a baby tiger in the pen, er, display, I assumed it belonged to him. Or her. The mother looked sad. My husband indulged me by returning it to the owner. Or who I assumed the owner was. The kitty. Cub."

"She looked sad?"

"I just wanted to return it to her. I meant no harm."

He exchanged a glance with the other two men.

"I've noticed she seems sad, too." This came from the younger man, a sturdily built guy with dark hair.

"She's not sad," the third man snapped. He had short, blond hair that was retreating from his forehead. "Animals don't get post-partum depression."

"You're not around her every day. How would you know?"

"Gentlemen." The curator gestured toward the unbeliever. "This is Harry Reed, one of our veterinarians. This young man, Jose Alvarado, is the tiger's keeper." He rested his forearms on the desk and tented his fingers. "It would be interesting to know if you're right, Jose. Maybe Sylvia has some thoughts on the matter."

Harry scoffed. "Why don't we get the animal a psychiatrist, too?"

"Her name is Suri." Jose looked at me. "It's short for Permaisuri. It's Malay for queen."

"I understand your intentions were good, but we can't have people endangering themselves or the animals." Mr. Sabata clasped his hands on his desk. "I'm afraid you're banned from the zoo."

Chapter Four

Frankie: Dinner with the Harlow Brothers

By the time we returned to the hotel and changed for dinner, me in a short-sleeved dress in lilac blue and Bowers in a brown sport coat, tan slacks, and a brown tie, the silence had become unbearable.

"I didn't do it on purpose," I said.

He sighed. "I know that, Frankie. What bothered me was what you did after your, you know—thing. You didn't behave responsibly. You put yourself in danger and . . ." He threw up one hand as if it would crank the words out. "You embarrassed me."

Everything inside me froze. Even my heart stopped beating. Not that it actually stopped beating. If it had, I'd be dead. But it felt that way.

Was this the first time I'd shamed him? A quick review of our history together made it clear there had been plenty of cringe-worthy moments.

"Why is this time different?"

"Before, it was just you. Now it's us. What you do reflects on me. And vice versa."

Jeepers. I thought I could be my own woman, at least until I gave birth. But he was right. We were a couple. Bonded by law, God, and my fear of his seven sisters should we decide to part.

"So, I should ask your permission the next time I have an impulse?"

"No, but a heads-up would be nice. Just so I can see it coming and duck."

I rubbed my forehead and added a sniff for effect. "This is so stressful. I'm thinking for two. Weighing each decision before I move on it." I looked down at my dress. "Is this all right? Does it reflect well on your brown jacket? Maybe you should dress me."

He shoved his wallet into the inside pocket of his brown sport coat. "Forget I said anything."

I gave him my broadest grin. The one that showed all my teeth. "Okay."

His eyes narrowed. "Did you just play me?"

Hooking my arm through his, I said, "Like a piano."

When he lifted me off my feet and threw me over his shoulder, I yelled. "Don't wrinkle the dress!" Bending my head toward his ear, I whispered, "Unless you want me to take it off."

He set me down and gazed into my eyes. "Later, my love. I'm starving."

In deference to my high heels, we skipped a stroll on the beach and followed the sidewalk from our cabana to the front of the hotel. They were only one-and-a-half inch heels, but anything higher than ballet flats comes with a danger of tripping.

Our reservations were for the Sheerwater, which billed itself as beachside dining at its best.

This was the first night of the convention, and the

instructions said all the attendees would dine at the same restaurant. It took some wrangling to convince my husband we should eat on site rather than in San Diego's Gaslamp Quarter, but when I insisted we'd be closer to our bedroom, he relented.

Bowers told the hostess we had reservations for two. Since the convention tickets already accounted for the reservations, I'd pretended earlier to call the restaurant to secure our table. He squeezed my hand. "They're under Bowers I assume?"

I nodded.

"Here you are. There is limited seating with the convention. You'll have to share a table."

Drat. The letter that arrived with our tickets mentioned we'd all eat in the Sheerwater. However, I imagined we'd dine like normal people. At separate tables. My plan was to spring my surprise on Bowers when he had a full, happy tummy.

Bowers turned to me. "Is sharing a table all right with you?"

"It's great. Perfect. We can meet new people."

His intimate knowledge of me prompted a frown. I didn't care for people. Not in a phobic way, but given a choice, I'd choose the company of animals.

Leave it to my detective husband to notice anomalies. My surprise might be toast.

The hostess picked up two menus. "Wonderful. You'll find this a friendly group. This way, please."

As she glided around white planters overflowing with green foliage, I spotted a battered tool bag peeking out from under the leaves. The weekend's agenda included a treasure hunt, so I assumed the bag was on the list and tucked the location into my memory bank.

The sound of the surf rode in on a gentle breeze. A chilly breeze. Already I regretted my choice of dress.

Most of the tables were full, but in the corner, getting the full brunt of nature, were two empty seats.

"Please, no," I whispered. But she led us straight to the corner and gestured. Bowers, after a moment's hesitation, pulled out my chair for me, which gave me time to gather my thoughts. And to stop blushing.

Our table mates were the guy whose butt I'd pinched and a second man who was bigger, maybe a little older, and, with his trim goatee, handsomer. I might be prejudiced against the first guy because I'd embarrassed myself with my impromptu butt-pinch and hug.

Both men stood on my arrival. Once we were all seated, the larger guy spoke in a deep baritone.

"Good evening. I'm Edward Harlow, and—"

"We've already met," Nicholas mumbled.

Edward raised his eyebrows. "Oh? Perhaps you could introduce us."

"I didn't catch their names."

"Martin Bowers, and this is my wife, Frankie."

Edward bowed his head in my direction. "Pleased to meet you, and this is my brother, Nicholas."

"Go easy on the names," Nicholas snapped.

My husband froze with his gaze fastened onto Edward. "Wait a minute. The Edward Harlow who wrote *Monday Morning*?"

Bowers had taken the seat next to Nicholas, so when he stood, he had to reach over me to shake Edward's hand. "I loved that book."

"Thank you. I'm pleased you enjoyed it."

"You captured the spirit of the bicentennial and Rick

Monday. I felt like I was there. After reading your book, I wished I had experienced it."

I scrunched my nose. "That would make you too old for me."

"If he gets his wish and ages a couple of decades, maybe I'd do in a pinch." Nicholas grinned at me.

"Hilarious," I responded in lofty tones, meaning it wasn't funny at all. Even as I met his gaze, my face burned at the memory of my latest act of public idiocy.

"Nicholas."

The younger brother glared. "Would you like me to get you a megaphone? That way, everyone will hear you."

I couldn't see why that would matter.

"It was an inside joke. How's your chest?"

Nostrils flared, both Bowers' and Edward's.

"Explain at once," the older brother demanded.

"There's no need—" I began.

Nicholas shrugged. "She pinched me in the lobby. And then she wrapped her arms around my middle."

"And then you hit me."

The transformation in Edward astonished me. A low rumble came from the back of his throat, and he seemed to inflate. "What's this?" he said in a silky tone.

Nicholas leaned away from his brother. "I reacted. I didn't know who was sneaking up on me."

Edward deflated, and his look turned to one of concern. Not for me. For his brother. "I didn't realize the affect this, er, situation was having on you."

"I'm fine." Nicholas slipped me a glance. "You okay?"

"My collarbone is fine. Just a little bruised."

"Apologize at once."

Edward's words snapped out, making me jump, but they didn't affect Nicholas one bit.

"I already did as soon as it happened."

"You still need to apologize for referring to, er, a body part that a gentleman wouldn't have brought up." To Bowers, he said, "He's in training."

"For what?" I asked.

"To be a grown up."

"No offense meant," Nicholas said, including Bowers in his half-baked apology. "To either of you."

"None taken." Bowers answered for both of us and jumped back into a conversation about *Monday Morning* with the author. In fact, he asked to switch places with me for easier access to Edward. Obviously, Nicholas Harlow was no longer a concern.

Once seated, I took the opportunity to study the menu. It was a group menu limited to a few choices in each category. The Harlows had already received their appetizers, though I noticed neither man touched his plate.

Nicholas had the corn chowder, but Edward's plate looked interesting.

"Excuse me. What did you order?"

He glanced down. "Charred Spanish octopus."

Yikes. With the briny smell of the ocean surrounding me, I could almost see the little guy frolicking in his natural environment. "How do they know it was Spanish?"

Both men stared.

"I mean, couldn't it be Moroccan? Or Algerian? He might have been minding his own business and strayed too close to the Spanish coast."

Bowers rested his hand on mine and leaned close, turning his head so the others couldn't see his mouth. "You could ask him, but he's dead. Do you know what you want?"

"I'll stick to the soup."

Once the waiter had taken our orders, I insisted the Harlows dig in while we waited.

"What brings you to the Hotel del Coronado?" Edward asked. "Or The Del, as the locals call it."

Bowers struggled to keep his grin in check. "We're on our honeymoon."

"Newlyweds. How nice."

I felt the need to clarify, since I always imagined honeymooners as hysterically cheerful, unable to keep their paws off each other, and generally obnoxious. I didn't want these two men to worry.

"We've been married about a month now, but we had to recover first."

Edward stopped cutting his Spanish—possibly Algerian—octopus. "Recover? From the wedding? I understand many brides overdo it, causing themselves stress."

"From our injuries. Bowers suffered more than I did. It was only my ankle whereas he fractured his tibia and broke his collarbone and a few ribs. We both tumbled down—"

"Frankie." Bowers squeezed my hand. "We don't want to bore these gentlemen."

He meant the gentlemen who were now gaping. To change the subject, I asked Edward—because I was ignoring Nicholas—if he was married. Nicholas answered.

"Just a girlfriend, but she's a pip."

The way he said it, a pip was something I should avoid.

"It's a long-distance relationship," Edward explained.

"She's in Illinois. Claudia and her brother run Inglenook Resort. They converted the family mansion into a delightful getaway."

"You can skip the commercial, Edward. They've already booked their honeymoon."

The waiter set Bowers' and my starters on the table. We all took advantage of the opportunity to end the conversation.

While I ate, I checked out our fellow convention attendees. Most of them were in their sixties and above, and no one had worn a costume this first night. At least not to dinner.

A large woman tore her chicken apart with her fingers. She slipped her hand under the table, and when she brought it up again, it was empty. Curious, I opened my mental doorway a crack and twitched when a high volt of energy snapped at me. Something was living under her chair. Closing the door with a firm mental hand, I told Curious Frankie to go away, or I'd be plagued all night by thoughts of rats and mice in the room.

When I moved my gaze to the woman next to her, my left eye twitched. It was Miss Flirty Pants from the lobby. The one who had rubbed against Bowers as she threw herself on the counter in front of him. Naturally, she nibbled on a salad. When she looked up and made eye contact, I averted my gaze to the table across the room.

A woman in her seventies wore a pink polyester pantsuit with a matching pink brimmed hat. Ribbons and flowers ran along the band.

The man at the table, his back to me, held her attention. He could have been telling her the story of how he made his first million. Whatever the topic, she hung on to every word.

He wore a white captain's hat, a blue blazer, and when he turned and showed me his profile it revealed a pair of glasses with thick, black frames perched on his nose. Fancy dress or costume? I couldn't tell.

The savory aroma of my tenderloin hit me before the waiter came from behind my chair and placed it in front of me. He'd arrived with four steaks—we had all ordered the same thing—and I gave up learning about my fellow attendees.

As soon as Bowers finished saying grace, he returned to his conversation with Edward Harlow.

Nicholas waved his finger at me. "What do you think of the Coronado?"

"It's beautiful."

"There's supposed to be a ghost. Room three-three-two-seven. She arrived on Thanksgiving Day in eighteen ninety-two and allegedly killed herself."

"Allegedly?"

"I think they found a gun, but as no one saw it happen . . ." He shrugged. "I'm a suspicious guy."

Ghosts. That's all I needed. "Hopefully she'll stick to her own room, which we aren't staying in, thankfully."

"Marilyn Monroe stayed in the Presidential Suite, which is a coincidence, seeing as how she was sweet on the president."

"Ha, ha. Very clever. Is that where you're staying?"

His expression turned dark. "We've got a room here in The Victorian."

"We were supposed to, but we got an upgrade courtesy of my husband's coworkers. We're in one of The Cabanas. It has a covered patio on the beach and an outdoor fire pit and . . . It's amazing."

The younger Bowers had nothing to say to that, and I

wondered if I'd gushed too much about my good fortune. But why shouldn't I?

Bowers, finally aware he'd spent the entire dinner talking to someone other than me, wrapped up the conversation. "It's been a pleasure to meet you. They say everyone has a book inside them, but I don't have that much to say. Mine would be a pamphlet."

The author waved away the compliment, but I could tell it tickled him by the way his broad chest expanded under his suit. Why couldn't people accept praise as their due? I'd love to tell a client, "It was all me, and you're welcome."

Edward's modesty annoyed Nicholas. He leaned back in his chair and gazed at his brother with a wicked gleam in his eye. "Edward usually has to settle for being the errand boy for a much more successful author."

"Who's that?" Bowers asked.

Edward glared. "I'm sure Mr. Bowers isn't interested."

Nicholas took a moment to savor Bowers' ignorance. "He might not be, since the books have nothing to do with sports. You've heard of Aunt Civility?"

"Aunt who?"

At this point, I thought Nicholas would climb over the table and kiss my husband, but he brushed his hand through the air as if the answer wasn't important.

"Aunt Civility. She writes about etiquette. Manners."

"I don't know anything about etiquette," I said, letting Edward know our ignorance wasn't personal.

He darted a glance at me. "I can tell. You used your dessert spoon on your soup."

"My what?"

I stared at my table service, wondering if I missed the labels.

Bowers came to my rescue. “That’s because she didn’t need it. We’re going to try Sundae’s for dessert. In fact, we should get going to beat the crowds.”

He stood to leave, but it was not to be.

Chapter Five

Frankie: Meeting Bowers' Competitive Side

As Bowers scooted back my chair, a woman in an old-fashioned silk dress with a microphone called for our attention.

"Good evening. For those who haven't met me yet, I'm Susan Sweeney. Many of you already know me as the head of the *Some Like It Hot* fan club. Welcome."

The diners acknowledged her with cheers. One woman yelled, "Sweet Sue!"

We joined in the clapping. Leaving in the middle of her talk would make it awkward if we ran into Susan again.

"I hope you are all settled in. Did anyone reserve room three-three-two-seven?"

An elderly pair of women raised their hands.

"How brave of you. You'll have to let the rest of us know if you experience anything . . . otherworldly."

Obligatory laughter followed.

"First, a gentle reminder from the management. If you are walking on the beach, the Coronado's beach villas and cottages are still undergoing remodeling. No peeking, please. We don't want to get in the way of the workmen, get injured by stray nails or paint buckets, or get thrown out. All right?"

The diners nodded.

"Good."

She unfolded a sheet of paper. "I thought we could warm up for this weekend with a bit of trivia about the movie."

"What movie?" an old man yelled. Everyone giggled.

She placed a hand over her heart. "Is there any other movie than *Some Like It Hot*?"

Bowers turned his head. "Frankie, what's this about?"

"Um . . . the people at the hotel are super friendly?"

As if she heard me, Susan's next words were, "We are all friends here, right? So, we will make this an informal, fun contest. The first person to call out the right answer wins."

"What are we playing for?" That came from a different old man.

"Fun."

A few people booed, but it was a good-natured razzing.

"Let's jump right in." The fan club president cleared her throat and read from an index card. "What did Detective Mulligan order from the speakeasy?" She lowered the card and winked. "I'll give you a hint. It was a drink."

Bowers and Edward murmured at the same time. "Scotch."

"Coffee," a woman called out.

Sue shook her head. "I know some of our hardcore members haven't arrived yet but come on. This is an easy question."

"But they were hiding the booze," the woman protested. "So, everything was coffee."

"The question is what did the detective actually order. What did he say?"

A woman closer to middle age than death raised her hand. "Whiskey and soda?"

Nicholas covered his face with one hand and pointed at Bowers. "This gentleman knows the answer."

All eyes turned toward my husband. He shrugged like it was information all of them should have at their fingertips. "Scotch. Make it a demitasse. Soda on the side."

"Finally," Susan said. "I don't recognize you. What's your name?"

Bowers looked back at the faces staring at us, some of them ticked he got it right. "We're not part of—"

I clutched his arm in my hands and yanked him down to his seat. "It's Martin."

"Well done, Martin."

My husband raised his eyebrows at me. I pretended I didn't see.

Other members easily answered the next questions. Edward and Bowers didn't find them worth the bother. But then the lady stumped her audience.

"Who did director Billy Wilder originally want to play Jerry?"

People called out names. "Bob Hope." "Danny Kaye."

The guy in the captain's hat said, "Cary Grant?" and they all giggled.

"Is Cary Grant in the movie?" I whispered.

"Sort of." Bowers tucked my hand into the crook of his elbow and patted it.

Sue got impatient. "Those names were rumors. Who did the director want to play the part? I'll give you a hint.

He arranged to meet the actor at a restaurant, but the famous person stood Mr. Wilder up."

Voices shouted in competition.

"Humphrey Bogart!"

The old lady hiding something alive under the table said, "Gary Cooper?"

After a moment of silence, Bowers and Edward both said, "Frank Sinatra," loud enough for Susan to hear them. The two men exchanged a glance of camaraderie. Or it was competition. It's so hard to tell with men.

"Very good." She seemed impressed, but I think she had lowered her standards.

Polite clapping followed. The kind that expresses criticism. I leaned over.

"Maybe you should let the old folks get one."

My husband kept his gaze on Susan. "They had their chance."

Ever since I'd known Bowers, he'd been cool, calm, and collected. Not one prone to let emotions get in the way, which was a helpful disposition for a detective. But I was learning something new. My husband had a competitive streak.

"This next one is even more difficult, but I have faith. Who played the character, Nellie?"

Again, Bowers and Edward answered at the same time, not giving the other participants time to think. "Barbara Drew."

"Bingo."

"I don't remember a Nellie," an elderly man mumbled.

"Let it go, Edward," Nicholas hissed. "You're drawing attention to our table."

Susan held up her cards. "This is the final question.

Are you ready? What foreign film was the movie based on?"

After a moment of silence, Bowers said, "Fanfaren der Liebe. A German film."

Once I picked my jaw off the floor, I said, "When did you start speaking German? Not that your accent was anything to brag about."

His eyes opened in surprise when Susan rejected his answer with a raspberry. "Wrong."

"Fanfares d'Amour." The correct answer came from Edward Harlow in perfect French.

Susan let the crowd hang in suspense before announcing, "That is correct." The room erupted in applause.

Nicholas muttered, "Show off." His gaze scanned his surroundings, and he started in surprise. "Is that . . .?" He shook his head as if he'd seen something too strange to believe. "I must need sleep."

Bowers accepted defeat with a handshake. He wanted to head directly to the beach for a romantic stroll, but I convinced him we needed to return to our room first for my sweater. Being a gentleman, he agreed.

I'd hung my costume dress on the door underneath a dry towel before we left for dinner, so I excused myself and slipped into the bathroom, locking the door after me.

Once I'd struggled into a white dress identical to the one Marilyn Monroe wore in the lobby—the zipper was a bugger—I added some drop earrings and applied red lipstick I'd purchased for the occasion.

"Are you okay in there?"

"Fine." Another thing I'd have to get used to as a married person. Someone monitoring my bathroom time. As I reached for the doorknob, I remembered the shoes I'd squirreled away under the sink. They were two-inch heels. A record for me.

When I stepped out of the bathroom, I put one hand on my hip and said, "Do you like it hot?"

Bowers looked up from the activity card. His expression didn't alter, but he set down the card.

This was a mistake. I should have warmed him up to the idea of playing dress up. Some women pulled off sexy just by blinking their eyes. The seduction gene wasn't in my DNA.

"It's a surprise. When I saw they were holding the conference, I bought tickets. I hope you're not mad."

Silence.

"We don't have to do it if you don't want to. A surprise you hated would be more of a nightmare, right? So . . . What do you think?"

Still, he just stared. I averted my eyes and realized I didn't have enough front to fill the dress. I clutched the bodice shut. "This was a terrible idea."

"Take it off."

Bowers' voice sounded strangled.

I pulled the pleated skirt out to the sides. "It looks ridiculous, right? I'm such an idiot."

He moved close and placed his hands on my shoulders. His thumbs massaged the fabric. "I said, take it off."

This time, I understood. "Oh. You mean that in a good way, right?"

"A very good way."

Chapter Six

Nicholas: Meeting the Fans

A pleased Edward is an insufferable Edward. Once at the mixer, his trivia victory over Martin Bowers had him doling out benevolent wishes and hearty chuckles to every gushing fan who approached him. Even the non-fans. Not once did he flinch when someone asked who he was. When the ego bender wore off, he'd regret all the invitations to share a drink and a chat at a later date.

Since it would be my job to send his regrets to any who took him up on the offer, his generosity disgusted me. I left him in search of better company, meaning myself. The snack tables drew a crowd, so I avoided them and moseyed along the edge of the room, studying the attendees.

Tonight's guests dressed to live up to the classy ambiance of the Crown Room. Some women wore what I call Mother-of-the-Bride suits in muted colors and long skirts. A few wore evening dresses, mostly black and all with sparkles. One man wore a tuxedo.

Those who dressed in costume fell into two categories: the Renters, and the Authentics. Those who rented costumes looked like an audience's idea of the prohibition era, with pressed, pristine outfits. I understood the company providing the costumes regularly outfitted theater groups.

The Authentics were comprised of people who had pulled their outfits from closets or great-grandma's casket. A few who had widened with age had made allowances. The double-breasted jacket that remained open. The drop-waisted dress that looked like it had a high waistline, usually covered with a wide belt.

One woman wore a striped dress with broad lapels. I could envision her unwrapping the packing paper and holding it up, a rush of memories flooding in. Maybe not. If she'd been twenty in the twenties, she'd be over a hundred years old now.

Though I wouldn't be caught dead in a costume, I looked fine in my charcoal gray suit and navy-blue tie with a burgundy pattern. The pattern consisted of beer steins, but they were small enough that Edward had never noticed.

About to slip back to the safety and silence of our room, a brunette in her thirties caught my eye. She sat alone. Not that I was looking for that kind of company. Still, it never hurts to be friendly.

She may or may not have been in costume. Her ankle-length black dress had a slit that exposed thigh-high leather boots with four-inch-heels. She held a black cigarette holder between her fingers, though it wasn't currently loaded.

"Is this seat taken?" Once I read her name tag, I added, "Cynthia?"

"Yes."

"My mistake."

"Excuse me." An old lady pushed me aside and dropped into the chair. She had something living in the large bag she set on the floor. Her name tag read: Edna.

Cynthia smiled. She hadn't been lying. Neither had she explained that all the other chairs at the table were free, so I nodded and moved on.

The lady in a pink polyester suit sitting by herself was more receptive. When I asked if I could join her, she fluttered her hand toward an empty seat. As I pulled back my chair, I looked her over.

"I'm amazed that a lady as charming as yourself is sitting alone." Edward wasn't the only one who could pour it on thick.

"But I'm *not* alone. Or I was. My friend injured her ankle and couldn't make it. We went to school together from first grade on. It's a shame. She loves *Some Like It Hot*. But I've made new friends."

"That's wonderful," I said. "I don't remember most of my classmates' names. Except Karen Dunnahoo. She used to steal my pencils and pull my hair."

"She probably liked you."

"Then why did she keep tearing up my math homework? I almost failed the class. She could have ruined my future college prospects."

"You're a card," Pink said, laughing.

A card. I liked the sound of that.

"Are you ready for a fun weekend?"

"It's so exciting." She looked around the room. "So many people to meet. And did you know there's a famous author here? Well, not Aunt Civility herself, but her nephew is here. He shows up on her behalf. She has one of those awful diseases where she can't leave the house."

An Edward fan. I should have guessed. I slumped back in my chair. "Agoraphobia. She has agoraphobia. It's not a disease. More of an affliction."

"That's it." She nodded. "A terrible affliction. Can you imagine being afraid to go outside? And she has to miss all this. Meeting her fans." She raised her glass. "Having a drink or something to eat that you didn't make yourself. I'd starve."

"I believe her housekeeper does most of the cooking." It was true. Mrs. Abernathy did an outstanding job of keeping my brother and me fed.

She grinned. "That doesn't sound so bad. I wonder why she doesn't meet her fans online?"

If my feelings made it to my face, I wore an expression of surprise and dread. Surprise that someone her age knew about the Internet. Dread because I'd been waiting for someone to ask the question and still had no response ready.

"Nicholas."

I turned my head. Edward glared down at me. His high had worn off. Grateful for the interruption, I jumped to my feet and introduced my brother. Her powdered face blushed. Not that she wore powder, but I always expected women over seventy to do so.

Edward bowed to her. She asked the usual questions, so I zoned out until I spotted the man from the registration counter this morning sans backpack, though he still wore the khakis, a blue-and-red plaid shirt, and leather sandals.

He stood in the doorway and scanned the room. Funny, but when his eyes met mine, he didn't flinch or scream. The effect of my glare must be short-lived. He sauntered away without hooking up with anyone.

"Pardon us," Edward said, catching my attention. "We need to discuss, er, something."

"Are we discussing our route out of here?" I murmured. "Because I'm ready when you are. I feel like an insect in a ten-year-old's science project. Any second I'll have my legs torn off."

A man in his mid-thirties dressed for a night of yachting replaced me at the table. Pink greeted him like an old friend.

When I turned to follow Edward, my eye was drawn to a large Black man in a dress and blond wig. He had his back to me, but the way he held himself seemed familiar. He reminded me of my brother. I started across the room, but Edward blocked my way.

"Not that way, Nicholas."

"I thought I saw Sykes."

He turned to look. "Where?"

But the man had moved.

Someone yelled, "Conga line!" As people joined in the fun, we followed them out the door in search of Detective Jonah Sykes.

Chapter Seven

Frankie: Making New Friends

An hour later, we had dressed in jeans and sweaters. I'd explained how I'd rented Bowers the manliest outfit available—a gangster's suit—and that he wouldn't be required to wear it until the dinner dance on the last night.

"A gangster? That doesn't sound so bad." He grinned. "It might be interesting to be on the other side of the law for once."

The convention mixer was in the Crown Room. As we entered, I drew in a breath. It was a beautiful space with arched wooden ceilings that invited guests to embrace their inner royalty with the addition of several crown-shaped chandeliers that gleamed from the ceiling. There were small tables with chairs scattered around the room with a flickering candle in the center of each. The tables, not the chairs. Two snow-white couches had glass tables in front of them for setting down drinks and snacks.

Most people ignored the furniture and stood in groups, chatting loudly about all things *Some Like It Hot*.

A few devoted fans had dressed in costumes—an

amalgamation of boas, fur-lined jackets, and feathered hats. Slinky dresses for the women, and baggy suits for the men. And vice versa for the braver folks.

One thing they all shared was excitement, the kind that makes people gesticulate a lot, talk loudly in an unnatural voice, and cackle with laughter. The kind of environment that makes me surly. A quick glance at Bowers told me we wouldn't stay long. If I wanted him to enjoy this weekend, I would have to drag Social Frankie from the dark, dusty corner where she hid most of the time.

Three steps in, the happiest couple on earth accosted us. They were African American, she with most of her hair under a pink turban that brought out the red highlights in her bangs, and he with short hair and a graying beard that framed his broad smile. She wore a pink, sequined flapper dress and matching high heels; he wore black jeans and a long sleeve t-shirt in a matching shade of pink.

"Isn't it exciting?" she squealed with a smile that showed her dimples. "*Some Like It Hot* is our favorite movie, and to be here where they filmed it." Her hand fluttered over her chest. "It's almost too much to take. I feel like Marilyn Monroe." She gazed up at her man.

"Coming to this convention and walking into this room was the best moment of our lives." She stared at him and sent some invisible message, and he added, "Except the day I met you, Sugar Cakes. I'm Willie. This is Rhonda." Together they grinned and sang out, "We're the Fishers!"

Would Bowers and I someday sing in public? Would we send each other invisible messages? We could do it now, but he wouldn't let me into his head. And he couldn't respond. I touched my lower lip. Or could he? To my knowledge, he'd never tried.

"What's on your mind, Frankie?" His tone held a warning. Maybe he *could* read my mind.

"Frankie." Rhonda beamed at me. "What an unusual name. Sounds like a character Marilyn Monroe might have played. Sexy. Kind of sassy." She demonstrated sexy and sassy with a shoulder wiggle that made her dress shimmer.

Me? Sexy and sassy? Surely one look would tell her my personality wasn't up to it. If I mimicked Marilyn's lip action, I'd be mistaken for a fish.

Picking up on his faux pas, Bowers introduced us properly. Edward Harlow had rubbed off on him.

"We're on our honeymoon." I skipped explaining the time lapse between the wedding and this weekend as Bowers hadn't appreciated it the first time.

Rhonda clapped. "How fun! And you decided to spend it celebrating one of the most romantic movies of all time." She gazed at her husband. "We should have done that."

"We could always get married again." He made a show of searching the room. "Is there a minister in the room? A priest?"

She smiled so broadly that her nose scrunched up, and she shushed him.

Bowers studied them without comment. Perhaps he feared that's what we'd become in a few years. They did seem to be trying too hard. Or they were naturally enthusiastic. My husband didn't have to worry. With my natural pessimism, an infusion of pure joy would only bring me up to moderately pleasant.

A waiter approached us with a tray of hors d'oeuvres.

I took a bacon and shrimp skewer for myself, and Bowers chose a wild mushroom tart. Before he walked away, I grabbed a caprese bite. "Gotta have my veggies."

Just as I finished chewing, a large woman, both in height and bone structure, shuffled past. With her gray hair and deeply lined face, she had to be in her seventies, yet I'm sure she could have pummeled me into toothpaste if she chose. It was the woman who slipped pieces of chicken under the table, and her name tag read: Edna.

She wore the same brimmed hat that half the older women wore, the band covered in flowers and bows. I counted five similar hats in the vicinity.

Her long nose supported a pair of silver-framed spectacles, and her wide mouth trembled, as if fighting off a frown.

I was more interested in the straw carryall she had over her shoulder. The head of a Chihuahua stuck out the top—the recipient of the chicken, I assumed. He studied his surroundings through narrowed eyes. What a relief. No rats.

"Isn't he cute?" When Rhonda reached to pet him, the little imp growled. Her quick reflexes saved her from a nasty bite.

"Tanner is on duty," Edna explained in a timorous voice, one that didn't match her powerful presence. "He's a service animal. A comfort dog. I'm prone to anxiety."

He ducked his head inside the bag and came up crunching something between his tiny but sharp teeth.

"Is my darling hungry? I always have kibble in the bag in case he wants a snack."

The dog's angry vibe didn't suggest anxiety reduction.

Tanner stared at me through bulging Chihuahua eyes as if judging me. Animals often put on postures to protect themselves. He must have a loving side. Didn't Edna refer to him as a comfort animal?

It took me seconds to build a quick path between his mind and mine. He stiffened, growled, and sent me a flurry of images that nipped at my brain.

Tanner snapping at a cowering lion.
Tanner's bark sending a wolf fleeing.
Tanner's mere presence forcing a grizzly bear into a bow.

The dog raised his nose in a smug posture, proud of his fearless reputation. What a little Napoleon. He ducked back inside his bag for more crunchies. Edna's bag reminded me of a mother's carryall that included cereal for their toddlers.

Her zeal undaunted by the unfriendly pooch, Rhonda made introductions, which were necessary as Bowers and I hadn't put on name tags. The woman's full name was Edna Tartwell, unfortunate thing, and she was traveling for the first time since her husband died five years ago.

"Alone?" Rhonda said. "You're brave."

"Not alone. My niece is traveling with me."

Just then, the brunette Amazon from the lobby, the one in need of a pen, walked up with two drinks and handed one to Edna. She had on a clingy black dress and spiked-heel boots that put her at Bowers' height. And her name tag, written in the same bold hand as Edna's, perched on one full breast.

"Thank you, Cynthia." She gestured at the woman in case any of us were blind. "My niece, Cynthia."

Auntie's little darling spread her full lips into a smile and looked us over with sharp, green eyes that paused when they reached my husband. He merely nodded at her, bless him.

Once Bowers discovered drinks were on offer, he took my order for a margarita and went in search of the bar.

"Are you fans of the movie?" It seemed like a safe question.

"Naturally," Edna said.

Her niece had other ideas. "Auntie needed a chaperon."

"Oh, stop." Edna swatted her arm. Cynthia winced. "I thought you might enjoy yourself. You need to get out more. Meet people your own age."

Cynthia's gaze wandered the room. "Not really my contemporaries." She smiled at me, the only other woman in her thirties. "Or my speed. Though some people like it." Suggesting I was a fuddy-duddy.

My cell phone rang. I fumbled it out of my purse and checked the screen. Mother. Whose parents call them on their honeymoon? If I didn't answer, she'd assume our plane had gone down. I excused myself and took the call as I walked away.

Chapter Eight

Frankie: Bowers' Performance

"Yes, Mother."

"You made it to San Diego?"

"I need to hang up, now. The stewardess just asked us to put on our oxygen masks."

"What?"

"I'm fine, Mother. I'm standing in the Hotel del Coronado as we speak."

"That wasn't nice."

"You're right. I apologize."

The noisy group next to me erupted into raucous laughter, so I stepped into the lobby.

"Have you done anything exciting? It's been a long time since I've been to San Diego. Such a nice place."

"We went to the zoo."

"On your honeymoon? That's not very exciting."

I nodded to a passing duo of men, pointed at my phone, and rolled my eyes, hoping to dispel the impression I was one of those technology addicts who chatted in public toilet stalls. "Sure, it's exciting. We saw a rare white tiger."

The lead man checked his step.

"What's a white tiger?" my mother asked.

"Same as a regular tiger but white instead of orange. There was a baby." Recalling the sadness that enveloped me outside the display, I missed my mother's next words.

"Pardon me?"

"I said I hope you don't spend your entire honeymoon looking at animals. We expect grandchildren by the end of the year."

"Mother!" Good grief. "We'll go back and see if the tiger has any tips. I have to get back to Bowers. We're safe and snug in the hotel. No need to call again."

When I disconnected, the guests who had passed me strolled over. The leader was a bit under average height, stocky build, had thin lips, a receding hairline, and a nose like a ski slope. He wore a dark suit, as did the big guy with him. In fact, it may have been the same suit, except the short guy also wore a pair of white spats on his shoes. Good grief. Another convention attendee.

His large friend had a jagged scar across his cheek, adding to the intimidation factor, and wary eyes that kept scanning the lobby.

"I couldn't help but overhear," the shorter guy said. "You were talking about a white tiger." He slipped a quarter from his pocket, flipped it in the air, and caught it. On the third flip, he dropped it.

"Heads or tails?" It just came out.

The man without a scar retrieved the coin and handed it back.

Shorty didn't appreciate the comment. I was going by his narrowed eyes and frown.

I dropped my phone in my purse and answered his question. "I was."

"I'm a big fan of wildlife."

Somehow, it didn't surprise me he was attracted to predators. Even though his words were polite, the man gave off a dangerous vibe. The air seemed heavier in his presence.

He sensed my discomfort, put the quarter away, and held out a hand. "The name is Jimmy."

Jimmy seemed like a harmless name, so I took his hand. He had surprisingly soft skin. People usually say soft as a baby's bottom, but since I hadn't had my hands on an infant's rear end since I babysat for an aunt, I dismissed the thought.

Once the handshake was over, he didn't let go. Not even when I tugged. The little girl inside, the one whose parents had raised her to be polite, refrained from kicking his shin or yelling. He might just be a lonely man in his fifties who wanted to chat. Or Heaven help me, he might be from Arizona, know who I was, and want to arrange a reading for his cranky cat.

"Are you interested in wildlife in general?" I said to distract him from that last possibility. "Or do you work for a rescue?"

He grinned, but it wasn't a pleasant smile. More like that of a hyena. "Of sorts."

"Then you would know more than me. I don't have much experience with wild animals. Except a pregnant Mexican wolf, but I only met her once."

I'd convinced her to stay calm while her rescuer removed jumping chollas from her fur.

"Mexican wolf. Is that the endangered one? I've got one of those." When my eyes opened in surprise, he added, "On my list. I like to keep track of endangered species. Like the white tiger." He moved a step closer.

I wrinkled my forehead. Penny pointed out that I do that when puzzled and said I was on my way to permanent furrows. I relaxed my eyebrow muscles, the culprits behind the crinkle. "I don't think it's endangered. It doesn't occur often in nature, so it's not really a thing."

"I should have said endangered and rare. My mistake."

I tugged my hand again with no results. "Well, if it's white tigers you like, you can see one at the San Diego Zoo. She just had a cub around a month ago. It's the cutest thing ever."

"Only one? Don't cats usually have litters?"

Had there been more than one? I shrugged. "I don't know for sure. One is all I saw. You can ask at the zoo. The vet's name is Harry, and the keeper is Jose. I'm sure they'll tell you."

Something flickered in his brown eyes. His gaze studied me with an intensity disproportionate to the conversation. I took a step back to get leverage for my hand. If I had to, I'd fall backward to the floor. Surely my body weight would be enough to break his hold on me.

The door to the Coronet Room opened. Another man in a dark suit stepped into the lobby. "They're waiting for you." The censure in his voice made me want to apologize for keeping Jimmy.

The latter turned his head slowly. His face flushed, and he raised his voice. "I'll be there when I'm good and ready. Capisci?"

His harsh words didn't faze the man. "I'll let them know." He returned to the room, closing the door behind him.

The guy with the scar nudged his friend. Or was it his

boss? "Jimmy. It wouldn't be smart to keep Enzo waiting. Not now."

Jimmy moved his sneer to his friend. "Now you're telling me what to do?" His volume was back at a yell.

"Not at all. I'm looking out for you. That's my job."

An employee, then.

Jimmy let go of my hand, tugged his jacket lapels, and straightened his tie. Now that he was leaving, I cheered up. "Nice meeting you. I need to get back to the party."

"I'd like to continue this conversation, but I have business to take care of first." He nodded at his friend. "Take her to my room."

"Is that a good idea?" Scar said.

"Don't question me again," Jimmy snapped.

When I took a step back, it made no difference. Scar gripped my elbow and propelled me in the direction of a hallway.

Suddenly, Willie and Rhonda tumbled out of the Crown Room, leading a conga line. Rhonda careened into Scar, loosening his hold on my arm.

Willie glanced into the open door of the Coronet Room, open because Jimmy had stepped inside and left it open. "A private party? We're in! Shake it, everybody!" He wiggled his rump and led the way.

"Did someone say private party?" The young woman behind Rhonda turned to the man behind her. "Hey! There's a party in the Coronet Room. Pass it on."

Word spread fast, and soon guests grabbed entire trays from the snack table along with bottles of booze and soda, ignoring the protests of the buffet staff and bartender. When Jimmy's friends blocked the doorway, guests thought it was part of the game and ducked under their arms. One woman tickled Scar.

Edna hobbled out the door to the Crown Room, took one look at the parade into the Corona Room, and turned tail. I guess Tanner wasn't up to keeping her calm in the rowdy environment. After an interested glance, Cynthia followed her aunt.

As the crowd poured into the room, they pulled me along with them.

The Coronet Room was a smaller version of the Crown Room. They even had a crown chandelier.

The tables made a U shape, with one along the top and two down each side. A number of somber men in dark suits sat on the outside of the conference tables, facing each other, and doing a fair imitation of a wake. A single man with white hair occupied the table at the top of the U.

Floor to ceiling windows lined one side of the room, and in front of each window stood two large men, one facing the window, and one facing the room. Though they stood like statues, their eyes moved, taking in each guest.

The men around the table didn't appreciate the party, and they addressed their concerns to the head table.

"What's the big idea?" one said, rising from his seat. The men on either side of him followed suit.

"This wasn't on the agenda," the man opposite the one standing complained. "I don't like surprises."

When a pair of women in flapper dresses climbed onto the head table and shook their shoulders and bottoms while belting out *Running Wild*, the men ignored the show and kept their gazes fixed on their opposites across the room.

"Add some heat to it," someone yelled, and the rest of the uninvited guests cheered.

Rhonda waved her arms like she was directing musicians, while Willie clapped in time.

A cork from a bottle of champaign popped. As one, the men along the windows shot their hands inside their jackets. At a head shake from the white-haired man, they relaxed and stepped back. He motioned with his hand, and two men stepped up and helped the women off the table.

"Jimmy." I'd swear the white-haired man hadn't raised his voice, but I heard him clearly. So did Jimmy, who snapped to his side. "Is this your idea?"

"No, Enzo. They weren't invited."

"Maybe if you hadn't wandered off, they wouldn't have found a way in. Make them disappear. Nicely."

At a look from Jimmy, four men started with the far side of the room and attempted to herd the guests to the door.

When Bowers walked in with two mixed drinks, I hurried to him and squeezed him tight. The Harlows followed close behind.

"Hey there." He smiled down at me and handed me my margarita.

I took a large swig. "Perfect."

While he sipped his gin and tonic, he scanned our fellow guests, especially the faces of the men seated around the table. Jimmy had mentioned he had business to attend to, but the hostile vibe told me this wasn't a friendly board meeting. Maybe it was some kind of takeover.

I tugged on Bowers' cuff. "We've all been invited to leave."

When he didn't answer, I looked up. He had his gaze riveted on a large Black man with trim facial hair standing across the room. He looked like a football player. A football player in drag. He wore a curly, platinum blond wig and a fur-collared, long, black coat over a conservative, black dress. Instead of nylons, he had on long, black exercise pants and tennis shoes.

"Hey," Nicholas said with a snort. "I told you it was—"

My husband clamped down on Nicholas' wrist, cutting off his words. The younger man frowned at him but kept quiet.

I found Edward Harlow's next move just as interesting. He stepped in front of Nicholas, blocking his brother's view of the room.

Jimmy, flipping his quarter again, wandered close to the Black man with his large friend in tow. The way they surrounded him, the phrase "closing in" came to mind.

"Stay here," Bowers said. "All of you."

Edward nodded, and when Nicholas voiced his objection, his older brother threw back an elbow to his ribs to shut him up. It might have been an accident. A muscle twitch. But I didn't think so.

Bowers strolled over to the group and clapped the guy in the dress on the shoulder. He greeted him with a loud, "You made it."

My husband waved his drink at our unwilling host like a man who was on an alcoholic high. "It took me three weeks to convince Reggie he'd look good in a dress. Where's the wife? She ought to see this."

"Reggie" said he'd left her at home. "No need for Wanda to witness my shame."

Bowers pointed his drink at me, and I wiggled my fingers. "If I'd known we were going stag, I would have left the ball-and-chain at home."

Jimmy stared at me, making the connection.

Bowers acknowledged the Black man's dress. "This will learn you. Never bet against me when I've got a royal flush." He threw back his head and laughed.

I'd seen my husband—before he was my husband—put on a personality when dealing with bad guys. I wondered if the men in the room were bad guys and how he knew.

Next to me, Edward pursed his lips in thought. Suddenly, in a decisive move, he grabbed his brother's elbow and pulled him over to join the conversation. Bowers covered his surprise and stretched out an arm to welcome the Harlow brothers.

"Reggie, I want to introduce you to the guy who wrote *Monday Morning*."

Reggie's jaw dropped in awe. "Oh, man. Edward Harlow in person. What an honor."

After the two men shook hands, the author turned to Jimmy. "I am Edward Harlow, and this is my brother, Nicholas."

Jimmy shook hands with both men. It was a reaction rather than a pleasure.

"You'll have to excuse us." Bowers wrapped his arm around "Reggie's" shoulder. "Mr. Harlow and I have been disagreeing on a point about dining etiquette, and you're the tiebreaker. I expect you to back me up."

He steered the man out of the room with the Harlows—and me—close on his heels.

They stuck to their roles until we were back in the Crown Room, where Bowers dropped his arm and the act and held out a hand.

"Detective Martin Bowers. You looked like you needed help."

"Detective Jonah Sykes. San Diego Sheriff's department. And I did. I'm not sure what made them notice me."

"You were staring at them."

"Was I?"

"Nice dress," Nicholas said.

"I thought you were leaving town," Detective Sykes said.

Nicholas glared at his brother. "According to some people, Coronado is out of town."

Bowers clapped Detective Sykes on the shoulder and said in a loud voice, "I think you've learned your lesson. Let's get you out of that dress. It's starting to creep me out."

When I turned my head to see what set Bowers off again, the guy with the scar stood in the doorway, watching.

Chapter Nine

Frankie: What Jimmy Wants

Out of deference to my feet, Bowers took me up by way of the elevator, while the other three men tackled the stairs. We arrived at Detective Sykes' room just as he unlocked the door.

The detective invited us in and went to the bathroom to change, leaving us with the Harlow brothers. They'd been hissing at each other in the hallway, but now their volume rose to argument level.

"And so, you thought it was a good idea to bandy my name around in a room full of criminals."

"You don't know they were criminals," Edward chided.

"Oh yeah? Did you see the way they went for their guns when they heard the champaign bottle pop?"

Edward gave him a tolerant smirk. "Did you actually see a gun? No? It's your imagination running away with you. And that's precisely why I did it. Ever since we've arrived, you've been cowering at loud noises and sudden movements. For goodness' sake, you even knocked Mrs.

Bowers down. It's not in your nature to quiver with fear. And it's unbecoming. I decided to end it. Compare it, if you like, to yanking the bandage off. It's over now. None of those men showed the least curiosity when I introduced you."

The discussion ended when Nicholas noticed us listening. Edward invited Bowers and me to take a seat on a padded storage bench at the end of the bed and exchanged pleasantries with Bowers. As he droned on, Detective Sykes stepped out of the bathroom.

He wore a pair of sweats and a San Diego Chargers t-shirt that hugged his muscled arms and chest. He was drying his face with a white hand towel. The motion made his biceps pop.

I stared.

Bowers patted my thigh. "Enjoy the view because you're only getting this one pass."

It flickered through my mind to protest, but since I was still gaping, I murmured, "I'm almost through."

"What brought you to the conference?" Edward asked the detective, oblivious to Sykes' muscles since he had an impressive set of his own. In fact . . . I looked from one man to the other. The same height and build. The same dark hair, though the detective had tighter curls. The same trim goatee. Only their skin color differed. And their eyes. Edward's were intense gray. When the detective lowered his towel, I gazed into eyes the color of a cat's. Orange brown with flecks of black.

Nicholas, seated on the edge of the bed, caught me looking. "If two different mothers could give birth to twins, it would be Edward and Sykes."

"If you had come for rest and relaxation," Edward mused, "you would have brought your wife. That is, if

Wanda is your wife? I seem to remember her name is Shauna."

"And you'd be going home for the night," Nicholas added. "Unlike me, who is forced to stay here against his will and mingle with nuts instead of exercising my right to slump in front of the TV, flipping through sports channels with every other American male. Baseball; basketball; football; hockey. I love October."

He sighed along with the other men in the room.

Nicholas stood, grabbed the remote off the television, and flicked it on. "Today's highlights should be on in a few minutes." Until then, he muted the news anchor.

Detective Sykes studied me. "What was Jimmy's interest in you?"

Bowers' hand was back on my thigh. "In Frankie? And who is Jimmy when he's at home?"

"Jimmy Bianchi. The guy you rescued me from. One of the Southern California families."

The way he said family, he didn't mean a pack of relatives eager to play corn hole.

"Well?" Bowers said.

With them all staring, I got self-conscious. "He wasn't interested in me. I was talking to my mother and—"

Bowers crowed. "You owe me ten bucks."

"Congratulations. You were right. She called us on our honeymoon. Once she realized our plane hadn't gone down, she wanted to know what we were up to." I squeezed his hand. "By the way, she expects grandchildren by next year."

When he didn't express the shock I expected, I removed my hand. "I told her about the zoo and the tiger."

Bowers lowered his voice. "All of it?"

"Obviously not. I just mentioned we'd seen a white

tiger. After I hung up, Jimmy said he had an interest in wild animals. I told him to check out the zoo and to ask for Harry or Jose. He said he wanted to talk to me and was, um, escorting me to his room when Rhonda and Willie came out of the Crown Room with a conga line."

"Are they an African American couple?" Detective Sykes asked. When I nodded, so did he. I'd seen that expression before on Bowers. The detective was tucking the information into a mental filing cabinet.

"They must have assumed the guys in the Coronet Room were having a party because they yelled, 'Party in the Coronet Room.' That's how it all started."

"What else did he ask you about?"

"There was a lot of jostling. You know. People with drinks and food pushing their way in. He didn't get the chance to talk to me after that."

It hadn't slipped my notice that Detective Sykes hadn't answered Edward's question about why he was here, but I didn't know the man well enough to push.

Nicholas Harlow had no problem pushing.

"Back to why you're at The Del in a dress . . ."

The detective considered his answer. "I'm assisting local law enforcement."

"With what? Crowd control?"

"The job isn't all glamor, Nicky."

Nicholas folded his arms and glared. He wasn't a fan of his nickname. I'd have to remember that.

"Jimmy said he had business to attend to in that room," I said, repeating what I'd heard.

Detective Sykes nodded. "It's a business meeting of sorts. A family-owned business."

"Who's the guy with the white hair?" Nicholas asked. "He looked lonely at the head table."

Sykes gave him a broad shrug. "Got me."

"Jimmy was called back into the room by some guy. He didn't want to go, but his employee, the one with the scar, said he shouldn't tick off Enzo. I assume Enzo is the guy with the white hair." I offered the information for what it was worth. To me, nothing.

"Do you expect a problem?" Edward asked. "I would hate for anything to interrupt the conference."

"Why would there be a problem?" Detective Sykes smiled at me as he asked the question in my mind. "Still, it would be better to leave those men in peace. Much better."

Chapter Ten

Frankie: A Whisper in the Night

On our way back to The Cabanas, we ran into Edna Tartwell and her mighty dog, Tanner.

"Are you staying at The Cabanas, too?" I asked after offering to carry her bag and receiving a polite declination.

"Oh, no. Cynthia and I have rooms at The Views."

The Views were the condos next to us, farther down the beach.

"They're so comfortable, and we have a balcony. Tanner is able to sit outside and listen to the ocean."

"I'd be afraid he'd try to catch a bird and jump."

Then again, I can find something to fear in most situations.

"He's too smart for that. Tanner has a high sense of his value and would never endanger himself. He knows how much mommy depends on him."

Tanner looked at me with contempt.

Back in our room, Bowers and I discussed what happened in the Coronet Room. At least, I discussed it, while Bowers avoided discussing it.

"Why did those men need a policeman in their room?"

"I think he just happened to be in there. You heard him. He followed the conga line."

"But why did Jimmy and his friends approach Detective Sykes?"

"You heard me. He was staring at them. They probably wanted to know why."

"I guess so. But couldn't he have explained he was a cop? That would have put their minds at rest."

"Yes." Bowers sat on the edge of the bed. "But maybe he didn't want everyone in the room to know who he was."

"Okay. But why did Edward keep blocking Nicholas' view of the men?"

A flash of interest sparked in Bowers' eyes. "He did?" He kicked off his shoes. "Nothing those two did would surprise me. I'm more worried about the attention Jimmy gave you."

"He wanted to see some animals, which was natural since I'd just mentioned a tiger." I sat down next to him and scooted close. "Are you jealous?"

He pushed me back on the bed and kissed my neck. "Incredibly."

I flashed him a smile and wrapped my arms around his neck. "Then I guess you'll have to stick to me like glue."

Sticking to me led to other things that didn't involve talking. We fooled around. Though it's not fair to call it that. Bowers takes his duty seriously and does it well.

Afterwards, we fell asleep in each other's arms, but a few hours later, I woke with a start, gasping for air. After listening for a full minute and hearing nothing but

Bowers' even breathing, I slipped out of bed and went to the glass doors. Through them, I could hear the gentle, repetitive roar of surf on sand. Beyond the patio was darkness.

Nothing moved, though I'm sure critters crawled, and hunters hunted. I focused on the noises but heard nothing unusual. Besides. I didn't remember a sound on waking. Just a feeling.

Fear. And a pit of loneliness that threatened to make me scream. My hands covered my mouth before I acted on that desire.

When I shivered, I threw on my bathrobe. Not a sexy covering but a fluffy, warm blue thing with matching fuzzy slippers, which is exactly what I slipped on my feet. The trembling continued, but it wasn't caused by the cold.

With utmost care, I opened the glass door and stepped outside. Bowers shifted his position in bed but remained asleep. Stepping into the cold, damp air, I closed my eyes and listened. Silence. The awful feelings came from somewhere . . . and something.

The dark expanse of ocean in front of me and the knowledge that creatures were chomping on other creatures under the surface freaked me out enough to send me back inside.

"No animals allowed," I mumbled. Once I brought up the image of my mental doorway, the one that kept the thoughts of animals from slipping into my head, I closed it firmly, jiggling the handle to make sure it stayed closed.

Satisfied that I'd taken care of the problem, I dropped my robe, kicked off my slippers, and slid back under the covers. Unfortunately, with my cold hands and nose, I had to resist snuggling up to Bowers.

This was my honeymoon, and my only concern was for my husband. Though he wasn't near death as his coworkers and doctors allowed me to think at the time, Bowers' injuries were serious. His recovery was a work in progress, and I hoped he would relax and stop willing himself to heal. Even though he never complained, I knew from his frown when he thought I wasn't looking, and the way he attacked the exercises the doctor had prescribed, that his slow progress concerned him. Not slow in a normal way but slow in the mind of a man who had enjoyed perfect health.

We would visit Old Town, eat great food, and walk on the beach. We'd have a wonderful time making memories, taking pictures, and enjoying our first trip as a couple. He'd have no choice but to kick back and let his hair down, figuratively speaking.

If I'd known how the next day would turn out, I would have stayed in bed for the rest of the weekend.

Chapter Eleven

Frankie: The Honeymoon Takes a Turn for the Worse

Some people are morning people. Me . . . not so much. Bowers popped out of bed as soon as the first rays of light penetrated our curtains.

He slapped my bottom and said, "Rise and shine, sleepyhead. We've got a full agenda."

After several attempts to stay under the warm covers, attempts that included moaning about how vacation and sleep were synonymous as well as comparing early rising to spousal cruelty, I crawled out of bed. When I reached for my white dress, intending to take it into the bathroom with me for a quick, post-shower dressing, he hung it out of reach. "Dress up is for the final evening. We wear normal clothes during the day. Unless you want to wear it to Old Town."

My husband had a point. He had already dressed in jeans, a navy-blue plaid shirt with a white accent that he wore untucked, and black tennis shoes. He held out his arms and did a slow turn.

"This is what I'm wearing. Memorize it. If Nicholas

Harlow has a blue plaid shirt, I'll arrest him. While you dress, I'm going to take a quick walk to get my bearings."

After he left, I stretched like a satiated cat before padding into the shower. When I stepped out of the steaming bathroom ten minutes later, The urge to put on my snuggly robe and lounge outside on the patio in the morning sun overcame me along with a desire to listen to the waves hit the shore.

I reached up and, grasping a panel in each hand, whipped the curtains open to embrace the morning. An unseasonal morning fog had settled over the coast, making the view a sea of gray. Creepy. But then I saw that Bowers must have had the same idea. He'd turned one chair, so his back was to me. Funny, but I didn't remember the straw hat. Giant sunflowers lined the band. It looked exactly like the kind of headwear a beach bum might favor. My husband had finally embraced this vacation.

His shirt seemed different. I'd thought it was blue-and-white checked, but I must have had sleepers in my eyes. This shirt had red and blue checks.

Opening the door as quietly as possible, I tiptoed to him and wrapped my arms around his shoulders. "Caught you."

When his head dropped forward, I yanked back my arms and held them up. Tacky red marked my hands and wrists.

"Bowers," I whispered, praying he would claim a practical joke. The red must be jam from a donut, right? But Bowers was not a slob. My breath became louder and faster until I panted like a winded bulldog.

One of the flowers, a purple carnation, had come loose and rested on the ground next to the chair. I picked it up and stared at it, willing the plastic decoration to explain.

The door opened behind me. "What are you—who is that?"

"He won't wake up." My shaking voice rose in pitch. "Bowers, make him wake up."

My husband placed his hands on my shoulders and pulled me back inside. When he saw the blood on my hands and forearms, he swore.

"I—I thought it was you. Playing a practical joke. But it wasn't. And now there's a dead man on our patio. Our honeymoon patio," I wailed.

Bowers bent his head to look me in the eye. "Listen carefully. You need to wash off that blood as fast as possible. Do it in the sink. Then dress in as many layers as you can."

"But it's not that cold. Not like a Wisconsin winter."

"Trust me. Just do it. Now."

He moved to the room phone, dialed, and introduced himself to a person I assumed belonged to the Coronado police department.

In a daze, I tucked the flower into the pocket of my robe and wandered to the bathroom. My robe had blood on the sleeves, but just the edges. It must have pushed up my arms when I hugged the dead man.

I removed it and stuffed it into the tiny wastebasket. I'd never put that robe on again, which was sad. It was an extremely comfortable bathrobe.

By the time I returned to the room, my arms were red from scrubbing. Bowers rummaged through our luggage, throwing out clothes and instructing me to put them on. Exercise pants that I'd brought to lounge in. They'd never seen a gym. The pair of jeans I'd worn yesterday. Slacks over the jeans. A t-shirt. A sweater. Another sweater. My lilac dress over all that. By the time I finished, I looked like the Pillsbury Doughboy.

While I dressed, he returned to the patio for an inspection of our corpse and only came in when someone knocked and identified themselves as the Coronado police. He conferred with the uniformed officers before leading them to our patio. I sat on the bed's edge and fought to keep my balance. The sweaters made me top heavy.

The male officer spoke into his radio in subdued tones. The female came back inside and explained that we would need to leave the room but remain at the hotel, as we'd be wanted for questioning.

"But our things," I said with a helpless gesture.

"Ma'am. I sorry, but—" Her gaze paused on my outfit. "You need to leave everything behind."

"Can I take my purse?" When she gave me a doubtful glance, I shook the contents onto the bed. "See? Wallet. Chapstick. Tissues. Cough drop. Nothing to worry about."

"I don't think—"

The other officer called her over, and while he had her attention, I shoved my purse down my bulky front and stepped outside to wait for Bowers. When he joined me five minutes later, we headed for The Victorian.

Lithe beauties in bathing suits stared down from the outdoor pool area a level above us as I hobbled by, looking as if I had the inside track on a freak snowstorm coming to San Diego.

"I don't have a bathrobe. And I forgot my slippers." I gasped. "I didn't bring spare underwear."

It showed that I had settled into married life when

this observation didn't make me blush. Nor did Bowers cringe.

"We'll buy you some new underwear. In fact, I'll enjoy picking some out for you. Maybe a few pairs without wide elastic."

Granny underwear, as my best friend Penny called it.

His delivery lacked enthusiasm, which wasn't a surprise when I considered what had just happened.

I stopped walking. "Bowers, where are we going to sleep?"

He held the lobby door open. "That's what we're about to find out."

The young desk clerk smiled at my husband as we approached, a reaction most women had to Bowers. A smile that slipped when her gaze landed on me.

As he explained the situation, her fair skin paled until her powdered blush, modestly applied, stood out in splotches on her plump cheeks.

"Let me get the manager."

A small, fussy man with soft, brown hair like down feathers and a sparse mustache scurried to the counter and invited us into the privacy of his office. Once there, he invited us to sit in tan leather chairs while he settled behind his desk.

"I've heard the unfortunate news. We at The Hotel del Coronado can only express our regrets."

As he spoke, he stroked his mustache as if wishing it to grow.

"Thank you for your concern," Bowers said. "As you know, my wife and I are on our honeymoon, and not having a room makes it awkward."

"Yes, yes. Of course." He turned to the computer and

typed furiously at the keyboard. "The convention has . . . quite full . . . so distressing."

He came to a decision, lifted the phone receiver, and spoke in a voice so low I couldn't decipher his words. Ten seconds later, the young woman from the front desk entered and handed a key to her boss, bestowing us with an odd look as she did so.

With the little man leading the way, we found ourselves back outside on the cement path that ran in front of the hotel. "It is highly unusual. We haven't opened them to the public yet. Remodel, you know. But the work is finished for the most part. Just some touchups in some of the other buildings, but you shouldn't be disturbed. I mean, painting is not a loud occupation." He allowed himself a chuckle. "Yes, I think this will do nicely."

On the opposite side of The Victorian, a row of multi-occupancy cottages stood in succession. There were no guests lingering by the front doors or heading to the beach in swimwear. The place seemed deserted. It was deserted.

As the manager unlocked the gated entrance, he spoke over his shoulder. "Very private. Kind of desolate right now, but as you are on your honeymoon . . ."

He led us down a path that passed by the cottages. It resembled an upscale, beach-front neighborhood. When he unlocked the door to the second cottage and motioned us inside, a spacious room with an open floor plan greeted us.

The living room area had a sectional couch, an ottoman that doubled for storage, and an additional low-backed chair. These were on a floor rug in front of a fireplace.

An outside patio came with a fire pit and plenty of

furniture should we decide to throw a party. I could see the strip of blue past the gate and beyond the sand. Since our ocean front room at The Cabanas had given me a secret fear of a tsunami drowning us in our sleep, I was perfectly happy to admire the Pacific Ocean from a distance.

The other side of the room held a kitchen table and a countertop, stove, and refrigerator. I hoped Bowers didn't expect me to cook on our honeymoon.

The bedroom had a king-size bed and the usual furniture, and beyond that stood the shower. I'm sure there was a sink and such, but all I saw was the beautiful, tile, walk-in shower.

"I'll turn on the utilities right away. That way you can enjoy the fireplace."

There was an awkward moment when Bowers wondered whether to tip the man, but as he was management, my husband thanked him warmly and sent him on his way.

"It's chilly," I said with a shiver.

He cracked a grin. "Even with all those layers? You might want to shed some of them before we get the call."

"The call?"

"From the police. I gave them my cell phone number."

When my stomach started talking, it dawned on me I hadn't had breakfast. Once I was down to a peach sweater and jeans, we headed back to The Victorian.

Chapter Twelve

Frankie: Feathery Witnessses

We made it in time to eat at the convention breakfast buffet. I chose the SoCal Croissant with bacon, egg, spinach, and feta cheese, while Bowers had the Classic Morning Muffin. Sausage, egg, and cheese. We both took an orange juice, and Bowers accepted a Rainforest Alliance Certified coffee.

Once we settled at a patio table, I operated on my croissant. I don't eat eggs I haven't cooked. They are usually too mushy. My husband wisely waited until I'd wolfed down my last piece of bacon before he took my hand.

"This is not going to ruin our honeymoon. It has nothing to do with us. We're going to continue as if nothing happened. Well, the police will want to talk to us. Other than that, it will be like nothing happened."

His pep speech seemed intended for both of us, so I agreed in order to give his confidence a boost, though I had my doubts we could go on as before. Already the dead body took up head space. Who was he? I hadn't seen his face. Not that I wanted to see a dead man's face. Where did he come from? Who killed him? And, most important, why leave the body on our patio?

After breakfast, my husband led me to the beach. "We missed our romantic stroll in the moonlight." He was trying to distract me, and I loved him for it.

"There's always tonight."

And the next night. And the night after. I hadn't yet wrapped my mind around having Bowers with me every day. No more canceled dinners because of work emergencies. No more early nights because he had to go home to get some sleep. If he got tired, he'd just walk into the next room. Heaven. Unless . . .

What if he tired of me? When we were dating, he only had to make an excuse and leave to get a break from me. How did I know those emergencies that called him away were real? What if he'd arranged a signal with one of his coworkers for those moments when he'd had enough?

Do married couples need breaks? Would he get sick of seeing my face every day? Would I stop caring about the litter box and revert to my slob nature, driving him into the arms of a neater woman?

I picked up an imaginary stick and chased away Paranoid Frankie.

The sun peeked over the hotel's red roof, illuminating the Victorian architecture with a glowing halo, and sweeping me into the past. A simpler time, when Bowers, as the husband, would have taken care of every worry for me. Sounded a little boring. Most women stayed home back then and amused themselves arranging flowers and giving orders to servants. Or children. Maybe that's how murder mysteries gained their popularity. Vicarious living.

Besides. Flowers in my possession died horrible deaths just to spite me, and I didn't have any children.

"Ready to get your feet wet?" Bowers took off his shoes and socks, and I did the same.

As I walked, I kicked the sand, spraying it with the satisfaction of a child. "I've never seen the ocean before."

His eyebrows went up. "Never?"

"Not in person. There aren't any in Wisconsin or Arizona."

"That's true. I suppose you've never swum in the ocean either."

"How could I—ahh!"

Bowers threw me over his shoulder and carried me into the water. "The cold shock will pass in a minute."

I screeched.

"Here goes." He swung me in the air, but at the last minute, he twisted. When I landed, only my feet got wet.

We had the beach to ourselves, mostly. After taking a deep breath of salty air, I stared at the water running over my tootsies. "It feels weird. Like the sand is dissolving under my feet." I grinned up at him, and he rewarded me with a kiss.

"Did you know that most shark attacks occur in three feet of water?"

Thankfully, my husband was used to the way my mind seemed to relish pointing out the downside and merely said, "Should I find myself in three-feet-deep ocean water, I'll keep that in mind."

As we walked hand-in-hand in the direction of the hotel, I noticed Bowers' limp had returned. All that uphill walking at the zoo yesterday had taken its toll. About to suggest we take a seat on the nearest bench, I paused to say hello.

Edna Tartwell teetered past, led by Tanner. She carried his bag over her shoulder should he need a respite from walking.

"It's a beautiful morning," she called out, her voice quavering. Funny how she seemed intimidating until she opened her mouth.

The toe of her orthopedic shoe caught in the sand, making her stumble. Bowers held out a hand. "Do you need some help?"

"You are such a sweet, young man. Walking on the sand is wonderful exercise. Move it or lose it. That's what my Nona used to say. Not that you two need to worry about it for many years."

Under his mommy's watchful eye, Tanner tinkled on a seashell. As the old woman and her dog shuffled away, I wiggled my toes in the sand. "She better have some poop bags in that carryall. I don't want to step in something."

Bowers' head jerked up. "Is that who I think it is?"

Edward and Nicholas Harlow were headed our way deep in conversation. Or an argument. Nicholas waved his hands at Edward in an excited manner.

"We can't avoid them without being obvious. Let's get it over with. Say nothing about what's happened."

I suspected the real source of my husband's lack of enthusiasm came from Edward's victory at the trivia game last night.

As they approached us, I caught the tail-end of Nicholas' sentence.

"—and I don't think a march on the open beach is what Sykes had in mind when he suggested I get away for a few days."

"I thought you were past your paranoia. The fresh air is good for you. The beach is far enough away one can't pick out individuals."

"Unless one has a scope," Nicholas muttered.

"Good morning," Edward said with a slight bow in my direction.

"It's going to be a nice day," Bowers responded, keeping the conversation banal.

"I notice you're not in costume," Nicholas said. "We were just discussing management's desire to put Edward in a dress. Publicity for next year's convention. If they have one next year."

"Nicholas . . ." An undertone of warning accompanied Edward's smile.

"I thought he should go for it. I mean, I'm not pushing for makeup or nylons, but if it makes the fans happy, why not?"

"Why don't *you* wear a dress?" Edward snapped, his volume just this side of a roar.

"There seems to be some commotion at The Cabanas." Nicholas glanced over his shoulder. "Isn't that where you're staying?"

I followed his gaze to the men and women gathered in front of our late room. The room that held all my clean underwear.

"Yes." Bowers left it at that, so I closed my mouth.

Edward looked over his shoulder and back at Bowers. "If I didn't know better, I'd think there had been an accident. Or something."

"Or something," my husband agreed.

This had an astonishing effect on Nicholas. He spun on his heels to take in the activity, and then searched the grounds of the hotel. People milled around on the hotel's outdoor patios, but other than that, I couldn't tell what he was looking at.

"Is it a woman?" he asked with hope.

Edward tried to shush him, but my husband studied him through narrowed eyes. "That's an odd question."

"Maybe for you, brother. We're exposed here."

Edward clapped him on the back. "Nonsense. My brother is talking about my fans. They will seek me out at the most inconvenient times, but I refuse to give in. A brisk morning stroll is the best thing for one's constitution."

"The best thing for my health is not being dead."

"Is there a reason you're worried about death?"

"Doesn't everyone over thirty?" Edward added a loud, fake laugh.

"I meant my death of cold." Nicholas shuddered. "Brrr. I'm heading back inside."

Edward hooked his arm and pulled him back. "Just to the end of the cottages and back. Then we'll get breakfast."

He dragged his brother in that direction.

"That was strange."

Bowers agreed.

As we continued our walk, my husband asked if I'd gotten a look at the dead man's face.

"Gack! Are you joking?"

"It was Harry Reed. The vet from the San Diego Zoo."

"No! What was he doing here? Doesn't he have animals to doctor?"

"Did you see him around last night?"

"If I had, I would have told you."

"Sorry. Stupid question." He sighed. "At least there aren't any animals involved."

On that point, Bowers was wrong. Hovering at the edge of the sand, floating on currents of air, a flock of seagulls watched the crime scene with interest.

I stopped to admire the view. At least that's what I was doing as far as my husband was concerned. Inside my skull, I was having a spirited debate.

Bowers and I had made promises. While we honeymooned, he would ignore criminals, I would ignore animals. But a dead man on the patio negated the promise, didn't it?

And then I worried that, once the mental doorway was open, I'd be subject to psychic ambushes. Not that animals with something important—to them—didn't make it through anyway, but I needed a break from the majority who couldn't. But I also wanted information, and that decided it.

As the birds' piercing cries floated on the breeze, I imagined a large wooden door straight out of Frankenstein's castle. As I cracked it open to reveal the swirling light beyond, I attempted something new.

The gulls appeared fixed in place as they rode the wind, which made it easier to attempt a group reading. Instead of focusing on one bird, I widened my net and tried to catch images or stray ideas from the entire flock.

First one, then another drifted my way.

As I connected, I lifted my arms to let the light breeze flow over and under them. A sensation of weightlessness overcame me, and I stood on my toes to capture the feeling of flight.

At first, snatches of potential prey that included a donut held by a little girl on her balcony flashed through my mind. I made a subtle gesture toward our old patio and threw back an image of Harry as I had last seen him.

The gulls farthest away dipped their wings to join the group in front of me. I had their attention.

No one had screamed last night, so I assumed his body got there after dark. People walked the beach at night—

A moving picture of Harry strolling the beach.
It was dark, but not pitch-black.
A figure approached him.
In the twilight—or was it the dawn?—the figure's outfit shone green. It looked like a uniform, and it was worn by a man.
Suddenly, the green guy went berserk. He grabbed Harry, pounded him on the head, stabbed him with a shiny knife that resembled the one from our breakfast on the outdoor patio, strangled him, and, for a finishing touch, blasted him with a shotgun.

I broke the connection and gaped at the birds. These were innocent animals who merely showed me what they'd seen. There must be other injuries on the corpse.

As I turned away from the water, the brothers had turned back, and Nicholas Harlow had his gaze fixed on me.

How much had he seen? Had I done anything weird? I never knew how I might behave while reading an animal. I arched my back and stretched and waved my arms around as if this were part of my morning routine.

After exhaling a deep, cleansing breath, I turned to my husband. "Bowers."

"Hmm." He, at least, was enjoying the view.

"If I tell you something, will you promise not to get mad?"

He stopped short of rolling his eyes.

"You might want to mention to the police that they should look for a man dressed in a green uniform. I think."

The lack of evidence of the versatile, multi-weapon attack on Harry kept me cautious.

"Green?" Several gulls joined voices in an annoying screech. He looked up and over my shoulder, and chastisement entered his tone. "Have you been amusing yourself with the seagulls?"

"They volunteered the information."

"And the birds told you that a man in green killed Harry."

"They might have suggested it."

"I'm not about to risk my professional reputation on what a seagull might or might not have told you."

"You're right. I'll tell them."

Chapter Thirteen

Frankie: A Chat with Sergeant Ken

My interview with Sergeant Ken Bautista wasn't as intimidating as I'd feared. He didn't give off an angry vibe like Bowers' sometime partner, Juanita Gutierrez. He smiled and asked me to talk about the body's discovery in my own words, so I did.

An unnamed female officer in uniform took notes from her chair in the corner of the room. The interview took place in the manager's office, which was less luxurious than the hotel, but still better than a cold, dimly lit interrogation room.

"I wonder . . ." I tapped my lower lip as if deep in thought. I'd decided to focus on the uniform bit and not the green. "Maybe one of the hotel's employees noticed Harry doing something suspicious, and it escalated into a confrontation."

Sergeant Ken's intelligent brown eyes looked up from the papers on the desk. "And instead of asking him to leave the premises, he or she killed the man?"

I hadn't thought through my approach. "Maybe Harry attacked him. Or her. It could have been an accident. Maybe it happened so fast that the employee settled him into our chair for his comfort and ran to get help, but I discovered the body before help came."

"No employee of the hotel reported accidentally stabbing a man on the hotel grounds."

Note to self. Cause of death? Stabbing.

"Maybe they saw the reception clerks racing to get the police and figured it was taken care of. Or maybe they were embarrassed."

"I'll keep that in mind when we speak with the employees, Mrs. Bowers."

I turned my head to look for Mrs. Bowers before I realized she was me.

"I understand that it's difficult to think a fellow guest might be capable of violence." Bautista avoided a condescending tone, but I could tell he was trying to sooth the client of one of the island's most important businesses. "Or that an unbalanced stranger had access to the beach."

I hadn't considered either possibility. Not after my conversation with the seagulls. But now, an uncomfortable sensation crept up my spine. What if it hadn't been a random guest who committed the crime but one of the convention attendees? A horrible image of a man in an evening gown holding a bloody knife came to me uninvited. I shuddered.

The sergeant suddenly smiled. It was a friendly smile; the kind someone wears when they offer you a stick of gum. "You keep referring to the victim as Harry. You knew him?"

"No. Oh, no. Not knew. My husband and I saw him

at the zoo yesterday. The San Diego Zoo," I added, as if there were another famous zoo in the vicinity.

"You met with him?"

Did the gathering in Antonio Sabata's office count as a meeting? "Define met. I mean, we met him, but not intentionally. We didn't have a date. I was interested in the white tiger and, as one of the zoo's vets, so was he."

Sergeant Ken nodded. "Then you didn't really know each other."

"No. Definitely not. Just in the way you and I know each other. I mean, you'd probably say hello if you saw me on the street."

Civic pride took over. Sergeant Ken straightened his shoulders. "We're a very friendly city. I would certainly greet you if I saw you."

"Right. So, you know me well enough to speak to me, but you don't know my favorite color."

"Yellow?" he said.

When I made a face, the woman taking notes guessed Purple Pizzaz.

I narrowed my eyes. "One of Crayola's special editions? Lucky girl."

Sergeant Bautista slid a baggie across the table. "Do you recognize this?"

Leaning forward, I studied the pink flower inside the bag. The memory of shoving the flower in my bathrobe pocket flashed across my brain. I opened my eyes wide. "Did you go through my bathrobe?"

"It was covered in blood."

"Not covered, really. Just the edges of the sleeves got dirty. From the body. I explained how that happened. I thought it was my husband. And I threw it away. You went through my trash?" I replayed our first night, looking for anything embarrassing I might have thrown away.

"The flower?" he asked again.

"It was on the patio next to the chair. I picked it up without thinking."

Shortly after that question, Sergeant Ken escorted me to the door.

Bowers waited in the lobby. He'd already had his turn with the detective. "Do you want to go back to the room?"

"Is now really a good time for that?"

"A good time for—" His eyebrows rose in surprise, but he allowed a small grin to escape. "There is not an inconvenient time for that, but it's not what I meant. I wondered if you needed to relax after your interview. Regroup."

"No, thank you. How about you? You probably don't want to hang around a crime scene on your vacation." His eyes had the blank look of the undead. "You remember. Your honeymoon?"

He straightened his shoulders. "After all that excitement, I could use some fresh air. How about you? Didn't Edward Harlow say it cured everything?"

He was already steering me outside and in the direction of The Cabanas.

The police had surrounded our former patio with yellow crime scene tape that led to the water's edge.

"Excuse me. You shouldn't be out here."

A large-boned elderly man in a white shirt and dark slacks stepped in front of us to block our view. He wore a badge on his shirt, and his blue and yellow shoulder patch identified him as a member of the Coronado Senior Volunteer Patrol.

"Are you a detective?" I asked. Flattery never hurts.

He hiked his belt up over his belly. Any higher and it would be a bra. "I joined the force after fifty years as a stonemason. Most of the headstones in the cemetery are my work. But now my job is to aid the detectives. Keep the perimeter clear so the men and women in blue can do their job."

Bowers looked down at him and grinned. "We're far outside the perimeter."

My husband had a conflict. As a member of the force, he appreciated the work done by volunteers such as—his name tag read: Mike. But now he was experiencing that fine work from the other side of the proverbial fence. And he didn't like it.

Bowers stared intently at the officers, following their movements as if it were his very own crime scene.

Mike shook his head. "Custody of the eyes."

Bowers, a faithful Catholic, took this as a reference to lust. "Excuse me? I only have eyes for my bride."

"But you're staring at the crime scene. The perimeter extends beyond the physical. You're invading their space, optimologically speaking."

Optimologically. Was that a word?

"I would think we've earned the right to a peek," I said, rising to Bowers' defense. "After all, we found the body." I gestured toward the police. "That's our patio. At least, it was."

The old man gaped. "You did?" He lowered his voice. "That must have been a surprise to see someone face down on the cement first thing in the morning."

"Actually, he was face up on a chair."

A second goggle from Mike. "You mean he made

himself comfortable on your patio? And you never noticed?"

"I don't know how comfortable he was," I murmured.

Detective Bautista joined us. "Mike." He grinned. "Are you keeping them in line?"

"Just doing my job, sir. These people were gaping at the crime scene."

"Where are your partners?"

"Probably lollygagging over a coffee. They have good intentions but no willpower. Do you have any suspects?"

Bautista glanced at Bowers. "We have a lot of witnesses. Not of the murder, but it seems everyone saw Harry Reed yesterday. Depending on which witness I listen to, Harry was at the conference, drinking in the bar, and darting around the beach in a furtive manner. One woman swears she saw him shopping for a purse in The Signature Shop."

"Sounds like he was busy," Bowers said with a smirk, acknowledging the cross of conflicting witnesses.

"I'm always ready to learn from other departments. Would you like to look over the scene with me and hear what Doctor Yu has to say?"

"Frankie . . ."

My husband had heard the seductive siren call of a murder investigation. But would it be good for him to get involved? The stress of a normal investigation came from the responsibility. This time, he was a mere observer. Limited stress, right? And I couldn't see the sergeant inviting Bowers to join a foot chase, so, his leg seemed safe.

I squeezed his hand. "I'll find out if the conference is canceled."

He kissed my forehead and assured me he wouldn't

be long. "Here." He dug his credit card out of his wallet and held it out. "Why don't you check out the shops?"

"Sure." He knew I ranked shopping right below having a mammogram, but it would be good to keep him on his toes. Holding the card between two fingers, I waved it in the air. "Don't be too long, darling."

Chapter Fourteen

Frankie: Two Unlikely Sisters

Of course I didn't put Bowers' credit card to use. I hate shopping. Instead, I wandered into the Crown Room, where Susan Sweeney held court from the front of the room.

There weren't many empty chairs, so, I leaned against the wall to listen.

The attendees hung on to her words. Now and then, someone asked a question. Call me paranoid, but after the first woman glanced my way, stared, and then nudged her friend, who also looked, it seemed every pair of eyes in the room found an opportunity to study me. Word of my involvement—however limited—must have spread.

Annoyed, I left, bumping into the large man with the scar in the lobby.

"Jimmy wants to know what's happened."

"Oh. Um, someone died."

His bushy eyebrows shot up. "What kind of convention is this?"

"It wasn't anyone from our group." Did I know for certain Harry the vet wasn't here because he was a fan of

Some Like It Hot? I did not, so I added, "At least, I don't think so."

When he moved aside to allow me to pass, his boss popped out from behind his employee's large form and blocked my way. I took a step back and bounced off Scar.

"We meet again," Jimmy said.

"It's a small hotel. Not small, but we're all staying here, so it's smaller than if we were wandering the streets of San Diego and kept running into each other. That would be a coincidence."

Even though I tried to dodge him, he got hold of my hand. "You seem to be in the middle of things. I find that interesting."

"Not on purpose. And it's really not interesting. Very boring." When I tugged, he didn't release me. Did this guy have a crush on me? Just in case, I explained I was married.

"To Detective Martin Bowers of the Wolf Creek Police Force. I won't hold it against you."

Chills shuddered through my body. He knew who Bowers was. How? More important, why?

Just then, Nicholas Harlow strolled past. "Nicholas!" I grabbed his arm with my free hand. When he saw who I was talking to, he tried to ignore me, but I dug my nails in. "We're going to be late."

The younger Harlow reluctantly caught on and went along with the charade. Being a smart mouth, he exchanged a few barbs with the men, but I had my hand back, and that's all that mattered.

The door to the Coronet Room opened, and the same guy in a dark suit stepped out. "Mr. Carpinelli is waiting for you."

Jimmy nodded at the guy, ignoring the implication

that everyone in that room was waiting for him. Again. To me he said, "Next time, we'll find somewhere more private."

I'd make sure there wasn't a next time.

Nicholas led me through the lobby. "Do you need a drink? Because I'm headed to the bar."

I released his arm and scoped out the surrounding guests. A family with a pale-faced teenage girl checked in at the front counter. As a child, I thought it was incredible to spend the night at a motel, playing with the ice maker. I couldn't imagine the thrill of staying at the Coronado back then. I couldn't even get over being here now. Other than a tinge of resentment, I found them harmless.

An important-looking man in a business suit rolled his luggage toward the elevator. He was so involved with his cell phone I doubted he noticed his fellow guests.

Marylin no longer shelled out flyers, but the table of convention goods still stood in the corner manned by volunteers. Since at least twenty benign people surrounded me, I felt safe enough to part company with Nicholas Harlow.

Most of the people milling about were my fellow convention attendees, passing through to the bar, beach, or other entertainments. Their initial shyness had worn off, and they were easily recognizable by their flapper girl dresses, suits with wide lapels, and old-fashioned hats.

"Do you think the zoo will close in honor of Harry's death?"

Drawn by the mention of Harry's name, I shamelessly listened to the two women next to me.

The woman's companion blew out a huff of air. "They never close the zoo. They didn't close it when Alvila the ape died, and she was pretty popular. They didn't even have a funeral. And then there was Carol, the elephant. She made an appearance on Johnny Carson. They didn't give her a memorial, either. What's a vet matter? He's not famous."

"Excuse me." When I turned, I faced the woman in the pink, polyester pantsuit. She had a friend with her. Purple. Purple had that kind of steel-gray, tight-curled granny hair that makes you want to attack her with a hair pick. She wore white tights with her two-piece skirted suit. She stood about my height and had the solid build of Penny's German grandmother. "I couldn't help overhearing you. Are you talking about the man who died?"

Purple had a hunted look in her eyes, so I introduced myself. She tugged at her jacket lapels and glanced at Pink, who took over introductions.

"I'm Dot." She put her arm around Purple's waist and squeezed. "And this is my sister, Polka. Those are the nicknames our parents gave us. We were always together, and they started referring to us as Polka Dot, like we were one person. We've been answering to them so long, they feel like our real names."

Dot had a petite figure, and her fine bones and silky white hair were probably the envy of her geriatric friends. Polka must have taken after their father, with her thick build, wide face, and heavy features.

"Pleased to meet you, um, Polka and Dot. May I ask how you knew Harry?"

Dot stared at me until I wondered if she needed a hearing aid, but then she pulled it together. "Oh, no. We didn't *know* him. My—my sister and I are lifetime members of the San Diego Zoo. We go on all the tours, including those that go behind the scenes. They once offered to let us hold a baby capybara. The largest rodent in the world."

Polka shivered her shoulders. "I declined the offer."

"That's great," I said. "About Harry Reed?"

"Harry was on some of the tours as a, well, not a guide." Dot put her fingertips to her lips. "As an expert."

"Was he good?"

"He seemed to know what he was talking about. But how would we know?"

"Good point."

Edna Tartwell, with Tanner peering out of her handbag, shuffled past. Was Edna's outfit a costume? I thought the buttoned cardigan, straight skirt that ended above her bulging knees, and orthopedic shoes were everyday wear for her.

Cynthia had on a pinstriped suit, black high heels with rose-colored spats, and a light-maroon fedora. Gangster, girly style. When she glanced in our direction, Polka spun to face me, almost knocking me over. She lifted her purse and stuck her face in it in her search for something. Maybe she needed glasses. She finally pulled out a tissue and held it up like a prize.

Dot sniffed, and I noticed her eyes were wet. She might have dry eye. Or she was holding back tears. She pulled out a tissue and dabbed her nose. "Goodness knows why I care that Harry's dead. I can't help it. If I were thirty years younger, I'd say I was hormonal."

"He wasn't very nice to you." Polka pressed her lips into a grim line, emphasizing the crooked application of her red lipstick. "From the stories you've told me, he was a rotten ba—" She bit her lip, getting lipstick on one front tooth. "A bad boy. He was rude to you. You didn't deserve that. You are the nicest lady in the world." She clutched

Dot's arm. "I'm sorry for being blunt, but sisters have to stand up for each other."

Dot patted her sibling's arm, and her lips quavered. "All love begins and ends there."

Love? Did I hear right? Did the septuagenarian have a crush on Harry? What was he? Forties?

"Um, sure." It seemed the best response to an overzealous fan of a man unworthy of such adulation. Looking back on our meeting, Harry Reed wasn't especially handsome, or even charismatic. The opposite, in fact. And he seemed a tad young for her, but who was I to judge?

I focused on the key point. Harry Reed was dead. It happened outside the Hotel del Coronado, but, unless he had seriously irked one of the guests—like Pink—the reason behind his murder must involve the zoo. Or not.

He could have come to the hotel with a friend and things turned ugly. Did I think Pink could have run into him and killed him? How would she have moved the body to our patio? Of course, if her sister helped . . . Purple looked strong, and Pink had strong feelings for the vet, which I've heard give you superhuman strength. That's what the magazines in the grocery checkout line say.

I dismissed the idea as too crazy to take seriously. There must be a reason in his personal life or work life that led to Harry's death. However, I had no access to his personal life, and as far as I knew, no one had seen him here before we found his body this morning. So, I'd start with the zoo.

My banishment might present a problem to one less creative, but I already had a plan. Unfortunately, it would take the cooperation of Nicholas Harlow.

Chapter Fifteen

Nicholas: Out of the Loop, Again

I was too mad to sit, so I leaned against the back wall and listened to Susan Sweeney break the news of the dead body to the waiting crowd. There were several good reasons for my anger.

One. I had to find out about the body from Pink and her sister, Purple. Otherwise known as Polka and Dot. They didn't look much like sisters. Dot had a delicate beauty and must have been a knockout in her day. Polka must have gotten the brains.

Others were gossiping about the discovery, but the ladies were nice enough to give me what details they had, which weren't many.

Someone had discovered a body without a pulse sitting in a patio chair. Said patio belonged to the room of a couple on their honeymoon, poor things. Poor things, indeed, as Edward would say.

Since Bowers and his wife were staying at The Cabanas with an ocean front view, and they were on their honeymoon, they must be the lucky couple. If so, why hadn't the Bowers mentioned anything when we ran into them on the beach? The hubby may have wanted to spare his wife, but she'd have to be pretty dense not to realize there was a body on her patio.

One important fact they shared was the name of the deceased. Harry Reed. I kept my strong emotions under control on hearing his name and merely said, "Life can be a bummer." Especially for Harry Reed.

Reason number two. When I'd passed on the gossip to Edward, he'd already known a man was dead and that the deceased's name was Harry Reed. But he hadn't thought to track me down and share this information.

I don't appreciate being the last to know, which is why my brother hordes information like a squirrel hordes nuts. Edward likes his secrets.

Three. Sykes and Edward had wandered off for a private conference, which set the chances Harry suffered a heart attack at nil. The guy was in his late forties and seemed fit enough. Not that you can be sure about someone's arteries from a quick look at their face at a hotel registration counter. I decided it must have been murder, yet my brother hadn't deigned to share that information with me when we discussed the dead man.

Since I wasn't invited to his and Sykes' *tête-à-tête*, I came to the Crown Room to kill time. And stew.

Once Susan greeted the faces staring back at her with an appropriately somber tone, she wasted no time.

"From the gossip I've heard, most of you know there has been an accident. A stranger turned up on the hotel grounds this morning. He kicked the bucket sometime during the night."

A few gasps came from those who hadn't yet heard.

"Who was it?" The man in the blue dress hadn't absorbed the part about it being a stranger.

"They don't know."

Susan might have been lying. Or the police might not have informed her.

The fan club president patted the air with her hands to quiet them. "The Coronado police department is all over it. We know you're eager to keep going, but we're not animals. Out of respect for the dead, we're holding off on panels until two o'clock this afternoon. By then, the officers should have done what they need to do."

One middle-aged woman raised her hand. "Are we in danger?"

Susan put her hand on her hip. "Heck, no. This poor man's death has nothing to do with the convention."

"Then why are the police here?" a male voice called out.

Sue narrowed her eyes at the questioner. "They've got procedures to follow, don't they? Nothing to worry about. During the delay, have fun exploring the site." She ticked off those sites with her fingers. "Stand on the porch and imagine Josephine and Daphne's arrival. Or why don't a couple of you rent a beach chair and role play Sugar Cane's first meeting with Shell Oil Junior. There are plenty of sites to see. Here's your chance to go crazy." She pulled a final ace out of her sleeve. "The good people of Hotel del Coronado gave each and every one of you a credit for a free ice cream of your choice at Sundeas. How's that for hospitality? You can grab yours as you exit."

After that, she lost the crowd as they moved in a herd for the exit, eager for a freebie. I left, too, but I wanted something stronger than ice cream.

Outside the conference room, Bowers' wife stood hemmed in by two men who I recognized as members of the Coronet Room contingent. As I passed, she grabbed my arm and clung to it.

"We're going to be late," she said, digging her nails in just in case I'd missed the hint.

Since "we" had no appointment that I knew of, I took it she wanted to escape her three fans.

No matter what my brother said, I knew the men in the Coronet Room were armed. It took an effort to stand my ground. Also, not being an ignoramus, I'd seen through Sykes' comment about staying away from their unhappy little meeting. The men in that room were dangerous. Dangerous enough to sniff out a cop.

Were they connected with Officer Hermes? I had no idea. It seemed unlikely, but since the detective hadn't explained who Hermes' accomplices were, caution seemed the better route.

They still showed no sign that they recognized me, so I let out the breath I'd been holding. My frustrations came out through a few pointed comments, but a damsel in distress is irresistible, so I complied with her request and led her away.

Frankie declined my invitation to join me for a drink, but I stuck to my original plan and went to the bar.

The bartender greeted me with the typical line, "What'll it be?"

Tempted to order a scotch, I stuck with soda water, since, as my brother's assistant, I never knew what miracles Edward would expect me to pull off: a complete set of signed copies of every book he'd written for an admiring fan, delivered to his or her room within the hour; his press kit for an interested party; the regurgitation of a pithy comment he'd made at a talk last year for use in a conversation he planned to have. All were possibilities.

Once Edward finished playing with the cops, I'd irritate him with a reminder of Susan Sweeney's suggestion that he wear a dress.

As if I'd summoned him, the event manager walked into the room.

"Nice speech." I held up my glass in a toast.

He grabbed his tie and fiddled with it. "Oh. Thank you. I'm just here to warn Ted that he may have increased business with the convention delay." He offered his explanation as if frightened I might accuse him of tossing a few back while on the job. In his place, I would.

My cell phone rang and cut our conversation short.

"Excuse me." Turning away from him as I answered, I failed to check the caller ID. "Hello?"

"Nicky. Is this you? I've never called your phone before."

"Hello, Zali. What can I do for you?" Claudia Inglenook's Aunt Zali. A woman with the logic of a five-year-old and the will to follow up with whatever crazy idea popped into her head.

"Everyone says Eddie's the polite one, but between you and me, he's never asked that question. I'll have to think of something. In the meantime, the favor is for Claudia."

I wouldn't do Claudia Inglenook a favor if she requested I save my own life. However, I had a soft spot for Zali. She and I shared a problem. Living with control freaks.

"Tell me," I said.

"I'd tell your brother, but he won't answer his phone.

It's making Claudia cranky, and you know how she gets when she's mad. All suffering saint. Drives me nuts."

That wouldn't be a long trip for Zali. I had a thought. "Zali, my dear, I must apologize."

"Goody. I love apologies. What for?"

"I once called you a nut."

Her voice sent frost over the line. "You did?"

I must not have said it out loud. "I take it back and beg your forgiveness. I have met the queen nut."

Zali wasn't one to hold a grudge. "Nicky! You met a woman? Three cheers!"

"She's married."

"Naughty boy."

"I'm not dating her. She and her husband are here at the hotel. First, she pinched my rear, mistaking me for her husband."

"He must be super handsome."

"Thank you. I heard a rumor the zookeeper banned her from the zoo. Something to do with attacking the fence outside a white tiger enclosure."

"Did she hurt it?"

I counted to three. "She didn't make it over the fence."

"Well, thank goodness for that. Course, I know something about getting ejected from places. It was never my fault. Except for Bill's, but I blame the bartender. He kept serving me. Maybe it wasn't this woman's fault, either."

The aged relative wasn't giving me the sympathy I craved, which was just as well, as someone else wanted my attention.

"Hang up. I wanna talk to you."

In front of me stood Jimmy, spats and all. Over either shoulder loomed a large ape.

It's hard to be brave when your knees are buckling, but I figured if my time was up, I refused to go screaming. So, I decided to respond to him the way I would if I weren't in fear for my life.

He needed a lesson in manners. If so, I didn't want to damage my phone, so I told Zali I'd call her back and set the device on the bar.

"Nice costumes."

The guy with a scar darted a surprised glance over his suit.

"Not that I'm dressing for the convention," I continued, "but if I were, I'd want what you're wearing."

Jimmy narrowed his eyes. "You couldn't afford it."

"You might be right. Still, I could take a few gigolo engagements. Donate a kidney or two."

"You're a wise guy. I don't like wise guys."

"Then don't dress like one." I stood. "Now, if you'll excuse me."

The bruisers with him stepped forward and left me with no choice but to back up against the bar. The one with the scar said, "Mr. Jimmy wants to talk to you. It's only good manners to listen. Wasn't you raised right?"

Aunt Civility fans. I altered my face to a friendly expression and turned on the polite button. "How may I help you?"

"You interrupted my conversation with that Frankie woman. Tell me about her."

"I barely know her."

He gestured to my phone. "That's not what you were telling your friend."

"For shame. It's rude to listen in on people's phone calls."

The two men grabbed an arm each and lifted me off

the floor. The bartender moved away, and when he reached for the phone, the guy with the scar shook his head. He grabbed another glass to clean.

"She knows something about the dead guy." Jimmy stepped close enough I turned my head to avoid his ski-slope nose. "Maybe you know something, too."

"Not me, but maybe *you* have something you'd like to confess?"

They lifted me higher and shook me.

"Why don't you fellas amuse yourselves elsewhere. My arms are getting tired, and I'm bored."

"Nicholas? Are you annoying these men?"

Edward strolled into the bar, which put the odds in my favor. The goons exchanged glances and set me down.

"Sergeant Bautista would like to speak with you."

At the mention of the police, my new friends melted out of the room. I rolled my shoulders and stretched my neck while Edward watched them leave. The bartender moved back to the center of the bar.

"Bautista has already talked to me."

"That was just an excuse to make them leave without violence."

The bartender stopped wiping his glass.

Before he asked, I told him. "They were interested in Bowers' wife. We should warn her."

"I'll tell Detective Bowers. You go home and get my chocolate brown slacks, socks, and shoes."

"What about the dangers of entering our home?"

"It's just a quick trip."

He shook his pant leg and sand dribbled out. That's what he got for forcing me to walk the beach this morning when he'd confiscated our casual clothes.

"And what will you be doing while I'm running errands?"

He gave me a smug smirk. "Assisting the police."

"I've been known to offer insights on an investigation."

"They asked specifically for me."

"By the way, Zali called. She had a favor to ask but didn't get the chance. It might have to do with you not answering Claudia's calls."

"I'll phone her later. Right now, I'm busy."

He floated out of the room under the lift of his big head. That's when I decided to go rogue.

Chapter Sixteen

Nicholas: Teaming Up with Frankie

As I headed for the lobby, my guilty conscience intruded on my thoughts. I hadn't told Edward about seeing Harry Reed in the lobby and how he asked for one of the guests. Not to mention the second time I saw him scoping out the Crown Room.

When I'd had my talk with Bautista earlier, he'd shown me a photograph of the blond man who'd tried to cut in on me at the reception counter yesterday. Since I hadn't yet touched base with my brother to find out if he wanted to get involved, I told the detective I'd never seen him before.

I'd been about to discuss the situation with my brother, but then Sykes had called him away. If Edward wanted to have secrets, so would I. Besides. The information might not be worth much anyway. At least that's what I told myself.

Was the person Harry tried to reach necessarily the killer? No. But in my experience, you only ignore coincidences if you want to end up on the receiving end of a deadly blow from a cane wielded by a mad woman.

It wasn't the first time my brother had abandoned me to play policeman. I'd done a good job before looking into crimes without him, though I admit one set of eyes isn't as efficient as two. That's how I wound up almost getting creamed by the cane. Only Edward's interference saved me from a humiliating death.

Big brother's rescue came with its own embarrassments, making it appear I needed him to finish a case. It was time to correct that error.

Before I could ruminate over possible next steps, Frankie Bowers stood in front of me with a fake smile plastered on her puss.

"Why aren't you with your brother?" She blinked a few times, affecting innocence.

"He's helping the police with their inquiries."

She gave an unladylike snort. "That's one way of putting it. It's frustrating being left on the outside looking in. But it doesn't have to be that way."

Her eyes narrowed and her lips puckered in what I supposed was an attempt at a sly look. Or maybe she was having a fit. I put her out of her misery. And mine.

"Look. You're not good at this. Why don't we stick to plain speaking, and you tell me what you have in mind."

Her cheeks puffed up with air and she blew it out. "Great. I prefer direct. I need your help. You won't have to do much. You're a decoy."

"A decoy for what?"

"You need to help me get into the zoo. The San Diego Zoo. The one Harry the vet worked at."

"Who is Harry the vet?" I hoped to make her squirm for omitting that information when we met her and her husband on our walk this morning.

"You don't know? You're probably the only one who

doesn't. Everyone's talking about it, though I'm not sure how they found out. He's the man who died this morning. At least, I found him this morning. I'm not sure when he died. I want to go to the zoo and—and find out more about him."

"Funny. You had nothing to say when my brother and I saw you on the beach this morning. Or maybe he wasn't carrying ID when you found him on your patio, and you only just now realized who he was. Or maybe you just forgot to mention it. Has it all come back to you?"

Her skin took on a greenish cast. "Fine. I found him on our patio this morning. There was a dense fog—"

"It's called a marine layer."

"Aren't they the same thing?"

She had me there.

"Anyway, I found him. I got his blood all over my arms and—" She shuddered. "You have no idea what it's like to find a corpse."

She had that wrong.

"He was cold, and the blood was sticky, and he wouldn't wake up . . . And then I had to leave all my clean underwear behind, and Bowers didn't have any time to grab some clothes before the police came . . . "

She struggled to keep her voice even. I'd wanted to make her suffer, but it wasn't as much fun as I thought it would be.

"I've got the picture. Now, why do you want to go to the zoo?"

"You have to agree it would help us understand what happened to him if we filled in Harry's background. That background is at the zoo."

"What you say makes sense. It might be interesting." And safer. And even rogue investigators had sidekicks.

She pressed her lips together and averted her eyes, which made her look furtive. She was the most transparent person I'd ever encountered. "Oh, no. It will just be a boring walk. Nothing unusual will happen. Nothing at all."

The lobby had emptied of people. "Okay. It's more interesting than hanging around here. I have to hit our house first."

"And I have to change."

My gaze scanned her. She had on jeans over her long legs and a peach sweater over the rest of her, neither of them too tight. They let you know she had a nice figure without rubbing your face in it. "You look fine."

"Fine isn't good enough. Not for what I want to do."

My mother taught me to never argue about a woman's wardrobe. We arranged to meet out front in fifteen minutes.

* * *

I'm not in the habit of bringing women home with me, which is why our housekeeper, Mrs. Abernathy, lifted her eyebrows when we walked through the front door of Edward's Spanish-style home. That and the platinum blond wig Frankie wore along with big, round sunglasses that made her look like a celebrity in hiding. The rest of her outfit remained the same. It was her idea of a disguise.

I lifted my eyebrows right back at her. "Edward said the house was empty."

"He suggested I take a vacation. Strongly, too. But it's easier to work without you two around, so I wanted to take advantage of your absence."

She took another look at Frankie. Ever the professional, Mrs. A merely said, "I wasn't expecting you back before Sunday afternoon. Will the two of you be staying for lunch?"

"No, thank you, Ma'am," Frankie said.

"Frankie and I are headed to the zoo, but Edward needed some replacement clothes first." The wig and the sunglasses were killing me. "She's part of the *Some Like It Hot* convention. That's her costume."

A look of relief passed over our housekeeper's face, and she nodded. "I heard about the discovery of a dead man at the hotel." She raised her shoulders and dropped them with a sigh. "Another body."

Frankie gasped. "Another one?"

I'm not ashamed to admit that Mrs. Abernathy is one of the few people to whom I can't lie. She's like a mother to me. A well-paid mother. Not that my own mother is dead, but her constant cruises—several a year—make her hard to reach.

In response to Mrs. A's unspoken question, I held my hand at waist level and pointed a subtle finger at Frankie Bowers, letting her know I wasn't responsible for this one. Mrs. A gave my guest a reappraising glance.

"Where did you hear about the, um, death?" Frankie choked out the words.

"It's all over the radio. The television, too, I assume, though I've not got time for that. They didn't say much. Just that he had been found on someone's patio."

After considering Frankie's dazed expression, she retrieved her cell phone and brought up a news site. We both looked over her shoulder at footage from a news helicopter's view of the police cordoning off the area.

Frankie blew out a breath. "That was my patio." She sniffed. "My honeymoon patio. A sweet gift from my husband's coworkers." A single tear squeezed out and rolled down her cheek. "And then we were moved to another room, an even better room, a cottage, but we had to leave most of our clothes and things behind. They let us take what was on our backs. Fortunately, my husband—he's a policeman—knew what to expect and told me to dress in layers. But he was so worried about me he didn't grab anything for himself. We saved for our honeymoon but . . . Buying him enough clothes to last the weekend will use up a lot of our savings."

"Oh, you poor thing." To my amazement, our housekeeper enveloped her in a hug. I wasn't aware the formal and efficient Mrs. A handed out hugs. She'd certainly never offered one to me or Edward.

She led my guest to the kitchen, clucking over her like a mother hen, and made her sit at the small kitchen table. "You need some sugar. It helps with the shock. Do you drink tea?" Before Frankie could answer, she waved off the question. "That will take too long to make properly." She swept a plate of cookies from the counter. "Caramel Chocolate Crunchies. My own special recipe. They were a surprise for the boys, but you need them more."

"If you insist," Frankie murmured, taking two.

"I could use some sugar, too," I said, and she reluctantly offered me the plate.

"It doesn't seem fair to let you get a head start on your brother."

I scooped up three more and put them in a sandwich bag. "I'll get these to him."

Mrs. A joined Frankie at the table. Another first. "If you don't want to talk about it, I understand. But, if it makes you feel better to get it off your chest, I'm here to listen. I make no judgments."

While Frankie poured out her tale, I made mental notes. My pulse quickened when she described the blood, but, to my disappointment, she hadn't gotten a frontal view of the corpse. I didn't know anything about the cause of death except it was messy.

Her recital was clear, but she included too many details of the room—both the original Cabana and the replacement Beachside Cottage—though Mrs. A appreciated them.

Mrs. A patted her hand. "Don't you let this setback keep you from enjoying your honeymoon. You only get one, if you're lucky." She stood. "Did your brother want a particular outfit?"

"Pants, socks, and shoes. Chocolate. And could you grab me a pair of jeans and some tennis shoes, please?"

She excused herself to retrieve the articles from our bedrooms.

We moved to the living room. As Frankie wandered through the space, it made me see our home through fresh eyes. It was a nice room, with an oversize white leather couch and two leather recliners on either side of the fireplace next to a large bookcase. Maple hardwood floors and neutral walls. Solid walnut furniture and not too many knick-knacks. I wasn't embarrassed to bring a guest here.

She took a seat on the couch, and I dropped down next to her. "You want to tell me the plan? What happens when we get to the zoo."

She got vague on me. "We walk."

"Okay. We walk. Are we looking for anything particular?"

"Nooo. I just want another look at the animals."

"Two sets of eyes are better than one. Are you sure you don't want to tell me?"

She turned a set of hazel eyes on me. "I appreciate your offer to help me, and you are by providing cover. I need to go to the zoo unrecognized, and no one will look twice at you."

"Thanks."

My sarcasm bounced off her.

"Women will, but not the staff. Unless they are women staff, but they'll be looking at you, not me, and that's what I want."

"I'm eye candy?" She flushed pink, so I skipped the comedy. "Why is it a problem if you're recognized?"

"It's not." She answered too quickly. "I don't want interruptions, that's all."

"The last time I was interrupted walking around the zoo was . . . never."

I'd led her to the point where she would either lie about what happened at the zoo, smooth over the incident, or give me the truth. Her answer would decide if she remained my sidekick.

Her hands twisted in her lap. "I've sort of been banned."

"Sort of?"

"Okay. I've been banned, but I need to get back in."

"Do I need to know why you were banned? You didn't murder anyone, did you?"

"Har-de-har-har. I got too close to the tiger. They didn't like it."

The rumors were true. "There's that tiger again."

"She's very popular, being white and all. It's rare."

I waited for more, but she proved she could keep quiet if it suited her. "Fine. We'll play it your way. But if you try anything funny, you're on your own unless I approve first."

Our housekeeper returned with several suit bags. She handed me one. "This is for your brother. This one is for you." Then she handed me the last and largest one. "I took the liberty of packing some of your clothes for Mr. Bowers. I don't know how big he is—"

"The same height as Nicholas." Frankie blushed as she said this, perhaps remembering how she mistook me for her husband that first day.

"Isn't that lucky?"

After asking if I needed anything else, she gave Frankie a final hug and returned to the kitchen.

We spent the first five minutes of the drive in silence while I guessed which of my clothes Mrs. A had packed. Knowing her, my best. I didn't know how to feel about another man wearing my pants.

I finally nudged my mind back onto the current situation. Jimmy Bianchi's interest in Mrs. Bowers rose to the top of my list. He thought she knew something about the murder. She preferred direct, so I was.

"Tell me about Harry."

She turned away from the passenger window. "Harry? Oh. The vet. What's to tell? He worked on the animals at the zoo, I assume."

"What do you mean, you assume. Didn't you know him?"

She dove into a garbled explanation that included the definition of "know."

"Had you met him before?"

"Before I found him? Naturally. That's how I knew who he was when Bowers told me."

"But you didn't know him?"

"No."

I clenched my jaw and spoke through my teeth. "But you met him at the zoo."

"Yes. After the, um, incident with the tiger. He was standing there and saw me. Two other men were there. Jose Alvarado, Suri's keeper, and Antonio Sabato, the curator of mammals. We went to Antonio's office and talked a while. That's when they banned me."

"Did anyone, anyone at all, say anything interesting?"

Taking her upper lip in her lower teeth, she shook her head. "Oh. Jose got mad because Harry didn't know the tiger's name was Suri."

Seemed like a silly reason to get mad, and not a good motive to kill a man.

"Let's review what we know about the murder."

She turned sideways in her seat. "Go ahead."

"Ladies first."

"Well . . . I don't know how he was killed, so, the killer could be a woman or a man. I mean, I know he was stabbed, but I don't know what weapon the killer used. Would a woman have the strength to stab a man if he were upright and ready to defend himself?" She looked at her upturned palms and wiggled her fingers, a move that was either cute or terrifying.

"I hate that this is happening," she continued, "but I do wish I'd had the presence of mind to, um, peek at him. I feel like a coward."

Her voice had dropped to a whisper. That made me feel kindly toward her, as I would any woman who admitted a weakness. It's so rare. "That's okay. When did you find out who he was?"

"My husband told me when we were walking on the beach."

That must have been when she'd turned to the ocean

and waved her arms around. She was shaking off the residue of murder. It was coincidence that the seagulls hovered in front of her while she did so. I wondered if she had food.

"How about you?" she asked. "Had you seen him before?"

A surreptitious glance revealed only curiosity on her puss. I felt no guilt when I said no.

"But you live in the area. Don't you visit the zoo?"

"Regularly, but I've never talked to the vets. And I've never spotted a wild curator, let alone an untamed keeper."

Usually, my humor charms the ladies. Frankie just sat back, deep in thought. She wasn't bright enough to get my references.

When we got to the gate, she turned to me with a flushed face. "I didn't bring my purse. I thought they might recognize it. You know, if some security guy is watching the cameras."

I pulled out the company credit card and tried to think how to expense the trip.

Chapter Seventeen

Frankie: The Story Behind Suri

For the second time in as many days, I found myself hiking the hills of the San Diego Zoo. Unlike yesterday, I had a mission. We would do a quick pass by some animal enclosures—I didn't care which ones—so I could do a brief survey to get the residents' opinion of Harry before returning to Tiger Trail to visit Suri.

It might be a waste of time. I had already witnessed Jose's attitude toward the vet. He felt Harry slacked off with the animals. Still, it's always wise to verify statements. I wanted the opinions of Harry's patients directly from the source.

Using a method I'd developed over time, I created an imaginary highway between my mind and theirs and sent each animal an image of Harry Reed.

The orangutans stared, surprised that I'd invaded their minds. The ape wanted to continue the conversation, going so far as to approach me, his powerful arms carrying him to the edge of his enclosure. I stumbled back when he hit me with an image of a key. One he wanted me to get for him. He knew how to use it and wanted to break out. When he showed me how he intended to express his appreciation, I fled.

"Wait up," Nicholas said, his long legs catching up in no time. "You shouldn't make faces at the gorillas. The one back there didn't care for it."

"You're imagining things."

As we walked, he pulled the plastic baggie from his pocket and removed a cookie.

"Aren't those for your brother?"

"What Edward doesn't know can't hurt him." He took a gigantic bite.

"Then you lied to Mrs. Abernathy."

He stopped chewing and studied me through narrowed eyes. The remaining cookies went back into his pocket.

When we reached the chimpanzees, I crossed my fingers and hoped for a direct response to my question. The orangutans and the gorilla hadn't shown much interest in Harry. He might not have tended to them.

After building the highway to the four largest monkeys atop a jungle gym of sorts, I sent an image of Harry. Oddly, one of them threw back an image of a pair of scissors.

The largest rose and bared his teeth. Big teeth. The one next to him—or her—held up a leafy branch and snapped it in two. I'd have to adjust my approach.

As soon as I finished a moving picture of Harry approaching their enclosure with bunches of bananas in hand, the four reached their hands back under their bottoms in unison. A wave of malicious pleasure flooded me.

"Run!" I double-timed it to the far side of the concrete

path. Nicholas reacted without question, making it to my side as the first lob splatted on the sidewalk where we'd stood moments before. Their "playful" gesture prompted shrieks from passing tourists.

"I wonder how they do that," Nicholas said. "Poop on command. It might be a handy talent."

His tone was conversational, but when he turned to face me, a warning reflected in his gray eyes.

"Are you ready to tell me what you're doing? Besides making faces at the animals?"

Drat. Bowers had been the first to point out the facial contortions I made when "talking" to my clients.

"I don't know what you mean. You can't make me responsible for animal behavior."

For emphases, I flipped my nose in the air and strode away. Time to head to the main attraction.

As we headed down Tiger Trail, I paused before the black-and-white tapirs to get the opinion of a non-primate. Without opposable thumbs, they couldn't retaliate like the chimps.

Once again, Harry approached the door to the enclosure. I made sure to omit anything that might hint at a painful checkup. No medical bag. No syringe. No bottle of nasty medicine. To make his image appealing, I went so far as to give him a bag of carrots. I hoped tapirs like carrots.

Startled, the tapir let loose a high-pitched shriek. I soaked up the anger, the fear, and a feeling akin to helplessness. A desire to let out my frustration built in my chest. Before I could disconnect, I let loose a matching shriek, stomped my foot, and snorted, slapping my hands over my mouth when I realized what I'd done.

Nicholas grabbed my elbow and hissed, "What in holy hell are you doing?"

"I'm not an expert on tapirs, or chimps, or any wild animal, really." Still fuzzy from my attachment to the tapir, I unwisely finished my thought. Out loud. "But it seems Dr. Harry wasn't well-loved by his patients."

My brain caught up with me, and I realized I'd shared my thoughts with a man other than Bowers. I let out a fake tee-hee. "At least that's my guess. They don't look sad that he's gone, do they?"

Nicholas couldn't resist another glance at the tapirs, and I took advantage of his distraction to pull away and head for the tiger enclosure.

Suri stretched to her full length in the mouth of her den, her cub between her paws. Harry might not have tended to all the animals in the zoo, but he was the tiger's vet. Why else would he have been there the night of her delivery?

"Everything looks peaceful here," Nicholas said from my side.

"Yes."

"Let's keep it that way."

Though I didn't want to trouble the mommy tiger with memories of the birth, that was the last time Harry had been with her. I needed to know if there had been anyone else nearby. Someone who might have had it in for the vet.

Before rolling out the mental highway, I thought through my approach. If I made the birth a joyful experience by tying it to the sweet thing gnawing on her toe, she could focus on the positive aspects of the delivery. I'd start there.

Just as I connected with the tiger, her cub wiggled close to her side and started to nurse.

"Ouch." When I instinctively rubbed the corresponding sore spot on my body, Nicholas yanked my arms to my side.

"Nice ladies don't do that in public."

His jostling didn't disconnect me. I could feel the tiger relax, and my own shoulders lowered.

Now for the image of Harry.

Suri shot to her feet and roared, sending her cub rolling like a tiny ball. She took three threatening steps forward and scanned the enclosure, searching for the enemy.

Harry was the enemy? Though I'd heard about women in labor who used language that would make a strong man blush, they got over it the moment they saw the beautiful result of all that pain. Suri hadn't forgotten.

As soon as my thoughts turned to the cub, the tiger let loose another roar. Anger, no, fury rose in my breast, and a raw cry burst out of me as I shook my fist at an unseen enemy.

A man in a tan outfit jogged over. "What's going on?"

Nicholas stepped forward. "You work here?"

"I'm Suri's keeper, Jose. Something has irritated her. Even before that woman yelled, she was stressed."

"Did you hear about her vet? Harry Reed? Maybe she senses he's gone."

The keeper's jaw clenched. "He wasn't her vet. Not exclusively. He didn't even know her name. He would stop by to look at her, but he never asked questions, like how she was eating, if she was behaving normally, her sleep habits. I had to offer everything."

"Sounds like a stinker. How did he get along with people?"

"His mother must have loved him," Jose grumbled.

"That bad. No wonder someone killed him."

The keeper kept his eyes on the tiger. "How did he die?"

With Nicholas keeping the tiger's keeper busy with details about the murder as far as he knew them, I returned to Suri. This time, I skipped Harry and focused on Suri's delivery. She let out a roar, this one accompanied by the weight of sadness. Mourning.

Something pulled at my breastbone, and suddenly, as clearly as if I'd been there, it was night.

My head swam; my thoughts fuzzy. But maybe that's what childbirth does to a woman.

Harry, crouched by my feet, caught something, and set it on a blanket.

He turned back as if expecting something to happen, and, sure enough, another cub came out.

He gasped and held up a pure white tiger, without stripes.

Harry whistled.

While I panted, he placed the first cub at my side. Then he wrapped up the white cub and carried it through the gate.

As the zoo came back into focus, the tiger gave another mournful cry. I couldn't leave her distraught, so I sent her images of the cub at her side. She pulled the little guy between her front legs and licked his face. My muscles untensed, and I let go of her.

As I returned to the present, my hand was wet. Probably because I was licking it.

"We should head back to The Del," Nicholas said.

"The Del?" Jose grinned. "Say hi to Darby for me. What am I saying? Chances are, you won't bump into him."

"Darby?"

"Older guy. Big. Was a groundskeeper here. At least until Harry got him fired. Now there's someone who's happy Harry's dead." He shared his smile with me. "Hey." His eyes narrowed into slits. "I recognize you. You're the lady we banned from the park."

"You're mistaken," Nicholas said. He grasped my hand in his. And I licked it.

As I caught myself, I noticed a man watching us from about twenty feet away. He wore a navy-blue double-breasted jacket with white piping on the lapels, a white shirt and pants, navy tie, and a dark captain's hat. A costume. Someone from the convention had witnessed the show, and now I'd have to explain it with another lie.

A sigh of relief escaped when I realized he wasn't watching me. He had his gaze fixed on Nicholas.

"What's she doing?" Jose demanded.

Dang it. I'd licked him again.

"It's our way of expressing affection, right darling?" He gave my hand a quick lick and barely controlled a grimace.

"Weren't you with a different guy last time? You're both coming with me," he said.

As we walked, Nicholas leaned his head close. "Are you okay?"

"I'm fine," I slurred, yawning wide.

"Are you sure? You seem—stop licking my hand."

Chapter Eighteen

Edward and Bowers: Assisting the Police

Edward Harlow, Detective Martin Bowers, Detective Jonah Sykes, and Sergeant Bautista studied each other in that surreptitious way men do before accepting new teammates. Accessing posture, tone, and words spoken to determine the natural hierarchy and any potential irritants. Deciding how much to say and what to hold back. Wondering where they stood with the others. And then pretending the evaluation never took place.

"Gentlemen," Bautista began. "I appreciate you staying behind. Your expertise is noted and welcome, though the Coronado Police Department is in charge of the case."

"What's his expertise?" Bowers asked, gesturing at Edward Harlow. "No offense."

"None taken. I've been fortunate enough to assist Detective Sykes on occasion."

"I wouldn't say assist." Sykes' wife had come to the rescue, sparing him the embarrassment of investigating in a dress with two suits, shirts, and ties. Her consideration left him feeling generous. "You have been helpful with your insights."

"I checked you out," Bautista said. "You also helped the police in Illinois with other cases."

"A private detective?" Bowers asked.

"No," Edward said with regret. "Just a sharp wit, unrivaled observation skills, and an ability to put people at ease."

"Not that you'll be working with us," Bautista clarified, "but I'm not shy about asking for your thoughts. You're both observant." He nodded at Bowers. "You from your training and experience, and Mr. Harlow from . . . let's say you're naturally observant, which is exactly what we need. For instance, I understand you're a writer and have attracted fans, so plenty of people have seen you and vice versa. Can you tell me if you've seen this man since you arrived?"

He held out a picture of Harry Reed. Edward glanced at it, then glanced again.

"Has anyone else recognized this man?"

The detective hesitated.

"My wife and I did," Bowers said.

Edward nodded. "Well, now you have three witnesses. I saw him come through the front doors to the lobby yesterday afternoon. He walked up to the reception counter. He spoke with the clerk for a few minutes. He left."

"Did you hear what he said?"

"I did not. I wasn't close enough. He spoke to the male clerk." He returned the photograph to Bautista. "You have me at a disadvantage. I assume that's the man who died on the premises." He spread his hands. "And, of course, I assume it wasn't a natural death or we wouldn't be here."

"You're right." Bautista set down the photograph. "This morning at approximately eight a.m., Detective Bowers' wife opened the drapes to their room. She saw someone sitting in the chair. It was Harry Reed, and he was dead."

"Good gad. That's terrible. How did the man die?"

"Someone stabbed him with a weeder. It's a long, metal tool with a split end, for pulling up weeds."

"I have one at home. How much force would it take to impale a man with that tool?"

The detective's gaze roamed over Edward's large build. "Quite a bit, I would think, but I'll let the coroner decide that. He also had a gash on his cheek. That's where most of the blood came from. I mean the blood your wife got on her arms." He glanced at Edward. "She thought at first it was her husband and wrapped her arms around his shoulders."

"I'm so sorry to hear that."

Bowers accepted his sympathy with a curt nod. "I'm not sure why she would think I'd ever where a hat lined with sunflowers, but she says she thought it was a joke."

Bautista tapped his desk. "He wasn't killed there. Not enough blood. If his murder occurred on the beach, it will be impossible to find footprints. I'd hoped there might be signs of a scuffle closer to the sidewalk, but no luck."

"It makes the most sense that he was killed on the beach," Bowers said. "Better than hauling a dead body from the parking lot or through the hotel."

"True. My officers went over the beach." He frowned. "It was pristine. Not a scrap of litter. Nothing."

Sykes put in a question. "Was the victim registered as a guest?"

"He was not. Harry Reed, DVM. Joined the San Diego Zoo six months ago after leaving a private practice in a rural area that handled both small animals and farm animals. They also served rescues, which is where he kept up his skills with wild animals. He'd interned with the zoo years ago but hadn't landed a position with them. No idea why not. He had the qualifications.

"Our information so far tells us the first time he showed up at the Coronado was the last. At least we thought so until you mentioned seeing him in the lobby. We'll interview the registration staff next. None of the bartenders or wait staff remember him, though they're extra busy with the convention. And we haven't had a chance to interview the zoo staff."

"I did wonder about the hotel's employees." When Bautista sent Bowers a questioning glance, he clarified. "The ones who might be on the beach as part of their jobs."

"I was just about to suggest that," Edward said.

The door opened, and an officer led in a man in a green uniform.

"Green," Bowers murmured.

Bautista nodded, and his slight grin held the hint of victory. "I was just about to speak with Mr. Darby. Mr. Clarance Darby. Your duties include maintaining the beach. Is that correct?"

Mr. Darby, a lugubrious man with gray hair and bushy eyebrows accepted the offer of a chair. "That is correct." He glanced around at the group standing over him. "Is this a party?"

"Detective Bowers and Mr. Harlow are consulting

with the police. I'd like to begin with any duties you have that take you to the beach."

"Someone has to clean up the messes the guests leave behind."

"You mean trash?" Edward asked. "Wrappers and napkins and such?"

"That, too. Sandcastles. People leave them up for everyone to admire. Do you know what a sandcastle looks like after a night of wind and water? A pile of sand. And there's those who like to bury their friends in the sand. I had a cousin that died that way. Suffocated. To be fair, no one has died on this beach until today, but they leave the pit behind for someone to fall in, which is worth at least a broken ankle. I rake the sand back in shape."

"You use a rake?"

"Well, sometimes a broom. We are environmentally aware here. I don't move the seaweed, unless it becomes a problem. Little critters count on it for food and such. I make the beach look good without tearing it up."

"Do you wait until the beach is empty to do this?" Bautista asked. "After dark, maybe?"

"No point in that. People stroll at night, too. I get to work early before the lazybones get up so everything's pristine. They all want a beach that looks like it hasn't been used. And though I'm only supposed to deal with the greenery and the beach, I find myself picking up after the guests like a common janitor. Paper cups and napkins. We have receptacles, you know."

Bautista sighed. "And you cleaned the beach this morning?"

"I did. Even had to clean up broken glass. People don't think."

"Broken glass?" Bautista asked sharply. "Where was this?"

"On the walkway leading to the beach from the Skating by the Sea Park. There's no skating now, but in the winter, the hotel covers the lawn with ice. Seems silly to me, but the hotel caters to all sorts."

"Do you still have the glass?"

Darby grinned. "As a keepsake? Course not. I threw it away."

After the detective pinned down exactly which receptacle and sent an officer to search it, he asked what time the landscaper had found the broken glass.

"Around five. Right after I dealt with the birds."

Bowers flinched. "Birds?"

"Those dang seagulls. I put up a kite with the face of a hawk on it every morning. Does no good. Little buggers peck at it. So, I shoo them off with a rake. Guests don't like to be pooped on or have their food snatched out of their hand."

Bowers sighed. "Revenge."

Sykes glanced his way. "What's that?"

"Sorry. I was thinking out loud. Possible motives for Harry's death."

Edward's thoughtful gaze remained on the Arizona detective.

Bautista pulled a picture out of a file and slid it across the desk. "Can you identify this?"

The old man paled. "Looks like my weeder. At least, I've got one just like it. Where did you find it?"

Which was a surprising question, since blood covered the tool. Bowers thought he should have asked: "How did blood get on my weeder?"

"When was the last time you saw this?"

"Yesterday morning. I was doing some detailed work on the roses. Then someone stole my tool bag."

Bowers cleared his throat. "You might want to check the planters in the Sheerwater."

"Now why would I do that?" But the expression on his face told a different story. His eyes stared at nothing as if replaying his movements yesterday. When he abruptly stood, Bautista asked where he was going.

He rubbed a big hand over his mouth. "To check on my tools."

"I'll send someone with you." Bautista opened the door and motioned to the officer in the lobby. They held a murmured conversation, and the woman and Darby walked away.

With the groundskeeper gone, Bowers explained. "My wife and I had dinner in the Sheerwater last night. I noticed an old tool bag in one of the planters."

"Thanks. That will save some time."

"Now, I know people are behaving oddly with the convention. Men dressed as women and vice versa. I've even seen a few in yachting caps. A lot of them are dressed as gangsters. They're living in a fantasy world, and some people can take that too far. Did either of you see anyone who might fit that bill?"

"In that case, wouldn't they use a tommy gun?" Edward spread his look among the men. "Or a facsimile?"

"In the real world," Sykes said, "criminals use whatever is handy. Gun. Knife. Baseball bat."

"Weeder," Edward added.

The uniformed officer returned just then, alone.

"Did you find the tool bag?"

"We did. I told Mr. Darby not to touch it. Marx is standing by until forensics retrieve it. It's an old canvas bag with pockets on the outside. A few tools are missing, including the weeder."

"Could Mr. Darby identify the other missing tools?"

"A trowel and some snippers, but he says he used them recently and must have set them down. He's had the bag for over thirty years, and it looks it."

Bautista pulled out his cell phone and issued instructions to cordon off the walkway between The Cabanas and the skating area. "Dozens of people have trampled any possible evidence, but it's worth a try." He then spread his hands. "Is there anything else of interest either of you have heard or seen in the last twenty-four hours?"

When the men offered no additional information, Bautista excused them.

"Please remain, Detective Sykes."

Once Edward and Bowers were out of the room, the elder Harlow brother asked the detective if he were satisfied with their interview.

Bowers grinned. "It's all ego, but I thought they wanted our help. So, I'm disappointed. Still, I don't know enough about what's going on to have any incites."

Edward nodded. "I'd better hunt down my brother."

"Same here. Hunt down my wife, I mean."

Five minutes later, the two men ran into each other in the parking lot. Bowers put his hands on his hips and grinned. "The zoo?"

"We can take my car. No need to put miles on your rental."

But when Edward approached the valet, he found that Nicholas had already checked out their car.

Chapter Nineteen

Edward and Bowers: A Trip to the Zoo with Surprising Results

On the drive to the zoo, the men pooled their information. Most of it.

"Was there anyone near Harry who might have heard what he was talking about?"

Edward turned on the car's blinker to signal his exit from the freeway. "I'll have to get back to you on that."

Bowers, an experience interviewer, recognized this as an evasion. "He could have been asking for a guest. If he wasn't registered here, why else would he approach the front desk?"

Edward agreed. "I wish I had paid more attention to who was in the lobby. The man left in a hurry, as if he'd seen something—or someone—unexpected."

"Another guest? Or someone who worked for the hotel?"

"I just don't know."

This time, Bowers sensed Edward answered with the truth.

"What was your point about the man in the green

uniform?" Edward slipped his passenger a glance. "Why green?"

"An assumption. Outdoor employees—the ones who deal with the plants and the landscaping—usually wear tan or green. I went with green. And I'd spotted the tool bag in the planter at last night's dinner."

"And that made you think of a gardener. That makes sense. Do you believe Mr. Darby was merely raking the sand this morning and not killing Harry Reed?"

Bautista had questioned Darby at length on the subject. Did he remember a spot near the sidewalk where the sand showed signs of a scuffle? Were the footprints on the path made from wet sand? But the landscaper couldn't recall.

Bowers answered the question. "It's unfortunate that he probably wiped away any signs of a struggle, but I think he was telling the truth. When he caught the implication that one of his own tools was used to kill someone, his reaction seemed genuine."

As Edward turned into the zoo parking lot, he blurted out a topic that had been on his mind. One that he'd found too awkward to ask. "You're wife. She thought Harry Reed was you."

"Because he was on our patio. Why should she expect anyone else?"

"She didn't notice anything unusual about him?"

"She was surprised I'd wear a hat with flowers on it, but she thought it was a joke."

"Did you, er, check his pockets?"

"He wasn't found in my jurisdiction."

"Naturally, you wouldn't want to take liberties. However, if it were a body on my patio . . ." Edward let the thought hang.

"The note had the numbers three thousand crossed off and replaced with fifty thousand. Then seventy-five thousand replaced the fifty thousand. My guess is these are dollars, and Harry was selling something he shouldn't."

"And Harry was the vet at a zoo where a white tiger recently gave birth. Interesting."

The first call was the Office of the Curator of Mammals.

So distracted was he by events, Antonio Sabato didn't seem surprised to see them.

"This is terrible." He gestured toward two seats. "I don't suppose there's any way to keep his murder from being linked to the zoo. No. Probably not."

"He wasn't murdered at the zoo," Edward offered helpfully.

"There is some comfort in that."

Bowers hoped Sabato wouldn't hold yesterday's kerfuffle with the tiger against him and launched into his questions. "Did Harry get along with his fellow employees? Yesterday, Jose seemed to resent him."

Antonio shifted in his chair. "Harry was—my mother would have called him a pill." Edward chuckled appreciatively, and the curator relaxed. "I suppose when you're good at your job, it's easy to become arrogant. But every vet we employ is good at their job."

"But Harry thought some jobs were more worthy than others?" Edward stroked his chin.

"Exactly. Jose is dedicated to the tigers. He's their keeper, and he knows them each. Their names. Their personalities. Their likes and dislikes. I've heard him say they are like family. Though, of course, they would rip him to pieces if there weren't bars between them."

Bowers grinned. "Just like family." He adjusted his expression. "Tell me. Is it usual to have veterinarians present at the birth of an animal?"

"Oh, no. It's much less stressful for the animal to give birth naturally. They've been doing so since the beginning of time. We only call in the vets if we notice something unusual. There are cameras that allow us to keep an eye on them."

"And the camera showed something unusual with the birth?" the detective persisted.

Antonio hesitated. "I don't know. What I mean is, I can't tell you. Someone tampered with the camera over the tiger enclosure. The one with the best view. Not directly, but—I wish people would understand that zoos aren't playgrounds. These are wild animals and serious business. Some hooligan was flying a drone disguised as a bird. The cameras are motion sensitive, so they focused on the movement. I'm afraid whoever it was planned to taunt the animals. If it were legal, I'd set up some type of cannon to blow them out of the sky once they entered zoo property."

Edward spread his hands. "Then how did Harry know the tiger was in trouble?"

"I'll give him credit for being a good vet. You don't always know a tiger is pregnant. They don't ovulate until they've, er, done the deed, and then they don't show until the last ten days or so. Jose pointed out to Harry that she was seeking solitude. Usually, Suri enjoyed watching the kiddies. Probably fantasized about hunting them down and eating them. That's one of the signs a tiger is ready to have her cubs. She hides. But there you go. There's that arrogance. Harry, afraid he was jumping to conclusions, didn't mention it to me or the other vets."

"Animal husbandry may be different with tigers than, say, cows," Bowers said, "but on my sister's farm, the animals need a father. That tiger was alone."

"About three months ago, the Heaven's Gate Wildlife Sanctuary in Ohio closed their big cat program. I dare say they didn't know she was pregnant at the time, or they wouldn't have let her go. Or they would have, knowing she'd get good care here. As it was, we were extremely lucky. Harry was on the spot. He had stayed late to do an analysis on hippo feces."

"Doesn't sound lucky," Bowers murmured. Edward snorted and covered it with a cough.

Antonio gave them a tolerant smile. "Harry supervised the delivery. It was the tiger's first birth, and she had trouble. He said once the baby was safely delivered, Suri collapsed from exhaustion. Thankfully, she didn't require intervention. I don't know how he would have handled it alone. He took quite a chance to make sure the baby came out healthy. I'll give him credit. She seems to have recovered from the event."

"Who's recovered?" A stocky Asian woman entered the room and halted when she noticed Bowers and Edward. "Oh. I can come back."

Antonio waved her in. "I'd like to introduce you to another of our veterinarians. Sylvia Yang. We were just discussing Harry."

"I heard about his death."

A simple statement unaccompanied by platitudes or regrets.

"These gentlemen were interested in Harry's role in Suri's delivery."

"Pure negligence." Her dark eyes snapped. "He should have alerted us as soon as he suspected she was pregnant so we could monitor her and set up a den where she could have the baby away from gawking tourists. I'm not happy Harry is dead, but I'm relieved he'll no longer work here."

Before Antonio could interrupt the flow, Bowers asked what she would have done in the same situation.

"Notified the other vets and her keeper of her condition as soon as I suspected something. And you, Antonio. Monitored her diet and movements closely. As I said before, set up a birthing den. We might have gotten an ultrasound if we'd had enough time."

"How on earth would you have done that?" Edward said. "Wouldn't it be dangerous to sedate a pregnant tiger?"

She nodded. "Vets have trained tigers to enter a small area, usually with meat as a lure, and then introduced them to the ultrasound device. Once the tiger gets familiar with it, the animal usually allows the vet to get the ultrasound. It's similar to clicker training a dog. The animal is never forced or pressured, so it doesn't get anxious."

Edward leaned forward, his elbows on his knees as if inviting a confidence. "Did you like Harry?"

"No. And before you think it's professional jealousy, I wouldn't have liked him if I'd met him socially. He was full of himself, dismissive of others, and, even worse, he let his self-involvement interfere with his professional judgment."

"That covers it," Bowers said. "Where were you the night Suri gave birth?"

She turned to him with a slight smile. "Here. One of the chimpanzees cut his hand on a pair of scissors some idiot had thrown into the enclosure. It wasn't deep, and, fortunately, it was Chuck. He's very good at showing us his hands and feet when we request it. I was able to take care of the injury with some antibiotic salve. I'll keep an eye on him."

"But otherwise, you would have been available to help out with the birth?"

"Harry knew I was here. He should have called me."

"But you were busy with Chuck."

"He didn't know that."

"Are you certain there was only one cub born that night?" The question came from Edward.

After a pointed study of the older Harlow brother, Bowers seconded the question.

The vet folded her arms. "Why do you ask?"

Edward spread his hands. "I don't know anything about tigers, but I am curious. Do they usually give birth to more than one cub?"

"The average is two to four cubs, but not every tiger is average. They can have as few as one or as many as seven. I haven't seen eight."

When the men were about to leave, Bowers turned back to the curator. "Do your vets ever wear green uniforms?"

"Green? Never, to my knowledge."

Once outside, Edward turned to the detective. "Do we look at the tiger enclosure?"

"Might as well."

They strode down the path deep in thought until Edward stopped walking. "Who the devil is that blond with Nicholas?"

Bowers followed his gaze. "Good grief. It's Frankie."

Edward raised his eyebrows. "Why is she licking his hand?"

Chapter Twenty

Frankie: Another Witness

The first thing I did on our return to the hotel was grab a courtesy bottle of water and step outside. I took a few slugs and sloshed the water around my mouth, then spit into the bushes.

When I glanced up, a woman watched my performance with a disgusted expression. It was the same Nosy Nellie who had witnessed my gum on the tennis shoe fiasco in the lobby. But I was too grossed out to care.

Pouring the water over my outstretched tongue, I scrubbed it with my available fingers. When I felt clean again, I finished off the bottle.

Bowers watched me, waiting until I could speak.

"Did you have to lick him?" He closed his eyes. "Never mind. I hate to ask, but was it worth it?"

I understood his meaning. "There was a second cub." He stayed silent so long, I added, "As in two."

"Just to be clear, you're saying the white tiger at the zoo—"

"Suri."

"Suri. You're telling me she delivered two cubs?"

"Yes. Harry wrapped the second cub in a blanket and took it away."

"He was in the enclosure? The tiger allowed that?"

"She seemed out of it. Maybe he drugged her."

"A dangerous thing to do with a pregnant cat, according to Dr. Sylvia Yang."

"From what I've heard about Harry, I get the feeling he wouldn't care. So, what did he do with the second cub?"

My husband gave me a pitying glance. "Maybe it didn't make it. That sometimes happens. Did you see it move?"

Unfortunately, he had a point. I'd been so wrapped up in what Harry was up to that I didn't notice the cub's movements. And Harry had wrapped it in the blanket, effectively hiding it from me. Had that been his intention? To hid the cub from its mother? Silly man.

"It was beautiful, Bowers. Pure white."

"A pure white tiger? I assume that's rare."

"Rarer than rare. What if Harry kept the cub for himself? He sounds like the kind of selfish so-and-so who might do that."

A spark passed through my husband's eyes. "We don't know his intentions for certain. And he's dead. And so might be the cub."

"You thought of something." I pointed at him. "I saw it in your face. You've had an idea."

"A rare tiger cub might bring a great deal of money from the right buyer. Maybe up to seventy-five thousand dollars."

"That's it! He stole the cub, brought it to the hotel for a trade-off, and the buyer killed him so they wouldn't have to pay. Cheapskate."

"It would be a good motive. However, there is no cub."

My mind raced. "And who better to do the dirty work than an employee here? No one would question him walking around the beach at night. The man in green. A workman who would carry a screwdriver. That's a tool you can stab a person with."

"About that." Bowers cleared his throat. "It wasn't a screwdriver. It was a weeder. I sat in on the interview with Mr. Clarence Darby, the head landscaper. Did you notice the work bag last night?"

"The one in the Sheerwater planter? But—that would make the murder premeditated. He planted the bag, and when the time came, he took out his weed puller and committed the murder." I shuddered. Thinking back to Jose's words, I had Darby's motive. "Revenge."

"Or it could be the man simply mislaid his tool bag. Oh. One of his jobs is to chase off the gulls."

I frowned. "Chase them? What does that have to do with—" The ball dropped. "Those sneaky birds lied to me?"

With a disgusted huff, I stormed to the water's edge and shook my fist at the flock as they hopped and scratched in the sand.

Once I had the connection, I sent an image of a guy in a green suit next to a dead body and drew a line through him. Their cries came short and sharp, and I felt them bounce around in my chest. They were laughing at me.

Suddenly, the leader, who I had named Amos, dove into the shallow water, coming up with a red crab in his beak. Twenty feet in the air, he dropped the poor critter on the beach.

"No you don't!" I ran for the crab and scooped him up

just as Amos came in for another grab. He veered off just short of nailing me with his beak. Holding the little guy close to my chest, I jogged to a scattering of rocks near the grassy edge of the path and tucked him under the largest one.

As I crouched in front of him, we made eye contact.

The sun disappeared.
A deafening thud came from behind me.
Two terrifying mountains moved my way, shaking the ground with each step.
I dove to my right, out of their path.
As they passed, I recognized them as two feet clad in a pair of dark dress shoes. And spats.

I gasped. Jimmy killed Harry? Common sense kicked in. We were at a convention where half the people dressed as mobsters. A small percentage of those wore spats.

"Nice save, though the gulls didn't appreciate it. Did you hurt yourself?" Bowers hooked me under the arms and lifted me to my feet. "Before you took off, I had something else to tell you. Harry Reed was seen in the hotel yesterday morning."

The gulls screeched and circled the crab's hiding place. I shot them an image of a bird on a spit browning nicely over a cozy fire. They scattered.

Bowers caught my glare at the gulls and changed the subject. "Nicholas Harlow was with you at the zoo. Did you, um, share what you were up to?"

"Of course not. And why were you and Edward Harlow at the zoo? I assumed you were looking for me, but your surprise when you saw me blew away that idea."

"Edward and I spoke to Antonio Sabato, the curator."

"And?"

"Harry wasn't a likable guy. He didn't alert the other vet when Suri went into labor, but she was busy tending to a chimpanzee with a cut and couldn't have helped him anyway."

"A cut?" I grabbed his wrist. "Were a pair of scissors involved?"

Bowers choked. I patted his back.

"I'll take that as a yes. But Harry should have sent for the other vet."

He coughed. "According to her, yes."

"But he didn't."

"No."

"Because maybe he knew there were twins and he wanted one for himself."

"Where is the evidence?" he asked once again.

"Oh!" I squeezed his arm. "Don't they have security cameras at zoos?"

"They do. Some smart aleck flew a drone into the park. The cameras are motion sensitive, so there's no recording of the birth."

That sounded suspicious to me, but it didn't damper my enthusiasm. I tapped my head. "There *is* a recording. Up here."

"One the police can use as evidence. So, we can't swear that Harry took the cub. And Darby's out as a suspect."

"About him," I began.

"I know you're disappointed because you thought you'd learned something valuable—"

"He only works at the hotel because Harry got him fired from the zoo."

Bowers tapped his fingers against his thigh. "You're source?"

"I overheard Jose tell Nicholas Harlow about it."

He reached for his shirt pocket. I poked his side with both fingers.

"You left your little detective notebook at home."

When my husband was on a case, he made notes in a small book. Detective Juanita Gutierrez had one just like it. They must be department issue.

"Anything else I should know?"

"Nothing important."

"Tell me anyway."

"It's silly. You know the older woman who dresses in pink? I was talking to her and her sister, Purple, about Harry. Their names are Polka and Dot if you can believe it."

"You brought it up how?"

"They were already talking about him. Pink—that's Dot—got worked up over him. You know. Tears and trembling lips. I heard he was rude to her at the zoo."

"Worked up?"

"The way Emily gets when she's in withdrawal and can't find her catnip mouse."

"Yikes."

"Anyway, Harry's death has shaken Dot up. It's shaken her up a lot." I hesitated. "They might have been having an affair."

"Who? Harry and, um, Dot? Isn't she in her late seventies? Early Eighties?"

"She quoted poetry, Bowers. That means love. If they *were* having an affair and he dumped her, shouldn't she be glad he was dead?"

"Or she might feel guilty about harboring bad thoughts about him."

I grinned. "Harboring. You're such a policeman."

He pulled me close for a long, slow kiss. When he raised his head, he mentioned something about handcuffs. Regrets that he hadn't packed his. Joking, of course. I think.

* * *

We'd missed lunch, so I convinced Bowers we'd find something to eat in the Crown Room. The hotel had set out a popcorn bar offering buttered, white cheddar, sea salt, and chocolate drizzle. Not a satisfying meal, but for once, I had something other than food on my mind.

As I wandered around the room, my gaze drifted to the floor. More specifically, to the feet on the floor. Someone wore spats to murder Harry Reed. If I could find a pair dirty with sand, I'd have the killer.

Susan Sweeney's announcement about a death turned some guests off the frivolity of costumes, but I still counted six pairs of spats encasing black shoes. Some of them were on men, some on women, but all on people in gangster outfits. And all of them were clean.

Since I wasn't looking, I bumped into Willie, with Rhonda at his side.

Willie had on a beige suit and wore a snappy fedora with a blue band. His wife looked spectacular in a gold, lace dress with a revealing, see-through yoke under which she wore a beige tube top.

"Did you drop something?"

"Just thinking."

"Girl, I do that all the time. Stare off into space when

I'm thinking. If we had cliffs by our home, I'd walk right over one when I'm deep in thought. What's on your mind?" Her smile lost a few watts. "The murder. You poor thing." She glanced up at her husband as if giving him a cue.

"If you want to forget your troubles, you've come to the right place." He patted me on the shoulder and led me to a table with open seats. "Where's your husband?"

I craned my neck, but Bowers wasn't at the buffet, and a quick scan of the room confirmed he'd left. I hoped he was scrounging up more substantial food.

"We missed lunch."

Rhonda took the chair to my right. "That's too bad. I had the Roasted Brussels Sprout Salad. Who knew Brussels sprouts could be good?"

"She's braver than me," Willie said, taking the seat on my left. "I stuck to the French Tuna Sandwich. I'm not sure what was French about it, but it was tasty."

"I'm not a cook," Rhonda confessed.

"I feel ya," I muttered. My inability to produce a delicious meal for my husband worried me. According to the advice book my mother had given me, my wedded bliss would end in an acrimonious divorce unless I mastered my kitchen skills. Then again, Willie still loved his wife.

"What were you doing that you missed lunch? Anything exciting?" She rested her hand on my forearm and shook it to add some enthusiasm.

If I relived my time at the zoo, I might lick her hand, so I gave a vague answer about touring San Diego.

"Where?" Willie's question shot out, but he followed it with a grin. "There's so much to see. Me and Ronnie were thinking about adding another day to check out the city, but it's hard to narrow it down. We'd love some recommendations."

Sounded reasonable. "I'd like to see Bob Hope entertaining the troops. And I've never been on a military ship. We're going to tour the USS Midway."

"How did you like the zoo?" Rhonda asked.

"From what I've seen, it's beautifully laid out. Very natural environments for the animals."

Had I told her about my visit to the zoo? The costumed man watching Nicholas must have had mentioned it. Oh, jeez. Had he mentioned anything else? Like my faces and licks, or our apprehension by Jose? If he had, I suspected their opening lines would have been, "*We heard you lick strange men when your new husband isn't around.*" Or, "*Do you find it amusing to taunt the animals with funny faces*?" I chased Paranoid Frankie away.

"Mind if we sit here, too?"

Dot and her sister, Polka, took the remaining chairs, and their first move was to take inventory of our home states. When Rhonda and Willie said Utah, Polka clapped.

"Go Mormon Tabernacle Choir."

Willie laughed. "Ronnie's tone deaf."

Rhonda clutched my arm. The woman had muscles. "Frankie here is on her honeymoon."

The ladies cooed and congratulated me.

"She also found that man's body. The one Susan talked about."

Dead silence.

Polka squeezed Dot's hand but kept her gaze on me. "Years from now, you'll certainly remember that. It's the little things. My only memory of my honeymoon was the best steak I've ever eaten."

"We saw Don Ho," Rhonda offered. "One of his last performances before he passed away."

After a moment of silence for the Hawaiian Mega-Star, everyone at the table agreed that would be an experience worth remembering.

The guy in the white-piped suit and captain's hat wandered past our table and bumped into Rhonda's chair.

"Pardon me."

Rhonda's surprise turned into curiosity. "You look familiar."

"Please, call me Oswald."

"Ooh," Rhonda said. "I get it. You look just like the man in the movie. The one who falls for Daphne."

The man rocked on his heels. "That's me. Osgood Fielding the Third."

"We're saving our costumes for the last night," Dot said with a note of apology.

Oswald pulled open his lapels. "It's surprisingly comfortable."

"And where are you from?" Rhonda asked.

"Mr. and Mrs. Fisher are from Utah," Polka said to prompt him.

Oswald clasped his hands together. "Home of the Mormon Tabernacle Choir. I'm afraid I don't have bragging rights. I'm from a small town east of St. Louis. Population twelve hundred and sixty-three."

"Go, Cardinals," Willie said.

"I'm not much of a sports fan." He dipped his head and—I swear it—he blushed. "I heard you had some excitement, young lady."

The young lady was me. He *had* noticed me at the zoo.

"It wasn't my fault," I began.

"I wouldn't dream of blaming you, but I'm afraid what I heard confused me. Did the man die of a heart attack?"

Oh. Harry. Not my favorite topic, but better than explaining why Jose dragged me and Nicholas Harlow away from the tiger enclosure.

When everyone waited with expressions of anticipation, I realized the police hadn't released Harry's cause of death. "Not exactly." They continued to stare. "I mean, he, well, he might have had help."

"Help?" Rhonda asked.

Dot's skin turned a paler shade.

Polka also changed color, but she chose pale green.

"It was probably an accident." I remembered the weapon. A weeder. "A gardening accident."

Rhonda frowned. "It was an employee? But then, how did he wind up on your patio?"

Just then, Bowers entered the room. I jumped to my feet. "My husband needs me."

Edna Tartwell's gorgeous niece intercepted him before I got there. She placed her hand on his arm and leaned her head close. And then my husband flipped her off. At least that's what it looked like until he pointed to his finger, and I realized he was displaying his wedding ring. Good golly. Was she deaf and blind? She had to know we were married from our encounter at the check-in counter. Some women are dense. Or evil.

I slipped my arm through his and gave her a bright smile. "Your aunt is looking for you."

She let her gaze linger on my husband before she left.

"What did Miss I-Need-a-Pencil want from you?"

"I'm not sure," he said, his gaze following her. Since it was his professional gaze, I watched her back as she wandered the room in search of Edna. I did so without a modicum of guilt.

"Don't give her another thought." I patted his arm. "I'll keep an eye on her."

He looked down at me, surprised, and grinned. "I'd rather you kept those hazel eyes on me."

"Done."

Susan Sweeney swept into the room, raised her arms, and waved her hands. "Ladies and gentlemen." She winked at a couple, he in a dress and she in a suit. "And vice versa. Enough of you have nagged us that we asked Mr. Edward Harlow if he could spare some time to answer any questions you might have. He has agreed to give us a half hour of his time in an impromptu interview in the Garden Room. Don't dawdle. You'll want a good seat."

"Shall we?" Bowers asked.

So, we did.

Chapter Twenty-One

Nicholas: Undressing Edward for the Fans

Susan Sweeney approached us after we returned from the zoo and asked if Edward would mind talking to his fans among the convention goers. Just a brief, informal chat. A freebie.

A corporate event had booked the Garden Room for their meeting last night and had left behind a small stage with three chairs.

White curtains hung as a backdrop, and in the preparation for this informal gathering, someone had set up a projector in the back of the room and splashed images from the movie on the material.

I retrieved a bottle of H_2O from the bar and set it next to one of the chairs.

Usually, whenever Edward gave a talk, I sat in one of the front row seats. Anyone who studied my habits, say, because they wanted to teach me a lesson for ratting on their friends, would know this. Under the circumstances, I retreated behind the curtains, joining Edward as he waited for his introduction.

My hand still tingled from the good scrubbing I'd

given it when we got back. Not that I suspected Mrs. Bowers of having cooties, but a strange woman licking your hand isn't as erotic as it sounds.

Thinking about Mrs. Bowers and hand-licking and zoos brought me to my conversation with Jose the tiger keeper. He had given me some intriguing points to ponder. Harry Reed sounded like a knucklehead. Any one of his co-workers, including Jose, would have been glad to see him gone, but would they have lured him to the Coronado to kill him on the beach? Would Harry have come? Under what pretense?

And I couldn't get past Harry's attempt to contact a guest. There must be a connection between that guest and his sudden death.

Susan approached my brother holding a huge, yellow dress. More of a tent. "You might want to put this on. Some of the more enthusiastic fans arrived today and . . . They have their expectations."

My brother declined.

Before long, fannies occupied the seats. Sue stepped up to the microphone. "Ladies and gentlemen. Going by the number of people who asked if we could get Mr. Edward Harlow to say a few words, most of you are familiar with Aunt Civility's books and advice column. Well, we asked, and he said yes."

The applause died down the minute he stepped out from behind the curtain. Their silence had an ominous feel, like the eye of a hurricane right before the wind picks up again.

"Where's your dress?" The woman in the fifth row might have been a man from the way her voice boomed. A few other hecklers joined in.

My brother looked down at his suit and back up again. "I'm dressed as a gangster."

Edward was wearing the chocolate brown suit. Even I knew gangsters wore black or gray, usually with pinstripes. Never chocolate brown. The audience was onto him.

It started with booing, followed by hisses. My brother tried to talk over them but finally stepped off the stage.

A personal assistant is always prepared. I held up the dress Sweeney had picked out for him—a lemon-yellow linen sheath. "I think it will fit."

He growled.

I helped him out of his jacket. He insisted on wearing the dress over his shirt and pants. A couple of yanks got the material over his broad shoulders, but the zipper refused to cooperate.

I stepped back and gave him an admiring glance. "That color sets off your beard."

He snarled, turned away, and strode onto the stage. The crowd erupted. Naturally, the cheers included a few cat calls and whistles, but Edward did me proud. He didn't scowl. At least not with his face. Inside . . . that's another story.

My brother nodded a few times to acknowledge their victory and took the seat next to Susan, ready to answer her questions. Before the interview commenced, a voice from the back of the room shouted, "Take off the pants."

This started a chant. People clapped in time with the words.

I peered around the edge of the curtains. When I caught sight of the heckler as his new wife dragged him from the room, I grunted my disappointment at Martin Bowers. I expected more from a representative of the law.

Meanwhile, the chanting had grown to a frantic pitch. I smelled trouble.

Before Edward had refined his manners for his role as Auntie's public face, he'd been a diamond with rough edges. Snag on the carpet rough. Etiquette doesn't count when you're a college linebacker. Edward played inside the box because he had the speed to keep up with the receiver and the strength to plow through anything that got in his way.

That bone-headedness hadn't abandoned him. He just got better at hiding it. However, his college years also left him unwilling, possibly unable, to walk away from a challenge. Even if common sense floated by with a neon sign telling him whatever he planned to do was a dumb idea.

My brother stood, turned to the side for modesty's sake, and, after lifting the dress high enough to undo his belt buckle, dropped his drawers.

He wore black boxer briefs that fitted around his muscular thighs. The female voices went silent. For an added measure, since Edward never did things by halves, he kicked off his shoes, leaving him in the dress, white dress shirt, and chocolate-brown socks.

Once the female audience members caught their breath, they cheered like madwomen. My brother has that effect on the gentler sex, as he calls them. I've never found anything gentle about them.

I don't think most of them could have passed a test on the content that followed and wondered if I had enough signed copies of his book in the car trunk.

Susan gave my brother a nervous smile. She got no further when a man dressed as a man called out, "What did the police want with you?"

The man's buddy chimed in. "You didn't kill him, did you?"

A handful appreciated the man's humor. Other men. The women tittered in that embarrassed and irritated tone they use when their significant other belches in public.

"The Coronado police spoke with me because I have a certain amount of experience assisting law enforcement."

My brother was exercising self-control. I breathed a sigh of relief. But then the next question came from a middle-aged woman in the front row.

"How did he die?"

"Does it matter?" he snapped. He closed his eyes and took a deep breath. "I apologize. It's been stressful."

Smart. That got him the sympathy of the audience, and damned if he didn't turn it around to a lesson in manners.

"We're all curious when unusual events occur, but we must remember to keep from getting too personal. The point of civil discourse is to avoid causing either party discomfort with unsavory topics. That's why, in the excellent movie *Some Like It Hot*, the characters avoid confronting issues that would have shortened the story by a great deal and eliminated many fun situations."

A few heads nodded agreement. The rest looked uncertain.

"For instance, I'm certain, being men, Josephine and Daphne had stubble by the end of the day. It would have been rude for one of their band mates to bring attention to this affliction, as an affliction it would be for a woman."

"Excellent point," Susan said, hurrying to her first question before additional murder questions arose. "In the movie, the roles are reversed on Joe and Jerry. Joe, at least, goes from womanizer to woman, yet it's Jerry, as Daphne, who gets the most attention from men. Why do you think that is?"

"It is my belief that Jerry, in the character of Daphne, exhibited more of the traits we associate with the finer sex. His open friendliness. His ability to enjoy even tricky situations. And, on the negative side, his capitulations to Joe's schemes. Women tend to surrender to men if the fight isn't something they consider worthwhile."

The women in the audience nodded, and their rapt expressions credited him with looking into their souls. No wonder females made up eighty percent of Aunt Civility's fans. I don't think the old lady could have done a better job at connecting with her audience. If she existed.

"Which character do you think made a better woman, Joe or Jerry?" From her grin, Susan thought she had stumped him.

A few women answered for him, shouting out their favorite character from the movie.

Edward settled back and crossed his legs. "I see the ladies desire to count Daphne as one of their own. May I ask why?"

One attendee jumped to her feet. "She's funny. Women have a good sense of humor. They have to."

That got her laughs, and she sat down with a pleased smirk.

Another followed. "She didn't talk down to the other women. That's how Daphne fit in."

Edward raised a finger. "But did Josephine ever talk down to her band mates? Can you give me an example?"

The woman chewed it over. "I still say Daphne."

My brother smiled. "And I would never argue you out of your opinion. Daphne it is."

The audience cheered.

"I would suggest Daphne is the more likable character. She has more personality. We relate to her, and we like to think of ourselves as having those characteristics we admire in others." He spread his hands. "Which I'm certain every one of you do."

A standing ovation.

Susan held up her hand. "Some people in the audience would riot if I didn't ask if it's sexist to think women have a corner on those likable traits. I mean, there are mean women and there are nice men."

"But there are traits that are more prominent in each sex," my brother countered. "Women are by their nature more generous. Kinder. Less violent. William Golding expressed it best when he said that whatever you give a woman, she will make it better. Mere groceries become a meal. A house becomes a home. And so on."

I knew that quote, and I knew why he left it at *so on*. He'd never allude to sex in mixed company, even if it resulted in something as innocent as a baby.

Edward didn't have to raise his volume for the women to hear. They hung on his every word. Some might say they were trying to please a man and earn his approval, but I knew from experience it was because he made them feel good about themselves. He played with them. He admired them. He treated them with respect. That's something both men and women respond to. It's human nature.

As the crowd quieted down, a smug-looking man in a duplicate of the fur-lined jacket and cloche hat worn by

Tony Curtis raised his hand. He stood before Susan acknowledged him and took a slow turn to survey the room. He reminded me of a dog tinkling on a tree to mark his territory.

Susan recognized him immediately. Her smile faltered and she shot a glance at my brother. "Elliot. How wonderful to see you. For those who haven't met him, Elliot is a lifetime member of our club. That option is available on our website."

He bowed his head in acknowledgment of the few claps, took a deep breath, and fired his question at my brother.

"In the scene where Sugar Cane, played by Marilyn Monroe, sings *I'm Through with Love* from atop the grand piano, the scene begins with Josephine outside a door at the top of the stairs. What's on the wall behind her? Or him, if you prefer."

"Mr. Harlow is an expert in manners, not movies." Her excuses trailed off when my brother answered.

"It appears to be peacock tail feathers. Though I can't be certain that's what the set decorator intended, as I wasn't in Edward G. Boyle's confidence." He pulled out the name of the set decorator as if it should be common knowledge. Touché.

Edward, a fan of the film anyway, had boned-up on the movie before we came here. With his photographic memory, a useful tool in memorizing facts about both etiquette and sports statistics, Elliot didn't stand a chance.

"Very good, Mr. Harlow." Elliot raised a finger. "What was the sign outside the door?"

"I assume you are referring to the sign before the open door at the top of the stairs. It said: Sweet Sue and Her

Society Syncopators. The word Nightly was above a photograph of the band."

The super-fan narrowed his eyes, displeased. "How many steps did Josephine walk down to get to Sugar Cane and the band?"

"Fourteen. That's if you count the top step."

By now, Susan gaped along with the rest of the attendees.

"What kind of flower did Sweet Sue wear in her hair."

Edward flicked invisible lint off his knee. "She didn't. She wore a black ribbon, as did the other ladies. All except the star of the show, Sugar Cane. She wore nothing in her hair."

The men began to chuckle, and the ladies tittered, as if Elliot were the pain in their side and they enjoyed watching someone outgun him. He didn't like it.

"How many stars was the policeman standing next to Toothpick Charlie and Detective Mulligan wearing?

"Four. Two on each lapel."

When Elliot smirked, Edward added, "Five, if you count the star on his chest. As a policeman, that one would be assumed."

"What's the name of the dog Joe wanted to bet on."

"The first one? Greased Lightning."

Susan put an end to the duel by asking if anyone else had a question for Mr. Harlow. Several gushed about his unparalleled knowledge of the movie, which irked Elliot, but what could the super-fan do?

Afterwards, when Edward joined me behind the curtain, I congratulated him on his impromptu answers. He made a dismissive gesture.

"I'm starving. Let's get lunch."

Edward may irritate me at times with his pompous manner and older brother's arrogance, but he's tops at what he does.

Chapter Twenty-Two

Nicholas: Treasure Hunt Gone Wrong

"A treasure hunt?"

Never ask a grown man to play children's games. Not if you want that man to remain friendly for the remainder of the weekend.

"I agree it's infantile," Edward conceded, "but we have to put on a good face. At least, you do."

I stared. "Tell me you're joking. Why don't you make an appearance? You don't have to stay long. Just let them see you frolicking. Your fans don't even know who I am."

"I've opened myself up to answering questions. Stupid of me. I'd rather avoid the attendees for a while, especially Elliot. He gives me a headache. However, they've seen you with me. They will subconsciously connect you with Aunt Civility."

"I have some subconscious thoughts I'd like to share with you. What are you doing while I'm making a fool of myself?"

"There is one item I'd like to go over with Detective Bowers."

"Aw, leave him alone. He's on his honeymoon."

Edward's face creased with guilt, but it passed. "I'll keep it short."

As usual, he won the argument, and I got stuck playing pin the tail on Marilyn Monroe. Once we'd debased ourselves, Susan Sweeney handed out a prize to a woman who reacted like a *Price is Right* contestant when she received a certificate for a free dinner at the hotel restaurant of her choice. My ears are still ringing from the screams.

Everyone had forgotten about this morning's sad announcement. The only sign sudden death had intruded upon their festivities was the extra shot of enthusiasm with which they embraced the festivities.

Most guests were in suits and dresses of the era. A few brave men sported dresses, but most had chosen the gangster outfit. The ladies were divided between those that dressed as gangsters and those that aimed for beauty.

One had gone so far as to strap on the one-piece bodysuit worn by the dancers at the funeral home from the beginning of the film. She had black mesh tights on her legs and a decorative thingy on a headband. She wasn't bulging out in too many places, but her rump sagged. That didn't stop the men past sixty from ogling her.

The Black Ken and Barbie had their heads together. She looked fabulous in the flesh-colored silk dress with gold trimmings that Marilyn Monroe wore for her date with Tony Curtis, though Rhonda had worn a tube top under the see-through fabric covering her bust. Repeat viewings of the movie by my sexually frustrated teenage self had convinced me Marilyn had not.

Willie wore a fedora with his beige suit, which I suppose made him a gangster. They had smiles plastered on their faces, but their gestures weren't friendly—short and choppy like they were reigning in tension.

"Oh, drat!"

The large, old lady called Edna seemed extra cranky today. She might have been speaking to her tiny dog or the tall beauty at her side. Cynthia. Both reacted as if they expected a rolled newspaper across the snout. She wore her usual granny outfit, and the young woman wore a gangster suit with pink spats.

She wasn't the only one in costume. Edna had dressed the pup in a gray, pinstriped jacket and topped it with a tied-on fedora. No wonder that little imp was always trying to bite something.

I noted several scratches on the back of the hand that clutched her straw bag. "You should get peroxide on those."

"Tanner doesn't like to take his medicine. It's my fault. He needs his nails trimmed, and when he tries to wriggle away . . ." She tapped his nose with her finger. "Naughty, naughty."

She took a seat and bent over to situate the dog in his basket.

My new friend Jimmy and his two goons peeked into the doorway long enough to scan the room. As usual, they wore gangster outfits. Whatever they were looking for, they didn't find it and moved on.

I'd worn my dark-gray suit after deciding the convention polo shirt looked silly with dress slacks. I fit right in.

After a few minutes standing around and trying to come up with a scathing comment for the next time I saw Edward, a voice interrupted my thoughts.

"What's next on the agenda?"

Bowers' wife Frankie stood next to me. I angled my rear away from her in case she had her pinchers ready.

"Treasure hunt."

"That sounds, uh, fun."

"I take it Edward caught up with your husband?"

"Snatched him away." She frowned. "Though he went willingly, so I guess it's all right."

A young man in the hotel's uniform handed us each a sheet of paper. The list was items we were supposed to hunt for, I assumed.

"Light fixtures shaped like a crown. Do we have to take them down and present them to Susan to prove we found them?"

She gurgled a laugh from the back of her throat. "I'll hold the ladder once we find them."

"I don't even have to search." I pointed up.

"Ooh. You're brilliant. Crowns in the Crown Room. It says we must take a picture of what we find to prove it. Do you have a camera?"

I gaped. "What century do you live in? Don't you have a cell phone?"

"I only carry it when I'm expecting a call."

The logic of women. As I was working out a way to bow out of the treasure hunt, Frankie saved me the trouble. She got this weird look on her face and drifted away.

I wasn't the only one who noticed. Rhonda and Willie Fisher watched her leave. I'm not sure if their expressions of concern had more to do with Frankie's odd demeanor or the possibility that she had a head start on the clues.

I'll admit I jumped when someone tugged on my sleeve. It was a guy in his sixties in a navy jacket with white piping and a matching captain's hat.

"Let me guess. Osgood Fielding the Third."

"Very good. Just call me Osgood. Say. Everyone is paired off. Want to work together?"

It might be a good idea to have a partner. If someone were stalking me, they'd be less likely to try something if I weren't alone.

Ken and Barbie—I mean Rhonda and Willie—still huddled in the corner. When they glanced my way, I caught a flicker of interest. It was stronger than interest, and it wasn't friendly. In a second, it was gone. When they approached me, she wore a cautious smile. He gazed down on her like she was the second coming.

"Excuse me. Do you want to work together? Everyone seems to be searching in teams."

"It doesn't seem fair," Willie added. "But when in Rome . . ."

"Only if you include Osgood, here."

He held up his hands. "If you three are already partnered up, I don't want to intrude."

"The more the merrier," Willie said.

Rhonda read off the first clue.

"A starry crown." She studied the words with a concentration that promised an aneurysm if she kept it up.

"Follow me." I led them to the corner of the room and pointed up.

Willie's mouth dropped open. "Look, Babe. The lights. They're shaped like crowns. I never noticed." He laughed and shook his head. "You're a genius."

Complimented on my brain twice in ten minutes. I'd get puffed up if I thought either party meant it.

Rhonda snapped a picture on her cell and put a check mark next to the clue. "We're rocking. Next clue. A chilly place."

Willie turned to me with considerable expectations. "What do you think, Nicholas?"

They both stared at me with open, friendly expressions, but an odd sight distracted me. Over Rhonda's shoulder, I caught sight of Frankie Bowers, wandering the lobby like a zombie. "Ice House. Excuse me. I just remembered something I have to do."

Osgood made a move to follow, but Willie blocked him and insisted he remain and help.

The woman needed a keeper. Next time I saw Bowers, I'd give him a talking to, but for now, it looked like I was the only one available to keep an eye on his wife.

Because she was focused on her mission, I didn't need to hang back to keep from being spotted. The expression on her face was a combination of deep sorrow and confusion.

She took a few turns and stepped outside. Had I read her wrong? Was she focused on the treasure hunt? This way led to the Ice House.

My curiosity went up a notch when she stuck to the beach. At one point, she hesitated and cocked her head, just like my old dog Scoots used to do, and then she took off at a jog and disappeared behind a hedge.

When I caught up, her attention was on the nasty Chihuahua that belonged to Edna Tartwell. He shook like small dogs often do and bared his teeth at her. Maybe he was angry about the ridiculous gangster outfit he still had on. She stared back and made faces at him.

When she reached for him, I said, "I wouldn't do that. I've heard he's bitten three people so far."

And he did lunge and snap the first time she tried. She made some more faces, and to my surprise, the dog allowed her to pick him up and snuggle him into her sweater for warmth.

"Where's your mommy?" she asked the dog.

I looked over my shoulder at the empty beach. An exceptionally good question.

* * *

As we headed back into the hotel, a voice called out.

"No dogs allowed on the beach." Clarence Darby lumbered over and jabbed a thick forefinger at Tanner. "Guests run around barefoot, and I don't need to tell you what happens when dogs run free, doing their business willy-nilly."

"I caught him. He got loose from his owner."

"That's okay then. Good job."

"Nicholas, meet *Mr. Darby.*"

The landscaper eyed me. "Do I know you?"

Fortunately, the younger Harlow caught on. "Not personally, but we have a message from Jose. He says hi."

"Jose Alvarado?" Darby broke into his first grin, showing teeth like tree stumps. Short. Big. Square. "That young pup? Well, you can just tell him hello back from me."

"If we go back to the zoo, we will."

"I wondered," I began, glancing around the beach. Several tourists in shorts strolled; others in bathing suits braved the chilly water. The Taco Shack was doing brisk business, and I made a note to try it before we returned home.

"This place is nice, but the zoo is way more interesting. You have variety. Animals. Your good friend, Jose. Why choose the beach over the zoo?"

Clarence stared. "How well did you know Harry Reed?"

His question caught me off guard. My hand went to my loose curls and twisted one around my finger. "Who? Me? Not well at all."

"Did you ever meet him?"

"Once. At the zoo."

"What did you think of him?"

What *had* I thought of Harry Reed? In Antonio Sabatos' room, he'd been officious, sarcastic, and cold. Then again, I'd just tried to climb into the enclosure with one of his patients. "I didn't find him warm and fuzzy."

"That's for damn sure. To answer your question, I didn't leave the zoo. That ass Harry Reed got me fired. Turned out he did me a favor, not that I'd thank him for it." He pulled his shoulders back and sucked in his gut. "I'm not as young as I used to be. The Del is easier on my legs. No hills. No climbing around enclosures to pretty them up so the animals feel at home. Here, I've got routine. At my age, routine counts for a lot."

"But you're such a good worker. How could a mere vet get you fired? For what?"

It sounded like syrup to my ears, but Clarence bought it.

"The humidity had skyrocketed that day. I took a breather. We just happened to be in the same place. All I did was watch him work. Not very interesting, but Harry didn't approve. A mere landscaper showing interest in his high and mighty profession."

"What was he doing?" Nicholas asked.

"Giving a chimp a checkup. Chuck's girlfriend."

I pulled my eyebrows together. "Chimps have girlfriends?"

"You bet they do. Lots of them, if you get my meaning. Everyone knows Chuck took to his training like a monkey. Give him the right signal, and he holds out his hands and feet, sits still, shows his teeth. He's a vet's dream. Chuck and his girlfriend were next to the fence, and the doc was checking her out with a stethoscope. Her tummy. She must have had a belly ache or something."

He grinned. "I hoped something would happen, seeing as how Harry was the person on the receiving end. Maybe get his arms torn off. Anyway, Chuck points at me, Harry turns his head, and suddenly, the guy's all over me. Tells me to get out. Says I'm upsetting his patient. Bull. I don't know what he told Antonio, but suddenly, I'm packing my bags. I know a guy who works here. They hired me. End of story. Now, about that dog . . ."

"Yes, sir."

We hurried back into the hotel.

Chapter Twenty-Three

Frankie: Too Close for Comfort

Nicholas Harlow tagged along as I returned to the Crown Room. Vendors had set up booths along the walls and flogged t-shirts with convention logos or the actors' faces from the movie, coffee table books, mugs, blond wigs, signature lipsticks and false eyelashes, posters, and every type of ware bearing the convention name. Even bras and undies. Someone even had miniature cellos and saxophones stamped Joe/Josephine and Jerry/Daphne.

When I didn't spot Edna, I did another scan of the room for her niece. As much as I disliked Cynthia, she'd be the person most likely to locate the dog's owner. Except the dog, of course. However, when I'd sent a mental highway and connected to his wee brain, snapping teeth greeted me. A vision had never attacked me physically, but I wasn't in the mood to tempt fate.

Edna's niece wasn't around, either.

Our search led us into The Garden, where a wedding reception was taking place on the lawn. White balloons tied in the shape of a heart floated behind the head table.

Mauve tablecloths covered a dozen round tables for eight. Each boasted a stunning display of exotic flowers, and from the scattering of china plates remaining, the guests had already eaten.

I approached four women dressed in mauve satin gowns who I assumed were bridesmaids.

"Excuse me." They had their backs to me and ignored my hail. "Pardon me." I tapped the shoulder of the nearest one, and she turned her head just as the other three screamed. Really, dozens of women screamed. I hadn't noticed the guests surrounding me were all female, right down to a young girl in a frilly white dress. The flower girl, I assumed.

We had liftoff, and every pair of heels came off the ground as the bride's bouquet sailed toward us. The bridesmaid to my left reached her hand in front of the one who had turned to me and caught the prize.

"You made me miss!" The loser snarled, shoving my shoulder, and knocking me off balance.

While I clutched Tanner to my chest, Nicholas caught me around the shoulders before I hit the ground. He jerked his chin. "Here comes the groom's bouquet!"

The angry bridesmaid halted her attack and spun, searching the sky. By the time she realized she'd been had, Nicholas had dragged me back into the hallway.

"Thanks. Are you okay, Tanner?" The dog had burrowed inside my sweater for safety, and I had to turn my back on Nicholas while I pried the pup out. He didn't come willingly and left a few scratches on my stomach.

Safely back inside, we resumed our search, wandering until we came to the entrance of the Babcock & Story Bar. Nicholas jerked his chin.

"There she is."

Seated on a stool in front of the bartender, Edna Tartwell absorbed the menu like she was boning up for an exam. They say it's always five o'clock somewhere, and though my watch showed two forty-five, guests occupied every seat on the outside patio as well as the inside seating.

As we approached, she questioned the bartender in that quavering voice. "What is in a Sandy Bottoms?"

"Campari, bourbon, lemon juice, pineapple juice, and pomegranate juice."

He rattled the ingredients off with a smile and pointed to a spot on the menu in front of her face. Her glasses had slipped to the end of her long nose keeping her from reading the menu. Or, she was lazy.

"Excuse us," Nicholas said.

As soon as Edna noticed Tanner, she hopped off the stool with surprising agility and took him into her arms. "There you are, darling. What have you been up to?"

"I found him wandering the beach." He had only allowed me to pick him up when I'd played a movie of me tossing him into the ocean and ringing the dinner bell. Even before that, I had sensed the dog's fear. "Something scared him."

She tucked the little beast into her ever-present straw bag where he disappeared, having lost his desire to explore his surroundings. "In nine years, we've never been separated except for short potty breaks."

"Then how did he get away?" Nicholas gestured at the bag. "If you don't mind my asking."

She looked as if she did mind, though she answered. "Cynthia said she'd walk him for me." Her head wobbled as she looked over our shoulders. "Where is that girl?"

"I don't know. Nicholas and I searched for her first before we found you."

"But you should know," the old lady insisted.

"Maybe she went back to your room." I gestured toward the beach that led to her condominium.

"But she was going to see you."

"See me where?"

"I assumed in your room."

Nicholas snapped out an excellent question. "How did she know which room the Bowers were staying in?"

"I'm not one for gossip, but people have been talking. Everyone has been dying to get a peek at the remodeled cottages, but they're not open yet. You're the exception."

"I suppose I should look for her." Meeting Cynthia didn't sound fun. The only thing we had in common was an interest in my husband.

Nicholas crooked an elbow at me. "Shall we?"

From his solemn expression, Nicholas found something odd about the situation. I had to double-step it to keep up with him as he strode toward the cottages.

"Tell me what you talked about with Cynthia since you've been here."

"Nothing. She could have heard I have an animal behavior business back home and wanted to ask for advice on Tanner. He's a tad cranky. He's Edna's service dog. For anxiety."

"He certainly is. Just looking at him makes me anxious."

I unlocked the community gate, but Nicholas insisted on opening the front door to our home away from home and entering first. Even though I knew Bowers was with Edward Harlow, I still called out when I followed him into the room.

"Nice," Nicholas said, taking in our lodgings. "Does that couch fold out into a bed? Cause right now, I'm on a cot."

I ignored him and searched the rooms.

He called to me while I was checking the bathroom. "Maybe she left you a message."

I leaned my head out and snorted. "She would have had to break in to leave a note." He gestured at the phone across the room. "Oh. Of course." I strolled over and stared down at it. "How do I check the messages?"

He joined me. "The light would blink if you had one. Is there another way into this place?" He stepped outside onto our patio. "You're on the ground floor. It would be easy enough to . . ." He only had to swing a leg over the short fence and he was on the other side. After turning a full circle to take in the view, he suggested we take a walk.

The path led between our place and the cottage next door. From what the manager had told us, the remaining remodeling work was taking place in the Beach Village Villas behind us, so I wasn't surprised when we didn't meet anyone. They'd probably gone home by now, anyway.

The sidewalk circled in front of a barrier that surrounded a large swimming pool used by the Villa guests. We turned to our left and passed behind the cottage on the opposite side of ours. To my surprise, between that cottage and the next one over, the Beach Village Cottages had their own pool. I wondered if the hotel kept it heated. Then I wondered who'd thrown a sack of clothes into the water.

"What's that?" My voice squeaked out. Nicholas put a hand on the gate and vaulted over. He kicked off his shoes and shed his jacket in his race to the water's edge.

By the time I convinced my feet to move, he'd dived in and reached his target.

It took a few tries to get over the locked gate. Not an athletic vault, but more of a half-climb followed by a fall. Still, I made it.

"Help me get her up," he gasped, more from the temperature of the unheated pool than from exertion. While I pulled Cynthia's arms, he pushed the rest of her out of the water and hoisted himself out of the pool.

One look at her froth-covered mouth and nostrils and her dull, staring eyes told me she was a goner. Still, I asked. "Is she dead?"

He felt her pulse. "As a doorknob." He wiped his palms on his slacks. "Run back and call—" He pulled his cell phone from his back pocket and pushed a button. "Waterproof. Thank you, Lord."

Even though I hadn't gone into the water, I wrapped my arms around my middle and shivered. Two bodies found in as many days. And on my honeymoon. When I gasped, he sent me a sharp glance, but I waved him off.

I'd just had a horrible and selfish thought. Would the police take away our cottage, too? Would we spend the rest of our honeymoon at Motel Express? Or one of those places that charged by the hour? We'd never afford it. And the word for those places was yucky.

While we waited, Nicholas paced. He paused in front of a pool net on a long pole that someone had discarded on the cement. Then he scanned the water. An impulse overcame him, and he jumped back in, waded to the shallow end, and disappeared under the water. When he came back up, he held out his hand to show me a candy bar wrapper that must have blown there on an ocean breeze and a couple of brown pebbles. But they weren't stone, because they crumbled.

"Are those—"

Call me selfish, but I saved my thought for my hubby. It wasn't a competition to find the killer, but it felt like a betrayal to share my thoughts with Nicholas first.

He wiped his hand on the edge of the pool and climbed back out.

In a short while, a group of men came along the path at a run, led by Bowers. When I saw his solid, reliable, dependable person, my lips trembled, and I broke into sobs. He took me into his arms and swore, something I noticed he'd done more on this vacation than in the entire time we'd dated.

"Let's get back to the cottage."

Without another look at the crime scene, a move which must have taken him significant effort, he steered me back the way I'd come and led me through the front door to our cottage, where he halted.

"Someone's been here."

"Nicholas and I looked for Cynthia here first."

"And why would you look for Cynthia Ferrara in our cottage?"

As concisely as I could, I relayed the events of the afternoon, ending with a joke. "That's what happens when you don't stick to me like glue."

"I'm so sorry Frankie. I shouldn't have left you."

I rubbed his arm. "I'm teasing. The same thing would have happened with you by my side."

"Do you have any idea why Cynthia wanted to speak to you?"

"None. If she wanted to exchange words with anyone, I would have guessed you."

His look of surprise confirmed it. My husband didn't realize how attractive he was to women. Or he'd grown immune to the admiring glances and blatant flirtations that came at him daily.

"Oh, no." A wave of nausea passed through me. "Someone has to break the news to Edna."

My husband paced the room and ran his fingers through his hair. "The police will handle it." He stopped by the window and watched as two paramedics pushed a gurney down the path.

"Bowers. It's okay. Go join them and see if you can find out what happened."

"You shouldn't be alone."

"I'm fine. Really. Go."

He didn't wait for me to change my mind.

I stood and walked to the bedroom, my feet dragging. It was cool enough for a fire, but I didn't know how to turn on the darn thing, so I kicked off my shoes, pulled back the covers, and slipped under them.

Within minutes, I was asleep.

Chapter Twenty-Four

Nicholas: Theories Abound

"Well, this is another fine mess you've gotten us into, Stanley."

My quote from Laurel and Hardy—I forget which one was Stanley—went over Edward's head. He'd set his mouth in a firm line, narrowed his eyes, and crossed his arms over his broad chest. I called it my brother's Thinking Man pose.

"I wasn't the one who found the body," he murmured.

"Neither was I. It was that Bowers' woman again, though I was with her."

He let out a sigh. "Tell me again. Why did you follow her out of the Crown Room?"

"She was acting funny. Like she was in a trance. I was worried about her."

"Fair enough. Did she say anything or do anything to give you a hint of what she was after?"

"Nothing. She wandered in a daze until she found the dog."

"And when you brought the dog inside, Edna Tartwell said she didn't know where her niece was?"

"She said she was visiting Frankie Bowers, but that news came as a surprise to Bowers' wife. Frankie and I proceeded to her cottage. There were no signs anyone had left a note on the door or a message on the machine, so we decided to check the grounds."

"Who decided?"

"It was my idea. I felt uneasy. My unease could be because I recognized the signs of a female killer. You remind me often enough of my proclivity for mistaking evil minions for nice women. Why couldn't Frankie Bowers kill Cynthia? The dog got loose, and she tracked it down. Then she faked an eagerness to reunite doggie and mistress and saw her chance to clean up any clues when she heard Edna thought Cynthia was visiting her cottage. And I was a convenient witness to the body's discovery."

When he snorted, I held up my hands. "Whoa there. I'm the one who usually gives the beautiful woman a pass."

"I'm not biased by her attractions."

"What then? It's not like she's a great conversationalist, unless you want to discuss the origins of your octopus appetizer." I imitated a female voice. "*How do you know it's from Spain? It's Algerian and the poor thing got lost.*" I dropped the act. "I should have guessed that first night she was bonkers."

Edward stroked his beard. "There is something about her. Something beneath the surface. She tries to hide it under that insecure shell, but the woman has a force."

"A force? You mean like a jedi?"

My reference from *Star Wars* went over his head until he scanned his memory banks. "I get it. Yes. In a way. That's the best way I can put it. There's more to Frankie Bowers than meets the eyes. And if you are interested in one of my reasons for assuming her innocence, I believe a detective would know and disapprove if his wife was a murderess."

I gave a perfect martyred sigh. "So, will you finally admit I was right? We would have been safer in our own beds."

"No."

My brother had that gleam in his eye. He was enjoying himself over these murders. Edward is rough around the edges, but deep down, he's a romantic. He sees himself as the knight on horseback rushing in to save the damsel. Not that we had a damsel in distress, or a horse, but he'd make adjustments.

"Did you notice the pool net lying on the ground?" Edward was showing off.

"I did. I also spotted something in the water, but it turned out to be disgusting pellets that dissolved in my hand."

"Pellets? What kind of pellets?"

"Disgusting."

"But they weren't pebbles?"

"I've yet to meet a dissolving pebble."

He paused for thought. "Did Edna Tartwell have her straw bag with her when you found her in the bar?"

"Is she ever without it?" He waited. "Yes."

"Interesting," he purred.

Since I knew he'd never tell me what he found interesting, I changed the subject. "Funny, running into Sykes here. Oh. Hey there little guy." I made some kissy noises and wiggled my fingers at a chipmunk. He backed away.

"Stop playing with the wildlife, Nicholas."

"A chipmunk isn't wildlife."

"Anyway, Detective Sykes being here is a coincidence. There's nothing funny about it."

"It's bad mojo."

He raised his eyebrows. "Mojo? Are you of African descent?"

Edward prides himself on knowing about words, like where they came from. "No, but I got implied permission to use the term ever since they made a video game by the same name."

"Did they really?"

Then again, there are things my brother doesn't know. "So, what's our next move?"

"We wait for your interview with Sergeant Bautista."

"Seriously? I mean something useful. Like our next step in solving this murder. Murders."

"Nicholas, Nicholas, Nicholas. Always looking for action."

It took effort to control my foot. The one that wanted to kick his rear. "It's better than sitting on my keister."

"What would you have me do?" he roared. "We know next to nothing about either victim. We don't know the guests' whereabouts for Thursday night. We have even less luck with this second murder. Everyone was scattered around the grounds for the treasure hunt."

Turning slowly, I scanned the edges of the building. "If they have security cameras, they're camouflaged."

"Sergeant Bautista will find out about those."

"It would be interesting to—what the hell's the matter with the seagulls?"

Chapter Twenty-Five

Frankie: Eavesdropping and the Seagulls Attack

Bowers rejoined me at the cottage. I awoke to find him sitting on the edge of the bed and staring at me. I immediately sat up and rubbed my eyes.

"Do I have sleepers? Did I drool?"

He pushed my hair behind my ear. "Nope. You're just beautiful."

Our companionable silence lasted a mere five minutes. This second murder had both of us antsy.

We stepped outside more for something to do than any desire to admire the sand and surf, and we remained near the cottage for the police to call on me. At least until a shrill cry reached my ears.

Striding forward, I connected with the seagull leader, the one I called Amos, and sent an image of Cynthia's body in the pool, followed by a question mark. For good measure, I shrugged my shoulders.

In twenty seconds, the sky had cleared of seagulls. They had taken off rather than share their secrets.

"Argh!" I shook a fist at the empty sky. "Those jokers know more than they're telling."

To lure them back, I sent a wide broadcast showing a seagull with crossed eyes, his wing on his head in a 'duh' position, and me with my back turned and arms crossed. A clear message that I didn't think they had anything to tell.

They returned with vengeance in mind and dove at me, brushing so close I could feel their wings. And that's not all they were doing.

"Run, Bowers! Save yourself!"

I raised my arms to protect my hair and ran in a zigzag. That's what they tell you to do if someone is shooting at you. It foils their aim.

In a minute, it was over, and they'd flown away again.

"Frankie. Hold still."

Bowers took a napkin from his pocket and wiped bird poop off my arms. "You might want to shower before the police get here. And wash your hair."

My poor husband had a few splatters on his shirt and hair, but I'd taken the brunt of their displeasure.

"Those brats!"

My husband went to put his arm around my waist but pulled back. "Let's get inside."

As we turned, Bowers' glance strayed to the path where the Harlow brothers were deep in discussion.

"There's something off about them," Bowers said. "They're hiding something. I'd bet on it."

Movement caught my eye as a chipmunk dived into the low hedge next to us. I got an idea. When I connected with him, the little critter froze. I directed his attention to the brothers, said "hello" out loud and then said it again in my mind. After repeating this exercise a few times, I showed him a big bag of peanuts. I think he got the idea because he scurried to the brothers and planted himself right behind them.

When I requested Bowers rummage for nuts in the beautiful welcome basket management had sent over, he narrowed his eyes.

"Right now?" He waved a hand over me. "This has made you hungry? Don't you want to change first?"

"Yes please. And if they don't have nuts, see if there are some seeds or popcorn. But I prefer nuts."

His eyes widened. He took a tentative step forward. "Are you having cravings?"

"Holy smokes. No. I just need some nuts. I'll wait here."

He stared at me for a long minute before he left to grant my wish.

By the time Bowers returned, my little friend waited impatiently for his reward. My furry informant had stubbornly kept his thoughts to himself until he received payment. When I held out my hand, my husband turned my palm upward and emptied the remains of a small bag of shelled peanuts.

"Sorry. I opened them this morning."

After rubbing off the salt, I set the pile under the shrubs to protect the little guy's stash.

Misinterpreting, Bowers said, "Frankie, you have a good heart. Though they prefer you don't feed the squirrels, it's a nice gesture, and that little guy looks like he's won the lottery. If you can believe it, I thought—"

Bowers' words cut out as the creature filled my head with male voices. At first, they talked about the pool equipment and something gross Nicholas found. It took a few minutes for them to get to the good stuff.

We're still not certain why Harry Reed was killed here and not at the zoo.

When Nicholas responded, he had an uber casual tone. *There's something I've been meaning to tell you. While I was checking in, Harry Reed tried to cut in line. He asked the clerk to call a room.*

A choking sound.

And you omitted telling the police? Telling me? I saw him of course, and reported it to Bautista, but if you overheard a conversation, why, for goodness' sake, didn't you tell the sergeant?

It kept slipping my mind. I've been busy.

With what? Edward sounded incredulous.

Aside from doing everything for you but wipe your fanny, I've been looking out for Frankie Bowers. That woman needs a minder.

She's a married woman.

It's not that. She's all right if you like that sort.

Edward let out a full-throated laugh that popped my eardrums. *You mean well-mannered and attractive?*

The woman belongs on a funny farm. Seriously, Edward. You saw. For the love of Pete, she licked my hand. And pinched my derrière. She could be obsessed with me.

Another loud guffaw from Edward.

And she gets in these trances. That's why I was following her. And then she makes weird faces. It's embarrassing. And did you see how she shook her fist at the birds? No wonder they attacked her. She's out of her mind, Edward.

As the elder brother paused, I held my breath. Not that it should matter what Edward Harlow thought of me, but I like to keep the number of people who found my behavior certifiable to a minimum.

Perhaps she had a reason.

You're darn tooting I had a reason. What a wise older brother. I wondered if life would have turned out different if I'd had the guidance of an older brother.

Nicholas made a derisive noise and I promised to ignore him for the rest of our time here. I smiled when Edward took him to task.

Not only that, but she led me straight to the body. Or at least the dog, which led to the body. How did she know it was there? I didn't hear any barking.

Nonsense. You said she was wandering as if in a trance. You can't have it both ways. Besides. You should pay less attention to the pretty lady and more to your job.

Aw. Edward thought I was pretty.

Why didn't you stop the audience from forcing me to wear that dress? It was demeaning.

Nuts. What did you want me to do? Yell fire?

A snicker escaped. Nicholas might be a rat, but he was a funny rat.

You need to get in touch with your feminine side.

Edward's responding roar made me jump.

How much closer can I get than embodying an elderly aunt? For Heaven's sake, I live and breathe estrogen half the day while I'm writing the Aunt Civility books and responding to her—my—fans.

"What are you smirking about?" Bowers asked.

I disconnected from the conversation and hooked my arm through his. "I'm just admiring my husband's great instincts."

He removed my arm. "My instincts are telling me you need a shower."

I batted my eyelashes. "Will you be joining me?"

After running his gaze over my bird poop spattered clothing, he took a step back. "I'll sit this one out."

Chapter Twenty-Six

Frankie: A Missing Person

"You heard something?"

Bautista leaned back in his chair and studied me. The interview took place in our cottage in the living room area. Bowers sat next to me on the couch. "Like what? A bark?"

"Maybe."

My husband and I exchanged a glance, and the weariness around his eyes confirmed he knew what I meant by hearing something.

I shrugged. "It was just a noise. I thought maybe someone else from the treasure hunt had discovered a clue." A lie, but it made Bowers' shoulders inch down.

"Did you see anyone else on the beach?" Bautista asked.

"Nicholas Harlow." I couldn't resist but relented right away. "He showed up after I found the dog."

"So, you took the dog to Edna Tartwell."

"We looked in the Crown Room first and made a brief stop in The Garden." I tried not to wince at the memory.

"After more searching, Nicholas spotted her in the Babcock and Story Bar."

"And she told you her niece had gone to find you."

"Yes."

"Why?"

"I've been wracking my brain for something worth discussing with the woman, but our conversations were the usual fluff. You're a fan of the movie? Did you like your dinner? Nothing worth talking about."

"Had you told Miss Ferrara where you were staying?"

"Of course not. But Edna said it was common knowledge. Or at least a rumor."

And then I told them about our walk and how Nicholas tried to save her but knew it was too late.

Bowers had his own question. "Did you ever find out about the glass on the walkway?"

"It was one of the commemorative glasses from the conference."

"Interesting. I noticed you cordoned them off the walkways not long after interviewing Mr. Darcy."

"I'm keeping that to myself for now. I'm sure you understand."

Bowers didn't, but, finally, we were alone.

My husband pursed his lips, loath to ask the question. But he's a strong man and went for it. "Was it really the dog you heard?"

I clutched Bowers' hand. "It was the same sad feeling as last night, only this time, there were cries. Tiny, scratchy cries."

Rather than bail on me, he remained in place through sheer will. "You're sure it wasn't the dog?" He preferred a domestic psychic experience to a link with a wild animal.

"I'm positive."

He wrapped my hand through his arm. "I'm not doubting you, but couldn't this have been brought on by your, um . . ."

"Obsession?"

"Not what I was going to say. But you want to believe there's a second cub, and maybe that's influencing your interpretation."

My stomach flipped. "You think I imagined it."

"I didn't say that. I said, or was trying to say without hurting your feelings, that you need to look at what's going on objectively."

"A life is on the line. How can I not care?"

"I'm not telling you not to care." He sighed and wrapped his arm around my shoulder. "Every day on the job I have to step back and make sure my emotions aren't involved and that I'm keeping an open mind. If there's a suspect I don't like, I take twice as long to consider the facts. Just because someone does bad things doesn't mean they are responsible for this particular bad thing."

He squeezed my shoulders. "In your case, just because you're getting feelings and hearing things doesn't mean it's what you think it is. A second cub."

Could Bowers have a point? Was I so certain the mournful feeling I had belonged to a stolen cub? What if it had been the dog? No. He gave off a different vibe. Like a live wire.

I'd been so certain. The experience had been enough to make me leave the treasure hunt. I'd followed the lonely ache and the scratchy cry, and it had led me to the dog. Good grief. Maybe it *was* the dog. I had to order my thoughts.

"What do we know for sure? Harry Reed worked at the zoo. He delivered Suri's babies."

"We only have proof of one."

"I know there were two," I said with a dismissive wave. "Harry took one away. He tried to contact someone at the hotel."

Bowers jerked up straight. "What was that?"

Did I admit to listening in on the Harlow boys? From the way my husband reacted the few times I got into his thoughts, he might not approve. "He was killed here, so he must have. Makes sense, right?" I batted my eyelashes and parted my lips in the quintessential pose for dumb.

After a suspicious glance, my husband relaxed. "Not necessarily. He could have arranged to meet someone on the beach. Someone unconnected with the hotel."

"Oh my gosh." I clapped my hand over my mouth.

"Have you remembered something?"

I lowered my hand. "Not exactly. It's just . . . Dot knew Harry, and now he's dead. I wonder if she knew Cynthia?"

The murmur of approaching voices hinted at new arrivals. When Bowers returned from answering the door, he had Detective Sykes and the Harlow brothers in tow.

Nicholas, a towel wrapped around his shoulders and his hair a mess of waves, strolled up with his hands on his hips and looked down at me. "Are there any other bodies we should know about?"

"Nicholas." Edward's voice held a warning.

"Ignore him," Sykes said. "Are you all right, Mrs. Bowers?"

My laugh wasn't as steady as I would have liked. "Sure. Why not? Two dead bodies in as many days shouldn't throw a girl off her stride. Especially on her honeymoon."

"You have my admiration," Edward said, bowing his

head. "A woman's strength, internal strength of character and such, is often underestimated. If you don't mind, what were you saying about, er, Dot?"

"My, what big ears you have," I said with some admiration and a lot of concern. What else had he overheard during this weekend? "Just . . . she seemed . . . attached to Harry."

The younger brother made a face. "Define attached."

"All love begins and ends there."

Edward's gaze snapped onto me. "Pardon me?"

"That's what Dot said."

He rubbed his chin with his knuckles. "Interesting. Robert Browning."

"If we're finished with the poetry recital, I'd like to speak with you," Detective Sykes said. "If you don't want to do it here, we can go to Mr. Proctor's office."

"Here is fine."

"And if you want privacy . . . "

Edward and Nicholas avoided eye contact with me, as if I might not notice them. "At this point, why? They can stay."

They went back to watching me.

"Barnaby Putluck," Sykes said as soon as we'd gotten settled. He took the chair vacated by Bautista, and Edward sat on the extended leg of the couch. Nicholas, unwilling to drip on our furniture, slouched next to the fireplace.

"Please don't tell me there's another body," I whispered. Bowers pulled me closer.

"Not that we know. According to his sister, he hasn't returned her phone calls. He's registered for the convention, but no one seems to have seen him since the first night when he shared a dinner table with three ladies."

He held out a picture of a man in his early thirties with dark slicked-back hair, black-rimmed glasses, and a nice smile. In the picture, he wore a blue suit and a red tie.

"I don't think I've seen him."

Bowers took the picture and squinted. "Isn't that the guy who wore the yachting outfit the first night? With a white captain's hat?"

Another look confirmed Bowers was right.

"When did you move into missing persons?" Nicholas asked.

"I wouldn't be involved, but since I'm here, I've been asked to look around."

Nicholas shrugged. "Maybe he got bored with all the silliness and left."

"He hasn't checked out. A Do Not Disturb sign is hanging on his door, so housekeeping hasn't been in the room."

Nicholas tried again. "Maybe he doesn't like his sister."

"That's probably all it is, which is why I haven't asked management to open the room for me. Let me know if you spot him, and I can cross it off my list. He may look different if he's not wearing the yachting outfit."

The detective tucked the picture into his jacket pocket and rested his elbows on his knees. Here it came. I would have to relive the experience again. "What relationship can any of you think of between Cynthia Ferrara and Harry Reed? Or even Edna Tartwell and Harry Reed."

A new question. Joy. "Edna had a dog. Harry was a vet."

Detective Sykes' eyebrows went up. "That's true. And not something I'd considered."

"I don't suppose Harry registered for the conference," Nicholas said, sounding bored.

"He did not."

"Do Edna Tartwell and her niece live in San Diego?" Bowers asked.

"Her niece was also her chauffeur and companion. Edna doesn't have a driver's license. They live in Graton, California. It's a small, unincorporated town in Sonoma County." For my benefit, he added, "That's up north."

Edward chuckled. "You say that as if it's a quaint road stop. They have fine wine and restaurants there. Art galleries."

"Is it expensive to live there?" my husband asked.

The elder Harlow rubbed his beard. "I believe the cost of living is higher than average."

Nicholas exhaled a huff of air. "If she's rich, the old lady will be able to afford a nice burial."

Edward chided Nicholas for his lack of feelings, but his brother's body language told me a different story. He kept rubbing the back of his neck with one hand, and the other held the towel in a tight fist. That fist had a slight tremble. He shifted on his feet more than a pup who needed a potty break.

I scooted against Bowers to move him over and patted the couch. "You need to get off your feet. You've had a shock."

He protested about dripping on our furniture, so I got up and went to the bedroom. On my way back, I swung open the bathroom door and set out a fresh towel.

"Take a hot shower and change. I've laid out a clean towel. A set of your own clothes are on the bed."

Nicholas met my gaze with a puzzled frown. About to decline my offer, he changed his mind and shrugged. "Sure. Thanks."

"And I ordered coffee from a confused room service person and told them to bring lots of sugar."

At the mention of sugar, Nicholas dug into his pocket and pulled out a soggy baggie. He held it out to Edward. "Chocolate Caramel Crunchies. Courtesy of Mrs. A."

Edward declined the offer.

Bowers kissed the top of my head. "That was kind of you, but which clothes are you giving him?" Bowers wasn't protecting his turf. I hadn't yet told him about Mrs. Abernathy's generosity. As far as he knew, he had the clothes on his back and nothing else.

"The Harlow's housekeeper felt sorry for you and made a donation."

As the owner of those clothes left the room, Edward stared at his brother with surprise that quickly turned into concern, and I gave him a frownie face for not noticing his brother's condition sooner.

Detective Sykes picked up the conversation. "Nicholas said that Cynthia wanted to talk to you about something. That's according to Edna."

"My wife and I have discussed it. She said nothing to the woman that would have prompted her to seek Frankie out. We're as puzzled as you are."

Detective Sykes pressed his lips together and puffed out his cheeks.

I patted Bowers' knee. "I appreciate that you want to spare me, honey, but you'd have three fits if a spouse answered a question posed to his wife. But ditto what my husband said. We didn't talk about anything. Me and Cynthia didn't. Bowers and I did."

The detective accompanied his thanks with a laugh. "Was I that transparent?"

Bowers apologized. "At least now I understand why husbands do it. Maybe I'll have more sympathy next time it happens to me."

"I've seen her . . ." I counted off on my fingers. "Two—no, three times. Once when we checked in. She was at the counter looking for a pen. At dinner, I saw her seated next to her aunt. And I saw her—" About to say talking to Bowers, I changed it to coming in the room during the mixer.

"And you, Mr. Bowers?"

"Call me Martin. I saw her the same three times. I spoke to her as she came into the Crown Room last night. She. . . she may have been hitting on me."

I snorted. "Of course she was." I shook my head, sadly. "Men."

Just to show Bowers I wasn't the jealous type, I added, "I especially noticed her last night because she and her aunt declined to join the party in the Corona Room. I guess that's the fourth time I saw her. I'm afraid I assumed a widow traveling with her niece would have been thrilled to check out another event room at the hotel. Maybe her niece talked her out of it."

"I have difficulty finding a connection between Miss Ferrara and Harry Reed." Edward spread his hands. "Someone they knew in common, perhaps?"

"That's a good suggestion," Bowers acknowledged with a hint of reluctance.

It was. And if I could get Tanner alone, I could find out.

Coffee arrived. Bowers came with me and tipped the waiter, who peered around us with undisguised curiosity.

When we returned to the sitting area, Nicholas had taken a seat on the couch and had changed into dark slacks and a heather gray sweater that matched his eyes. His wet hair curled, and he wore the only pair of dress shoes Mrs. Abernathy had given us.

As if reading my thoughts, he said, "I'll return these after I grab a pair from my room."

I knew my husband was still curious about what the police found on the walkway, but he'd asked once and wouldn't bring it up again. So, I did.

"I noticed the police put yellow tape around the walkways leading to our Cabana. Did they find anything?"

Sykes sipped his coffee. He wore the unreadable cop face.

To prepare for my fit, I set my coffee down. "It's—it's just so troubling. So . . ." I touched my knuckles to my face like I'd seen the woman do in a fifties horror movie. "So, frightening. To think that a murderer killed a man on my patio while I was sleeping."

Holding my eyes open wide hurt my eyeballs, so I went with lowered lashes and trembling lips. Not only did Bowers gape at me, but Nicholas wore the expression of a teacher about to call out an unruly student. I narrowed my eyes at him. He frowned and decided to play along.

"There, there, Mrs. Bowers. I'm sure there's nothing to be frightened about."

I wished he'd stop helping me. His wooden delivery caused his brother to glance sharply in his direction.

Since I couldn't talk with my knuckles in my mouth, I moved the back of my hand to my forehead. "If only I could get the image out of my head. Me. Sound asleep.

And . . . " I lowered my voice to a whispered hiss. "*Death* stalking my patio."

When I shivered my shoulders, it set off a reaction until my entire body shook. I was afraid Detective Sykes might throw me to the ground and put a stick between my teeth, but I got it under control.

As I sucked in my lower lip in a final gasp, my only obstacle was Sykes. Or, rather, Sykes' wife. As a married man used to female company, he might recognize my theatrics as baloney.

He leaned forward and rested his elbows on his knees. "You can rest easy. There were snags of knit material on the walkway."

Bowers rubbed his chin. "Meaning someone dragged him there." He squinted as he ran scenarios in his head. "A beach towel?"

"Most likely."

I had opened my mouth to gush out my thanks, but Bowers silenced me with a hard squeeze to my knee, so, I stopped while I was ahead.

"Then are we decided?" Edward slapped his hands on his knees, reminding me of dad letting us know he'd made reservations for a cabin on the lake even though no one else fished.

"Decided about what?" Nicholas rubbed his eyes.

"On the motive. Was Harry Reed killed because of his involvement in animal trafficking?"

His brother dropped his hands into his lap. "That's a stretch."

With an imperious gesture, Edward invited Nicholas to come up with his own theories.

"What about the usual? Love, money, hatred, money . . . " He gave his brother the stink eye. "If I had a sheriff's investigator that I regularly gossiped with, I might know if Harry had any money in his wallet. If he didn't, I might guess robbery."

"By someone who carries a weeder with them on beach strolls? You can do better."

"Unless Darby killed him, the weapon was a convenience."

"One that anyone who entered the Sheerwater would have had access to," Bowers added.

Nicholas nodded. "Back to motive. Had Harry put his paws on someone's girlfriend? Or did he recently dump his own woman? We don't know anything about his private relations."

My husband's logical mind took over. "Then why here? If his murder had nothing to do with the Hotel del Coronado, why happen here?"

"An excellent point," Edward said.

"Fine." Nicholas crossed his arms. "Tell us your theory."

"We know Harry Reed was present for the birth of Suri's cub. We also know he didn't tell the other vets at the zoo about his suspicions, almost as if he hoped to hide her pregnancy. Suri is a white tiger. White tiger cubs are rare, which would mean a large payoff for our unethical friend. And Jimmy Bianchi, a man with unsavory connections, has shown unwavering interest in the animal. It's only an assumption, but Jimmy Bianchi strikes me as a man with money."

"But where's the cub? If he wanted to sell a cub, he'd need one to sell."

Bowers glanced at Nicholas. "I'm afraid I have to agree with your brother."

My husband and I would discuss his betrayal later. I raised my hand. "I vote yes."

As if sensing he'd made a marital boo-boo, Bowers added, "But it's the only motive we have right now."

Sykes cleared his throat. "I discovered that Jimmy Bianchi is known for his private collection of animals. He has paperwork that lists him as a rescue. Money must have changed hands somewhere because I don't connect him with altruism."

We drank in silence, each with his or her own thoughts. When Bowers began massaging the back of my neck, the men gulped down the rest of their coffee and said they needed to get back to The Victorian.

Nicholas stretched when he stood. "Why are you working on the murders?" he asked Detective Sykes. "I thought you were busy with crowd control."

"Sergeant Bautista has asked me to consult on the murder investigation. He didn't intend to call in the sheriff's department, but since I was already here, he decided to take advantage of it." He shook Bowers' hand and gave me a kind smile. "I sincerely hope this is the end of the excitement for you. The unpleasant kind, I mean. I wish we could have spared you the interview, but now you can return to normal."

Bowers stared, deep in his own thoughts. A place where he searched for the meaning of normal.

The detective winked. "Look after her."

My husband started and looked up. "I certainly will."

Once they left, Bowers apologized in earnest. "This entire vacation has been turned upside down. Instead of the romantic getaway I promised, you've been exposed to two dead bodies and a police investigation. I'm so sorry."

I giggled.

"What?"

"It has been unusual. Something I'll never forget."

He grinned. "It has been that."

"And some of it's my fault. If I hadn't booked us into the convention, we would have had dinner alone and never met any of these people. But at least you got a personal introduction to a famous author and his annoying brother."

"They're not so bad. All right. Nicholas is annoying, but he is lending me his clothes. I wondered how I'd dress for dinner."

"Oh. Speaking of Nicholas, when we were on the beach, we ran into Mr. Darby. Well, he ran into us. He wanted Tanner off the beach. But we asked him about how he left the zoo. I told you about that, didn't I? How Harry got him fired? I'll give you three guesses why."

Bowers' expression told me he wasn't in the mood to guess.

"Okay. I'll just tell you. Darby said he witnessed Harry examining Chuck the Chimp's girlfriend. He was examining her *tummy*, and when he saw Clarance Darby watching, he freaked out."

"You and Nicholas found this out."

He used his even, emotionless cop tone.

"Yes. We were together at the time. With Tanner."

"I see."

My husband, back when he was my fiancé, met my ex-boyfriend, Jeff. If anyone could drive a girl's beloved crazy, Jeff would be the one to do it, but I never caught a whiff of jealousy from Bowers. Not that he had reason to be jealous.

"Bowers! Are you jealous?"

The cop face scurried away, replaced by surprise. "Jealous?"

"Hmm. Nicholas *is* handsome—"

Bowers scoffed.

"But Jeff is darn good-looking, too. And, obviously, you trust me. So, it must be . . ."

"Frankie, you're imagining things."

But I wasn't. I gasped. "You're jealous that I was investigating the murder with Nicholas. But I investigated the last murder with Jeff, and that didn't bother you."

"Jeff's an idiot."

"And Nicholas, though annoying, is not." I grinned. "Bowers, sweetie. You don't like that I'm enjoying myself with another man." I scrunched my nose. "That came out wrong. What I mean is you love the excitement of an investigation, and you'd rather I share that excitement with you."

"If you say so."

He could pretend it didn't matter, but I knew I'd nailed it. "I'd much rather discover dead bodies with you at my side."

He pulled me close. "Don't even joke about it. I wish I could have saved you from the ugly bits this weekend."

It was a nice sentiment, but the only thing that would have saved me from what happened later was if I'd had eyeballs in the back of my head.

Chapter Twenty-Seven

Frankie: Nicholas Goes Too Far

Bowers' warm and fuzzy feelings about the Harlow boys didn't last.

One thing I hadn't shared with my husband. Two things. That Nicholas Harlow had seen Harry Reed trying to get in contact with a hotel guest the morning of the man's death, and that Edward Harlow was Aunt Civility.

I had both these items in mind when we seated ourselves at dinner across from our table mates.

After the many stares from the other guests as we entered the restaurant, I was happy to have the chair that faced the wall.

"Nice suit," Nicholas said with a nod at my husband.

The navy-blue suit's length was fine, but it hung slightly baggy off Bowers' leaner frame. It looked like he had dressed for the movie's time period, except for his tennis shoes. Nicholas had forgotten to return the dress shoes.

By unstated agreement, the chit-chat remained surface level until the waitress brought dinner. As soon as she left, Nicholas leaned forward to address my husband.

"How did you like Edward's interview? By the way, that's some set of lungs you have on you."

We all knew he referred to Bowers' call for Edward to take off his pants. My better half took a hearty bite of steak and smirked while he chewed.

"Not that I blame you. Edward's got good legs and should show them off more. The ladies certainly appreciated it."

Bowers speared a potato. "How did you like wearing a dress?"

The author considered his answer. "In some ways, it was freeing. But it was drafty, and I felt . . . exposed. Especially after I took off my pants."

Unbidden, an image of Edward Harlow without his pants came into my head. I shooed it away.

"I don't know how women stand it. They are made of sterner stuff."

Bowers laughed. "You can say that again."

"He has seven sisters," I explained.

Both Harlow brothers gaped. "Seven?" Edward rubbed his chin. "I'd love to get your insights. For instance, do you find a feminine commonality in their behavior? I imagine their personalities vary."

"Do they ever," I murmured. Bowers gave my ankle a light tap with his shoe. "Sorry."

They continued along that theme through dinner. When we had our dessert plates in front of us—Madeline cookies with pudding, fruit, and whipped creme—I decided it was time to force those brothers to confess all they knew to Bowers.

Sure, I could have given him the chipmunk's report,

but my husband's ego would appreciate the information more if it came from the guys. It must have been a dormant maternal instinct. I wanted my husband included. And I didn't want him viewing chipmunks with suspicion.

In my experience, people have a harder time lying when their focus is elsewhere, so I planned to use their weaknesses against them.

I rested my chin on my hands, which put my elbows on the table.

Edward paused mid-sentence and stared at my obvious violation of good manners. Even I knew I shouldn't have my elbows on the table. He looked away. Then looked back.

I twisted my head and fluttered my eyelashes at Nicholas. He recoiled as if I'd pinched him again. Good. Now I had them off balance.

"Did you men learn anything interesting today?"

"Define interesting," Nicholas said. He had better control than I thought. If I hadn't seen him flinch, I would have thought from his neutral expression that he hadn't just received a flirtation from a married woman he thought was "obsessed" with him, according to the chipmunk's report. I considered playing footsies under the table to drive him into a panic but dismissed it as creepy.

I decided to ease into my interrogation. "What was it you found in the pool?"

Bowers sent the younger Harlow a sharp glance.

"You dove back in to retrieve it. Then you wiped your hand on the side of the pool."

"A candy bar wrapper."

"No, not that. The *other* thing."

"Nothing important. I thought it was a button or a

pin, but it crumbled in my hand. I hate to think what it was."

Bowers stared thoughtfully. I could feel the heat from the wheels turning in his head and knew he'd get it sooner than later.

To guarantee it was sooner, I leaned over, put my lips against his ear, and whispered, "Kibble." When I leaned back and grinned, he ignored the stares coming from across the table and patted my knee.

"You know what it was," Nicholas said.

Edward barked out a laugh. "Of course she does. Dog food. Am I right? And Edna Tartwell carries a bag filled with goodies for that obnoxious Chihuahua of hers. Not that Cynthia couldn't have put a few bits in her pocket before walking the dog."

I'd lose my advantage if I gave him credit, so I didn't. "Interesting about Harry Reed," I continued. "No one seems to know what he did when he arrived at the hotel."

Bowers shifted his chair to look at me. He knew I meant more than I said. "Edward saw him approach the front desk."

"Yes, but what did he say? If only someone had overheard him."

I rested a pointed glance on Nicholas. He met my gaze with open frankness.

"Here's an idea." Edward leaned forward and lowered his voice to a rumble. "Why don't we *both* share what we've learned?"

My shoulder muscles tightened. How could I tell them what I'd learned from some seagulls and a tiger? And a crab? They'd never believe me.

Edward added in a silky voice, "Ms. Chandler."

Nicholas jerked straight. "They're not married?"

Edward tilted his head. "I thought I stressed the zzz sound. Mzzz. Mzzz. Meaning either married or unmarried." He raised his brows with interest. "Will you keep your professional name?"

"Your point?" Bowers said through gritted teeth.

"I did some research." Edward folded his napkin and placed it on the table. "You've both been in *The Wolf Creek Gazette* a few times. I thought, perhaps, with your wife's interest in the zoo, she might have discovered useful information from the animals."

Nicholas interrupted the silence. "What does *from the animals* mean?"

"She's an animal communicator."

"What the hell is that?"

"Nicholas. Watch your language. The point is, it's information I hoped the Bowerses would like to share with us."

Was that a threat? It sounded like a threat. But what could he hold over my head?

My husband, the detective, was about to say something in that cool, even voice he uses in his professional capacity, but Nicholas hadn't insulted him, so I got there first.

"Why don't you go first, Aunt Civility?"

Edward balked. Nicholas had an unreadable expression. Bowers gaped.

"Wait. What? What does my wife mean? What about your aunt?"

"Keep your voice down," Edward hissed.

Nicholas tossed his napkin on the table. "I've told you for years you should let it out." He scooted his chair to face me. "What I want to know is how you know and what you plan to do about it. My brother should decide for himself how much he wants fans to know."

"Do about it?" Was I supposed to do something about it? Like what? Nicholas filled in the gaps.

"Sell it to a newspaper. Leak it on the Internet. Don't play innocent. You're strange, but you can't be that dumb."

"Don't speak to my wife like that."

Bowers cool tone was more threatening than a yell.

"I never thought about doing any of those things. But now we're even with our secrets. Except for the bit about you standing next to Harry Reed at the reservation desk yesterday morning."

"You what?" This time Bowers yelled. Several heads turned in our direction.

"Are you following me?"

I narrowed my eyes at the younger brother. "I have a network of spies."

"The chipmunk," Bowers muttered.

"Which is exactly what we wanted to talk to you about," Edward said with a conciliatory gesture.

"Back up." Bowers held up a hand. "What did Harry Reed say when you saw him?"

"Ask your wife," Nicholas snapped.

"I'm asking you, since you're the one who will have to inform Sergeant Bautista of information you held back."

Nicholas picked his napkin off the table, folded it, and set it next to his plate. "He wanted the clerk to call a guest's room."

"Which guest?" Bowers swore. "Do you know how much time we've wasted?"

Nicholas leaned back in his chair and folded his arms over his chest. "Keep my shirt on. He didn't say. He tried to cut in front of me. I gave him a nasty look, and he changed his mind and left."

Edward covered his snort with his napkin, but his shoulders shook. "You think the man fled because of a look you gave him? Isn't it more likely he saw someone in the lobby he didn't want to meet and escaped before they saw him, too?"

"I wondered. It wasn't my most threatening expression."

Should I ask the gulls if they saw Harry during the day? Not that they'd answer my questions after I menaced them with a good roasting. But they'd retaliated. We were even.

Edward spread his hands. "And now you know all that we do. Your turn."

This wasn't going to be easy. Not telling them but telling them in a way that didn't send Bowers into fits. My husband skirted around the edge of believing. He'd seen too much for a straight denial. Still, he would never chat casually about my talent with two strangers.

"Well, it's like this. My animal behavior experience tells me that Suri—she's the white tiger—is depressed, and it has something to do with her cub."

"Post-partum depression?" Edward nodded as if he'd expected this.

"Nooo. Kind of the opposite."

His brow wrinkled. "You mean she lost a cub? I understand that happens often in the wild, but I would think the zoo, with all the veterinarians on staff and access to modern equipment, could avoid that outcome."

"Define lost. What if Suri had a second cub and Harry stole it?"

Edward caught on quickly. "Animal trafficking. Just

as I suspected. It gives the killer a motive, but only if he or she got their hands on the cub first."

And had they? Was the mournful cry I heard late at night the call of a cub, trapped in a lonely room, and longing for its mother? My heart broke until a thought popped up and waved at me.

"The cub is still here. We need to find it."

"Have you all lost your ever-lovin' minds?" Nicholas swiped a roll from Edward's plate, tore off a piece, and shook it at his brother. "Are you seriously considering placing our investigation in the hands of a woman who's guessing what a tiger thinks?" He turned his glare on me. "And what's with the faces?"

Bowers launched into a coughing fit.

"It was embarrassing. Every time we came to an enclosure or cage, you made these weird contortions."

My fingers went to my face in a subconscious move to hide the evidence.

"And then the animals went nuts. I dodged monkey poop courtesy of the chimps."

"Chimps aren't monkeys," Edward murmured.

"Even the tapir started screaming." He gestured with the roll. "And then the crazy lady screamed, too. I don't know if you give off an anti-animal vibe or if they just think you smell funny, but I didn't hear you say one word. You were *not* talking to the animals." He threw down the roll. "Okay. What did they say?"

"That's enough," Bowers said, and Edward sent my husband a wary glance.

"That they didn't like Harry Reed. It was unanimous."

"They said that did they?" Nicholas said in a derisive tone that made me want to slap him.

I floundered for a way to describe it and directed my explanation toward Edward, who looked genuinely interested when he wasn't keeping tabs on how close Bowers was to exploding. "They don't talk. Not in words. It would be easier if they did." As I struggled, Bowers grasped my hand.

"You don't need to explain yourself."

"I want to. It's only fair. We're asking them to believe me. It's just . . . images. Feelings. Sometimes a weird vibration. It depends on the animal."

Nicholas scoffed. "Sounds like a drug trip. Someone find a straitjacket."

After patting my lips with my napkin, I scooted back my chair and excused myself. I didn't want to cry in front of a room filled with *Some Like It Hot* fans.

"Frankie—"

Bowers moved to rise, but I placed a hand on his shoulder. "I'll be right back." With a final glare at Nicholas, I added my parting shot. "And I am not obsessed with you, you twit. Your brother had it right. I am a jedi."

Several diners stared at me, but it was worth it to see his shocked expression.

Chapter Twenty-Eight

Frankie: A Walk on the Beach Goes Bad

My steps quickened as I approached the exit, and I didn't stop moving until I stood outside at the water's edge. Confrontation wasn't my thing. I hated the roiled emotions that came with an argument. If I tried to defend myself, it usually came out with stutters and garbled ideas that made no sense. I wished I could communicate with humans as well as I did with animals. Not that I was great with animals either, but the tension wasn't there.

The breeze skirting over the ocean chilled me. Folding my arms for warmth, I headed down the beach toward our cottage. Bowers had the key, but a walk there and back would calm my nerves. In fact, the repetitive lull of the surf had me taking deep, relaxing breaths.

I forgave Nicholas Harlow. If someone had told me a few years ago they talked to animals, I would have written them off as certifiable. Or as charlatans, like I had been before Sandy the golden retriever broke through my mental barrier with an image of a murdered maid. An event that marked the end of my normal life.

But I had gotten better at dealing with the chaos that came with communicating with animals. Had I missed any signs on my visit to the zoo?

The tapir had screamed and shown a defensive, agitated posture. No hidden messages there. Chimps throwing poop. They might have been seeking amusement and I gave them a target. No. The bared teeth meant something more, and it came after I'd shown them an image of Harry.

And what about the image of a pair of scissors? One of the chimps had injured his hand after someone carelessly threw scissors into the pen. But who carries scissors to the zoo? Had Harry deliberately endangered the animal to keep Dr. Sylvia Yang occupied while he stole the cub? What a jerk.

Suri's reaction was the most important, and she had shown rage mixed with an empty pain. No one could tell me she wasn't in mourning for her cub. Through her, I'd seen it born. But had the cub moved after delivery? Even a slight twitch? The mother believed it was alive, and that was good enough for me. Mothers knew.

A clump of seaweed rested on the beach about ten yards away. Odd, but it didn't move like seaweed. It looked more solid.

When I got to it, I stared. It was a pink bunny, though in its current soggy state, it looked more grayish pink. But it was *the* pink bunny. The one Bowers returned to the tiger's cage. I recognized the missing eye and the tear in its belly.

As I bent to pick it up, something slammed me from behind, sending me sprawling face down in the water.

I rolled onto my back while I caught my wind. My

attacker hadn't hung around, an assumption I made since the shove wasn't followed by a kick or two.

The bunny. I crawled through the rolling waves, straining to see through squinting eyes. Finally, I used ocean water to splash the sand from my eyes and stood. I caught sight of a form running toward the walkway near the Taco Shack.

The urge to chase . . . I didn't have that urge. My soaked clothes weighed a ton, my teeth chattered from the cold and shock, and my feet felt leaden under the weight of wet sand. There was no chance I'd catch them.

A voice called out. "She's here!"

The voice belonged to Nicholas Harlow. He turned me around and brushed the sand off my sleeves. "Were you trying to talk to the dolphins?"

"Get him! Or her!"

"Who am I getting?"

I pulled away from him to see if my attacker was still in sight, but when I put weight on my left ankle, I collapsed against him. He wrapped his well-muscled arms around me to keep me from falling.

"What happened?" Edward asked.

When I turned my head, the movement made me wince. "I think I have whiplash. Where's Bowers?"

"He went to look for you in—Ah. Here he is."

Bowers charged across the sand at a full run. "Frankie!"

"He knows I'm not hugging his wife, right?" Nicholas said as an aside.

My husband pulled me into his arms, a warm and familiar embrace that set off tears. He brushed me off, including my sweater front and rear end, which Nicholas Harlow had been gentleman enough to skip.

I gathered my husband's shirt in my hands. "I found it. The bunny. It washed up on the beach."

Bowers made soothing noises, which meant he thought I'd knocked my noggin too hard.

"When is the last time we saw the bunny?" I demanded. "When you threw it back into the enclosure at the zoo. What's it doing here? Someone knocked me down and took it."

He swore.

I held his face in my sand-covered hands. "Don't you get it? That proves I'm right!"

A cross between a cackle and a cluck came from where the old pier rose out of the sand. Where the gulls gathered at night. Though they'd proved to be untrustworthy, I sent them an image of my face plant in the sand.

My vision turned hazy, and when it cleared, flying bunnies, all flapping their ears to stay airborne, packed the sky. The birds were mocking me.

I switched to an image of Harry carrying the bunny as he walked the beach at night. The flash came so quickly that I knew it was an involuntary response from one of the flock. A straw bag with flowers. The large kind mother used to take to the beach, except this had a lid.

The birds hadn't meant me to see. Their cries rose to a hysterical level. Nicholas sent a wary glance skyward. "Maybe we should move inside."

Edward cleared his throat. "It might be helpful to share the details about what happened tonight." I couldn't see Bowers' expression, but Edward added, "But you should take care of your wife first."

"You're damned straight I will." He lifted me into his arms and glared at Nicholas. "You and your trap. This is your fault."

The younger brother spread his hands. "What did I do?"

Bowers snarled.

Nicholas didn't sound worried by Bowers' anger. Just annoyed. "You sound just like Edward and Sykes."

"Two very smart men." With that parting shot, Bowers carried me back toward the cottage. I had so many conflicted emotions and thoughts running through my head that I didn't take time to chastise him about straining his leg.

When he set me down to unlock the gate, I gave the beach one last look. I was destined to never have my romantic, moonlit stroll.

Before he could pick me up again, I suggested that exercising my ankle might be best. My husband didn't argue, and the two of us limped our way to our cottage.

Chapter Twenty-Nine

Frankie: Whispers in the Night

I woke with a start that made Bowers groan and roll over. Placing my hand on my chest didn't slow my pounding heartbeat.

When the cry hit me again, I wrapped my arms around my middle and bit my lip to stop me from joining in.

"No," I whispered.

Bowers sensed something was wrong and stirred. "Honey? Why are you up?"

"It's nothing," I whispered. More than anything, I hoped he would go back to sleep. He hadn't complained, but I knew he worried about the setback with his leg. Bowers didn't need the additional stress.

However, he reached out for me and touched my face, sighing when he felt the tears. He scooted to sitting and pulled me to his chest.

"You heard it again."

It wasn't a question, so I didn't answer.

"Can you, um, hear it now?"

His waking had distracted me, but the connection was

gone.

"No."

"Could it be a lost cat? Someone's pet? And they finally let it inside?"

It wasn't a pet, and Bowers knew it. But it seemed easier to agree.

The next morning, we had a buffet style breakfast in the Crown Room. Overnight, I'd become a popular gal. The convention guests had somehow learned about my adventure last night and everyone wanted details.

Even Edna Tartwell and Tanner had come down for nourishment. She said it helped the grieving process to be around other people. "Nothing will bring Cynthia back. I'm sure she's in a better place, and she'd want me to go on with my life."

The way she attacked her ham steak, she took honoring her niece seriously.

"The beach isn't safe," one woman said to her companion, both showing wrinkled kneecaps under their flapper dresses. "Two deaths and now this attack."

"I don't think you need to fear the beach. Just exercise caution. Don't go walking alone." My husband, having delivered his Officer Friendly speech, speared a sausage, and chewed it with gusto. He'd spent last night comforting me to the best of his abilities, which were something to write home about. Not that I'd ever write a letter describing . . . Never mind.

An older woman's voice shook me out of pleasant thoughts. "Did they take your purse, dear?"

"No, ma'am," I answered, abandoning my pancakes.

The mention of a purse had me scanning the room for a large straw bag with a lid. Edna Tartwell's didn't have a lid. The rest of the women all had cloth or leather purses.

The largest bag I spotted was a cloth carryall on the floor next to a woman's chair. It bore the convention logo on the side facing me.

Rhonda and Willie hurried to my side. She clapped her hands together. "I knew you were fine. Someone said you'd been attacked."

"Well, I was. Last night on the beach."

Willie nodded. "But instead of crumbling, you're here, and you look one hundred percent. Even after finding *two* bodies. Isn't she brave, Ronnie?"

"So brave," his wife agreed. "I knew the good God above would not allow you to get hurt. That's why I refused to believe the rumors."

"Nor would He let your attack ruin the conference," Willie added with a chuckle.

His wife's mouth puffed up as she held in a laugh, but it was too much. She poked his arm as it escaped. "You're bad. You are so bad."

He pinched her arms. "No, baby, it's you who are bad."

"No. You're bad."

"*You're* bad."

They ended up calling it a draw and rubbing noses just like how my first-grade teacher told us Eskimos kissed.

"Maybe the person didn't mean it." That suggestion came from Edna. Polka didn't look as positive, and Dot looked ill.

Rhonda raised herself up on her toes. "I hadn't thought of that. This could all be an accident. Just a silly mix-up. Anyway, you look fine. All's well that ends well."

Ice packs and heat had helped with my headache and sore neck, and makeup bought at extortionate prices from the gift shop had covered the few scratches on my face. But Rhonda was wrong. The person had snatched the pink bunny, and I felt the loss.

"I hear you discovered another body."

Oswald Fielding II stood over me, dressed in his captain's uniform.

Bowers gave him a hard stare. If the guy had been a clock, my husband would have taken him apart and examined all the pieces.

"Leave Frankie alone," Rhonda said, her tone closer to snippy than I thought possible for her. "It's not her fault."

"I'm terribly sorry. I didn't mean to offend you. My choice of words wasn't the best."

"That's okay. And I wasn't the only one who found the body."

I dipped my head at Nicholas Harlow who had just entered the room with his brother. Oswald studied him with interest, and I wondered if the younger Harlow had a fan.

The brothers cut through the crowd of gapers—those who wanted to hear all about last night but didn't want to appear interested.

"How are you feeling this morning?" Edward asked. Nicholas hung back out of Bowers' line of site.

Before I answered, the older brother leaned down to position his mouth near Bowers' ear. "Perhaps we could find somewhere less crowded, and you could fill us in on the details?"

Bowers took my hand. "Are you all right with that, Frankie?"

I wasn't. This was supposed to be our honeymoon. Okay. That wasn't the real reason. What's a honeymoon except another name for a vacation?

Last night, Bowers had focused every scrap of his attention on me. I liked it. A lot. And, while I realized life came with distractions and interruptions, and to expect my husband to behave like a love-struck teenager every moment of every day was selfish, unreasonable, and a bit monstrous, I wanted it to last.

If there had to be a murder or two, I didn't mind poking into them with my husband. In fact, doing so played into my fantasy about working with Bowers as a team. A modern-day Nick and Nora Charles. That team did not include the Harlow brothers, but I was stuck with them. For now.

I let my fork drop with a clatter and dabbed my mouth with my napkin. "Sure. Why not?"

My husband was too professional to let his personal animus toward Nicholas get in the way of working on the murder, though when he backed up his chair, he "accidentally" barked the younger brother's shin.

Edward paused by Dot, rested his big paw on her shoulder, and squeezed. She glanced up, startled, but tears came to her eyes, and she squeezed his hand back. That gave me all the proof I needed that Edward was the sensitive brother.

As we headed out of the room, I went back to retrieve my purse from the back of my chair. When I passed through the exit door, the large man with a scar stepped into my path.

"Excuse me, ma'am."

Oh, my gosh. That's right. I was a ma'am!

"Yes?" I answered in a lofty tone, trying to do my new title justice.

"Mr. Jimmy heard about your troubles last night and wishes me to express his anger over any injuries you suffered and let you know you are welcome to his assistance. Any time. Just ask."

"Um." I supposed it was nice of him to offer, and I should take his disturbing invitation in that spirit. "I'm sorry. I don't know your name."

The big man blushed and stammered. "Stanley."

"What a nice name. Tell your boss—is Jimmy your boss? He is? Please thank him for his concern, but my husband has me covered."

The big man cast a doubtful glance toward Bowers' back as he left the room, obviously not confident my husband was capable of handling trouble. Then again, he didn't know my husband. "I will tell him."

When he glanced over my shoulder, Stanley's eyes widened. I turned to see what could surprise this man, but I didn't spot anything except my fellow guests still chatting about the incident. Rhonda and Willie stood next to Edna's chair. The sisters, Polka and Dot, had joined her at her table, as had Oswald.

By the time I turned back to ask Stanley what he'd seen, he'd disappeared.

* * *

Antonio Sabato wasn't happy to see Edward Harlow and Detective Martin Bowers when they strolled into his office. But juggling crises came with the job. Apathy from the lions bored by their enclosures. Aggression from the rhinos for the same reason. And prolonged infantile behavior from the elephants. Again, boredom.

Sometimes he felt as if he ran a daycare. As soon as the workers altered the environment for the tigers enough to satisfy, the gorillas would demand more amusements. A never-ending circle of upgrades, and all of it costing money.

At least these men wouldn't ask him to lay out a goat carcass so they could pretend to stalk it. He invited them to sit.

Edward tugged the seams of his pant leg straight. "We hoped we could speak with Dr. Sylvia Yang."

"Sylvia? What for?"

The author looked to the detective to explain. "We'll tell you when we tell her."

The curator summoned the vet, and while they waited, Antonio asked if the police had any suspects.

"It's early days," Edward said, repeating an oft-used phrase from British mysteries.

"Have you replaced Harry yet?" Bowers asked.

Antonio shuffled through papers on his desk. "We're interviewing. I have a friend who specializes in primates. He's helping. It takes some of the pressure off the others, but we need to hire someone soon."

The door opened, and Dr. Sylvia Yang walked in. She gave the visitors a cursory glance and said, "I'm right in the middle of a hoof trimming."

"This won't take long," Bowers assured her. "I wondered if there were any abnormalities in the number of babies who are, um, unsuccessfully delivered at the zoo. Specifically, ones Harry Reed oversaw."

At the mention of the late vet's name Dr. Yang forgot her rush and leaned against her boss's desk. "You mean, did Harry have an unusually high death rate in the pregnant animals he oversaw?"

"I can answer that." Antonio adjusted his glasses. "I keep a close eye on pregnancy to live birth statistics." He turned to his computer and input the necessary search criteria. "I'm pleased to say we haven't lost any babies since Harry's been here."

"How many births has he attended?" Bowers amended his question. "Alone."

Antonio's fingers paused over his keyboard. "None. That is, none that I'm aware of. It would be highly irregular. Sylvia?"

"We haven't had any high-risk pregnancies. None that would require us to interfere with the natural process. Why are you asking?"

Bowers smiled. "It's what we do. Check every possibility. Look for anomalies." He stood. "You could do me a favor. Could you check on Chuck the chimp's girlfriend to see if she's, ah, all right?"

The vet's eyebrows shot up. She said nothing but turned and left.

Antonio tapped a nervous beat on his desk. "I assume you had a reason for asking."

"My wife notices animal behavior. She was concerned."

"I see." But it was clear Antonio Sabato, Curator of Mammals, did not see.

Chapter Thirty

Frankie: Shopping Spree

Bowers and his new friends had gone on without me. About to look for them in Detective Sykes' room, it occurred to me the best way to get Bowers' attention back on me would be to bring him a big, juicy clue.

One of the downstairs rooms had been put to use as a costume room, accessible through The Garden. The door stood open. Inside, racks of pants, shirts, slacks, dresses, and shoes crowded the space, separated by type of clothing and further divided by those separators that are used to guide shoppers to the right size. Only these said things like gangster, casual, evening, yacht, and so on.

A large woman with purple hair piled on her head, her impressive arms exposed by her short-sleeved orange sheath covered by a full apron, stepped out from between the racks. I'd talked to her the night we'd arrived about Bowers' costume.

"Jen. I'm so glad you're here. I didn't know how late you were, um, open."

"What do you need, honey?"

I pulled my envious gaze from a lavender gown with sparkles. "I already have my dress."

"You can exchange the outfit any time, dear."

"I can?"

"That's what I'm here for. That lavender would go great with your hair, but it's a women's twenty-two. Too big for you, and I don't have time to take it in."

"That's okay." Really, it wasn't. I didn't often feel a connection to clothing, but married life had me seeing my outfits through Bowers' eyes. During our recovery period, I'd gotten away with my usual sweatpants and t-shirts, but it was hard to seduce a man when you looked like a homeless woman. My wardrobe needed a refresh.

"I wanted to ask you about shoes."

She glanced at my black flats.

"Those are fine for what you have on, but if you're going to wear a dress—Which dress do you have?"

"Um, the white one. It's a little large in front." I blushed at the remembrance of where that white dress had led me and Bowers the last time I tried it on.

She reached into her apron pocket, pulled out a safety pin, and handed it to me. "Fasten it on the inside and no one will ever know. Now, about the shoes. You want white pumps for the dress, I assume. What size do you wear?"

"Um, the shoes are not for me. I wondered about the shoes with spats."

Jen led me to a table with a small chest of drawers sitting on top. The scuffed wood made me think this was her private property. A relic from her grandmother's era. She slid open a drawer that held small pieces of folded cloth.

"The spats aren't part of the shoes?"

"Where have you been?" She chuckled.

Obviously, a place where people didn't wear spats. Like present day . . . everywhere.

"Can you tell me who rented them?"

She closed the drawer. "That's not possible."

"You mean you can't? Don't you have some sort of record?"

"I mean I won't. That's personal information you're asking for. Besides. If someone gave you their spats directly, my records wouldn't be worth spit."

Jen seemed like a nice lady. If I shared my reason with her, would she change her mind?

"You heard about the dead body?"

"Which one?"

She had a point. "Well, both of them, I guess. I'm helping the police, and they think someone wearing spats might be involved."

A small lie.

My insides did a happy dance when she reached for a binder and flipped through the pages. "If the police want to know, they can ask me themselves. I won't even make them get a warrant."

"Can you tell me if they're all accounted for?"

She glanced through her ledger and walked back to the drawer to take inventory. "I have eleven pairs, but only seven have been checked out. The remaining four are still in the drawer."

Pushing my luck, I asked if the spats went to men or women?

She pursed her lips. "Both."

I turned back before leaving. "Do you have pink spats?"

She chuckled. "Now *there's* an idea. But no. I don't."

So much for the spats. My next stop took me to a hallway of shops ready to take my credit card. I'd seen photographs of the downstairs prior to the renovation. Dark wood from walls to ceiling. Management had decided brighter is better and altered the ambiance, replacing wood with whites and lights.

The gulls, at least one of them, had let me see an image of a straw bag with flowers and a lid. Bautista mentioned one witness who had spotted Harry Reed buying a purse. Coincidence? I thought not.

My version of shopping is a drive-by. I know what I want. If I don't see it at first glance, I keep going. This was going to take more effort.

I passed by S.R.F, as the wares on display targeted sports enthusiasts. Surfboards, bikes, weights, and the clothing worn by those who ruined their vacations with strenuous activity.

I ducked into Speckles Sweets & Treats not because I thought I'd find straw bags on display but because I couldn't resist the chocolates. I bought two, one for me and one for Bowers. And yes. I ate them both.

Through the windows of Beachouse, I spotted several wicker baskets on display. This seemed the best bet. After winding my way around displays and not finding my quarry, I asked the blond woman in her fifties who stood behind the register if the store carried straw bags.

"The one I'm looking for is big with handles and it has a lid. And flowers on it."

She broke into a smile. "I know exactly what you want. It doubles as a beach bag and picnic basket. That's what the lid is for. To keep the seagulls out."

"Perfect. Can I see one?"

"Unfortunately, we sold the last one yesterday."

"Do you remember who bought it?"

She frowned and called to another woman who was arranging some knick-knacks that didn't look like they needed arranging. "Do you remember who bought the last Day-at-the-Beach bag?"

The Asian woman in her sixties, answered immediately. "A single man. I remember because it's usually women or couples who shop in here."

"Can you describe him?"

She crossed her arms over her flat chest. "Why should I?"

"Because I think he's dead." It just came out. What can I say?

Her eyes narrowed as she nodded. "I heard about that. Wait. Weren't there two people who died? Such bad luck."

For them, too, I thought. "I mean the first one. The guy."

She shook her shoulders and made a face. "The man who bought from me was in his forties. Short, blond hair. He had on a red-and-blue plaid shirt. I remember him because those weren't his colors."

A flash of that exact shirt on the torso of the dead man confirmed it for me. I mumbled my thanks and wandered out to the corridor. The police would never accept a clue I'd received from seagulls.

However, it was a fact, and it might lead to the killer. And I strongly felt that, until I recovered the cub, the killer might strike again.

Chapter Thirty-One

Nicholas: Dr. Yang Gets a Surprise

We followed Sykes to his room. He wore a suit—a cross between cornflower and powder blue that was his wife's favorite. My brother noticed, too, but for different reasons.

"What shade of blue is that?" Edward asked.

I shook my head. "Forget it. You'd never pull it off. It takes a certain personality."

"Are you saying Detective Sykes has more personality than I?"

"Yes."

We kicked around a few ideas until someone knocked on the door and Edward let Detective Bowers in. The newlywed gave me a look he thought I deserved and greeted my brother and his fellow cop.

Sykes gestured to the bed and single chair. "Get comfortable. I want to know what happened last night. The whole story."

"My wife went for a walk on the beach. An unidentified person attacked her. Knocked her down. She didn't get a look at them. There were no witnesses as far as I know."

Sykes filled his gaze with a sympathy he'd never bothered showing me in sticky situations. "You know the routine. Why was your wife walking alone? Why weren't you with her?"

Bowers didn't throw the television remote at me, but his jaw clenched a few times, and his gaze strayed in my direction.

Sykes nodded. "I understand. Once, in an unprofessional moment, I knocked him down." He grinned. "It felt good."

"Hey!"

"Let it go, Nicholas," Edward rumbled. "Detective Sykes was justified."

This was too much. I stood and gestured at Bowers. "All I did was refuse to believe his wife was Dr. Doolittle. That she could talk to animals."

This time, Sykes looked at Bowers with a healthy dose of doubt.

Edward raised a finger. "If you recall her words, and I'll repeat them verbatim if you wish, her experience in animal behavior led her to a certain conclusion. You misunderstood."

"What about the newspaper articles? You're not the only one who did research."

"I've been a victim of the press before. It sounds like that dastardly reporter has it in for Mrs. Bowers. His articles were clearly mocking her. I've been there."

"And all that jazz about feelings, images, and buzzing? Did I misunderstand that, too?"

My brother expelled a sigh of martyred tolerance. "You took what she said literally. Haven't you ever felt an animal was telling you something? We've all felt that from our pets."

Bowers face remained impassive throughout my brother's explanation, but I could sense his relief.

"Detective Bowers. Please repeat your theory to Detective Sykes." Edward gestured for him to proceed.

Bowers cleared his throat. "Frankie had the idea—purely through the animal's body language and behavior—that the white tiger was, in human terms, in mourning. Since the tiger had a healthy cub at her feet, Frankie drew a conclusion. She must be missing a second cub."

Sykes nodded. "Ah. One didn't make it."

"Not exactly. The—the depth of the tiger's mourning led her to believe the cub was still, um, available, but not with her."

"Where is it?"

I couldn't believe Sykes was taking him seriously.

"Wouldn't Antonio Sabato have known if there had been two cubs?" For Sykes' benefit, Edward added, "He's the curator at the zoo."

"I know. We've spoken."

"Not if Harry Reed wanted the white tiger cub for himself."

"For himself?" Sykes said.

"I would think it would be valuable, especially as it's pure—as it's young."

That wasn't what Bowers had intended to say. A few tags went through my noggin. Pure as the driven snow? Pure-blooded? He might have meant either, given it was a white tiger.

"So. Now we have an animal worth trafficking. It's an idea." Sykes stroked his facial hair with his knuckles. "An illegal sale of an exotic animal gone wrong? That would give us a motive. And Jimmy Bianchi has a private zoo."

"He overheard my wife telling her mother about it on the phone. And she did mention Harry Reed."

"You're talking about a cub that, as far as I know, doesn't exist. Where is the proof?" I thought I used my reasonable tone, but I got another glare from Bowers.

"There was proof. Or at least something to connect the zoo to the Coronado."

"What happened to it?" Sykes asked.

"It was taken last night. When Frankie and I were at the zoo, there was a stuffed pink rabbit on the ground near the tiger's enclosure. My wife thought it might belong to the tiger cub. To appease her, I threw it over the fence. Into the tiger enclosure. She saw that same stuffed animal washed up on the beach last night. When she reached for it, she was attacked. By the time she was back on her feet, the rabbit was gone."

Bowers' cell phone rang. He glanced at the screen, back at us, and pressed a button.

"Dr. Yang, I have you on speaker. There are other parties interested in your answer."

"Who?"

"Detective Jonah Sykes from the San Diego Sheriff's Department and . . . his assistants."

"I don't know what tipped your wife off, but Carla, that's Chuck's mate, *is* pregnant. About ten weeks pregnant, which is impossible. We track the menstrual cycle of the chimps, and she hasn't missed. But someone should have noticed the lack of estrus swelling. That's her rump. When chimps are fertile, their rumps swell up like two red balloons to signal the males."

"Good Gad," Edward hissed.

Bowers' lips twitched. "Who records that information? Who has access?"

"Different people."

"Could someone have changed the records?"

She was silent for a moment. "It's possible. The information is noted and initialed, but there isn't a reason someone would give the papers more than a quick glance. Are you saying that Harry changed the records?"

"I'm just learning how the process works. I hope the delay hasn't caused problems."

"Thank you. It hasn't, though the endocrinologist isn't happy. She would have liked to have gotten an early ultrasound."

"How did you confirm the pregnancy?"

"You mentioned something being off. We gave her a full checkup, and when we found nothing wrong, we gave her a pregnancy test. The same test a human woman would use. Then we checked her hormone levels against another chimp's to make sure. She's definitely pregnant. When we get an ultrasound, we'll have a better idea of how far along she is."

"Thank you for getting back to me."

With that, Bowers disconnected the call. "Nicholas and Frankie spoke with Clarence Darby to learn why Harry Reed had gotten him fired from the San Diego Zoo."

"Mr. Darby worked at the zoo? Nicholas! Why didn't you tell me?" Edward lowered his roar for Bowers. "Is that why you asked Dr. Yang about the chimp when we were in Mr. Sabato's office?"

The detective nodded. "Harry Reed had been examining," he cleared his throat, "her tummy. Frankie's word. Not mine. Darby saw, and that was enough for Harry to want to get rid of him, which seemed suspicious." He gave Sykes an apologetic glance. "I wanted to confirm it first before passing it on, since it was based on hearsay."

"I appreciate that. You've saved me time." Sykes turned his glare on me. "I don't appreciate how you've been keeping secrets."

"He squirrels them away like nuts," Edward murmured, which was funny, coming from him.

I gestured at Bowers. "You heard him. It was unconfirmed. Darby's word against Harry's, who isn't here to defend himself. Besides. It's a jump from examining a chimp to assuming she's pregnant."

"Considering the missing cub, it should have been obvious."

"*What* missing cub? Has the zoo reported one missing? Has anyone seen it? Mentioned it?"

"Still," Edward said, reluctant to let go of a win, "you should have made the connection."

"Sorry, brother, but I've had other things on my mind."

Sykes and Edward exchanged a look. If I hadn't known the two men, I might have interpreted it as pity, which ticked me off.

"Frankie Bowers thinks a chimp is pregnant. There's a tiger cub no one has seen, but I'm supposed to take her word that it exists. Then someone attacks her over a stuffed bunny." I blew out a huff of air. "Sounds like a movie I once saw." I flipped on the remote to make my point and landed in the middle of the Chargers game.

Chapter Thirty-Two

Frankie: A Group Share

When Detective Sykes answered the door to his room, his surprise at seeing me carried an infusion of guilt, and as I entered the room, I saw why.

Nicholas had kicked off his shoes and was leaning against the bed's headboard. Edward had the chair, and my husband sat on the floor with his back against the bed. The television set held them in thrall. Football.

"I feel so much safer knowing the four of you are hard at work solving the murder."

Bowers looked up, started, and jumped to his feet. "I was just about to look for you. You had me worried."

"I can see that."

Detective Sykes shrugged his jacket on. "I should get back to work."

"I thought you were going to stick to me?" I smiled sweetly at Bowers' guilty face. "No need to worry, though. Jimmy has offered me any protection I need."

The detective, halfway out the door, turned back and closed it behind him. "You talked to Jimmy again?"

Nicholas swung his legs off the bed and stood. "Are you nuts, lady?" He glanced at Bowers. "No offense, but the guy has an unhealthy interest in your wife. I wouldn't encourage him."

I ignored the younger Harlow and addressed Detective Sykes. "I didn't speak with him. He sent his employee, Stanley, to see if I was all right."

"Stanley?" Bowers said.

"Stanley Fabrezo," Sykes answered. "The guy with the scar."

"He's sweet." The men stared at me. "I think he might be shy. Anyway, he said Jimmy wanted to express his concern over my attack and to let me know I could call him any time I needed anything. Doesn't that mean he's not as bad as we thought?"

My question held an edge of desperation. I really, *really*, didn't want to attract the interest of a criminal.

"I don't think he meant help like give you a jump." Nicholas held a hand up. "I meant a car jump."

Bowers put his hands on my shoulders. "Do you remember his exact words?"

"Just what I said. He wanted to express his anger over my injuries and if I had a problem, I could call him any time." My voice might have shaken a little.

"Nice. Very nice." Nicholas threw his hands in the air. "How do you know he wasn't behind the attack?"

"You *must* be mistaken about him. You *have* to be. Otherwise, I'll be looking over my shoulder and sleeping with one eye open."

"Welcome to the club," Nicholas mumbled.

Detective Sykes studied me, pursing his lips in thought.

"No." Bowers pulled me next to him and held me

clamped to his side. "Don't even think about it. Frankie is my wife, not a trained investigator."

"You have to admit it's an opportunity to find out what's going on in the Coronation Room. With the parties involved, I'm not the only one who's interested."

"I agree. But you'll have to find another way."

Since they were talking about me, I felt entitled to join the conversation. "You want me to make friends with Jimmy?"

Sykes was blunt. "No. Jimmy is a killer, among other things. But if he talks to you, I want you to listen and remember. Good listeners are hard to find, so if you say little, he might keep talking."

I lifted my head to look my husband in the eye. "That doesn't sound so bad. I won't seek him out, but if he's talking, why not listen?"

"Then I'll make sure you don't have the opportunity for a conversation."

"That's exactly my point. You'll be there."

"Back up," Nicholas said. "What do you mean Jimmy is a killer?" He turned on his brother. "And you practically shoved me in his lap."

"Calm down, Nicholas."

Sykes put his hands on his hips and sighed. "I'll tell you this, Nicholas. As far as I know, Jimmy and his friends have nothing to do with your situation."

"Care to pinky swear?"

"There are other people who would be interested in what's going on in that room. That's all."

Bowers squeezed my shoulders. "Don't court trouble. Please? For my sake?"

"Do I ever?"

"It's up to you two," Sykes said.

"You're right about one thing," Nicholas said. "Women are naturally nosy."

I narrowed my eyes.

He shoved his hands in his pockets. "It's not a criticism. If it weren't for women, men would remain oblivious. How else would we know the neighbor is a serial killer, or the grocery store manager is having an affair? We rely on women to connect us with the outside world."

His gaze strayed back to the television, so I didn't bother with a rebuttal.

Bowers scratched his chin. "It didn't take you that long to exchange a few words with Stanley. What else have you been up to?"

When I lifted my eyebrows, he said we were sharing everything.

"Okay. First, I talked to Jen. She's the woman in charge of costumes. She can account for all the spats."

"So?" Nicholas kept his gaze on the television screen.

"She keeps very careful records."

Bowers wore a puzzled frown. "Harry Reed and Cynthia Ferrara weren't killed with a pair of spats."

I decided to skip the part about talking to a crab. "Remember when Bautista said one of the many witnesses saw Harry shopping for a purse? She was right."

Edward grunted. "Was he a guest at the convention after all? That would narrow down the field."

"He bought the last straw carryall with a lid."

Sykes rubbed his beard. "A good way to conceal something you wanted to keep secret."

"Like a tiger cub," Edward added.

A flush of pleasure ran through me. Were they taking my suggestion seriously?

"And no one would question him," my husband said,

"because he carried it on the beach at night. Or early morning. After most guests were in bed."

"Are we assuming the alleged buyer of the cub, if there is one, and, therefore, the murderer, is a member of the convention?" Edward waited for a response, which Sykes finally gave him.

"Not necessarily. But, based on the information Nicholas withheld—"

"Give me a break."

The detective glared. "I think we can assume the buyer is staying at the hotel."

"And maybe Cynthia saw something when she was walking Tanner." Sykes looked confused, so I explained. "Edna's therapy dog."

"I didn't see—"

"The Chihuahua. She keeps him in her straw bag. But it doesn't have a lid. I checked."

"I suppose it's possible. Though what does that have to do with Cynthia wanting to talk to you?" Sykes held up a hand. "I know you don't know what she wanted, but she was killed near your cottage, which supports Edna Tartwell's statement."

"Maybe she saw something and wanted to tell my husband. He's a detective." I didn't add that she'd use any excuse to flirt with him.

"Would she know that?"

"Jimmy knows."

The unreadable cop face came down over Bowers' face. And Sykes'. And even Edward's. Nicholas had his attention on the game.

"Jimmy seems to know a lot of things he shouldn't know," Sykes said.

Whatever that meant, it didn't sound good.

Chapter Thirty-Three

Frankie: Impromtu Talent Show

We left shortly after that ominous statement, and once we got to the lobby, Bowers steered me away from the Crown Room. "You won't have time to chat with your buddy Jimmy because we're going to Old Town."

"We are?"

"I thought we could visit the Kissing Statue to assure you it's still there. Then we can hit the shops and have lunch. I've heard there's a place with gigantic margaritas. Then, when you're properly drunk, I can bring you back here and take advantage."

"You've thought this through."

"Spur of the moment."

"As in the last five minutes?"

"Maybe four."

I kissed his chin. "An excellent plan."

Movement by the door caught my eye. "Is that Edna Tartwell?"

He looked toward the exit. "It is."

"Doesn't she look . . . different?"

The old woman wore the same type clothes as usual. Cable knit sweater, orthopedic shoes, and a dress that looked as if she'd worn it while cooking dinner for soldiers returning from World War II. She had her bag. Tanner's head peeped out as if he were leading a charge.

But she moved like a younger woman. No tottering. More like a confident stroll.

"Maybe she only acted helpless around her niece." Bowers looked at me. "You know. To manipulate her. Now that her niece is dead, she doesn't have to pretend."

"Do you believe that?"

He sighed. "No."

I grabbed his hand and pulled. "Let's follow her."

As soon as we made it out the door, I spotted Edna climbing onto a small tour bus. The scrolling sign above the driver's window said Presidio Park. It pulled out of the parking lot before I could suggest joining the tour.

"Is Presidio Park in San Diego?"

Bowers skipped the lecture and told me yes.

"Let's go."

"Frankie, wait."

But I was running to the parking garage where Bowers had left the car. I'd made it down the ramp before I noticed my husband wasn't with me and stopped to wait for him. A minute later, he loped toward me with a noticeable limp.

"Oh my gosh, Bowers. I'm so sorry. I didn't know your leg hurt that bad."

But he wasn't listening. He'd glued his eyes on something over my shoulder, and from their horrified expression, I was afraid to look.

There wasn't much I could do but turn around and

confront the scene that had Bowers reaching for his side where his gun holster usually rested.

A group of men stood with their backs to the wall. Among them, I recognized Stanley.

Facing them, another group of men in dark suits held guns. Not tommy guns, but weapons that looked just as dangerous.

"Just like the movie," Bowers whispered.

"Like the movie?" I whispered back.

"St. Valentine's Day massacre."

"St. Valentine's Day—oh."

When the guys holding the guns turned to us, all chance of leaving went bye-bye. In the past, I'd found feigning ignorance sometimes diffused situations. Like when my mother asked my teenage self if I'd been drinking, and I responded, "Who, me?" Bowers, hypnotized by the scene, reacted too late to stop me.

I strolled forward with confidence. "Stanley."

The big man jerked his head in surprise. "Hello, Mrs. Bowers."

"You fellas are really getting into the *Some Like It Hot* spirit for the convention."

"Convention?" one of the gunmen said.

"Sure. The celebration of a famous movie filmed *right here*."

"They filmed a movie in this garage?" A guy with a buzz cut lowered his gun.

"No, no, no. At the hotel. And the movie starred Marilyn Monroe." I clasped my hands together in a fair imitation of Rhonda.

"I like Marilyn Monroe," someone said. "A real lady."

"And here you are, reenacting the scene from the

movie. How wonderful. How authentic. You're all very good actors. Are you professionals?" I placed my hand on the closest gun-guy's arm, and he flinched.

"Especially you. That menacing look you just gave me? Brrr." I shivered my shoulders.

He lowered his gun and exchanged a glance with the other gunmen. "Yeah. Just like the movie. We were play acting."

Bowers stopped gaping at me, grabbed my collar, and swung me around so he stood between me and the fellas with the guns. "Quick," I hissed. "What's the movie's theme song?"

He tilted his head back and spoke out of the side of his mouth. "I don't know. Why? You want me to sing it to you?"

I jabbed his back.

"The most well-known song is *I Want to be Loved by You.*"

"Perfect. I actually know the words to that one." I stepped out from behind my husband, drew in a breath, and started to sing. "I want to be loved by you . . ." I let the note hang.

Another gunman swung my way. "You wanna what?"

"And nobody else but you," I continued. A few of the men smiled and nodded, and I rolled my hand to encourage them to join me. A chorus of raspy smoker's voices, basses, and one clear tenor tentatively stepped in.

"I wanna be loved by you alo-o-one."

As I moved into the second verse, the gunmen gradually relaxed and added their voices to the performance. And then the middle part came.

By now, every man except the head gunman had

joined in. He shook his head with disgust and barked out an order to his men. "Louder. Put in some effort." He gestured at the men lining the wall. "Don't let these mutts out-sing you."

They obeyed, and their counterparts against the wall responded in kind. It became more of a shouting match than a rendition of the movie's sexy number. They finished on an explosive note, and their combative postures returned.

At least until an especially gruff-looking gunman said, "Poo-poo-pee-doo."

The others gawked at him in surprise. He shrugged.

"What? That's how the song goes."

Stanley said, "He's right." He nodded at the gunman. "That was a nice touch."

"Thanks."

I nudged Bowers to join me in my cheers and clapping. "Wonderful. Are you sure you fellas didn't practice together? You're a shoo-in for first place in the talent show tomorrow night."

"What time's it at?" one of the gunmen said, and the head guy told him to shut his trap. They were losing the mood.

"That was great," I said, "but you should find somewhere else to practice. I heard a rumor that the police are on their way to cordon off this area. Something about a clue to one of the murders. I forget which one."

The gruff leader jerked his head at his friends, and they followed him up the ramp. As he passed, he offered a small wave. "Thanks for the tip, lady."

The men against the wall sagged with relief. Stanley lumbered over.

"I owe you." He gave Bowers an unfriendly glance.

"This is my husband, Martin. Martin, Stanley."

Stanley nodded. "Jimmy has a special interest in animals. Exotic animals."

"Okaaay."

"Let's call it a possessive interest. The entire family shares his enthusiasm. That's it. We're even." He motioned at the remaining men, and they followed him up the ramp.

"You're right," Bowers said. "He is sweet."

"That was weird." I dug in Bowers' pocket and pulled out the rental car keys.

"You're not seriously—"

"We've got to catch Edna." I searched the cars, clicking the unlock feature on the fob over and over like it was the crosswalk button. Our Camry's lights blinked from the corner. "I'm driving. That way, you can read the map."

I took advantage of his temporary disability to get to the driver's seat first, just so he couldn't argue.

As he slid into the passenger side and buckled his seatbelt, he asked if I wanted to spend my honeymoon this way.

I gave him a raspberry. "Right. As opposed to how we've spent it thus far?"

"Thus?"

"Edward Harlow must be rubbing off on me. Anyway, we're just checking up on Edna. Something's off. After that we can visit the sites. Do you want to let it go?"

He rubbed his hands over his face. "No."

"Great. We're in agreement. Now, how do I start the car?" I'd never driven a hybrid.

He pointed at the dashboard. "Push that button and press on the brake."

I jabbed at the button and stomped on the break. "It's not starting."

"Then you're doing something wrong."

"Come on, car. Start. Start. Start you damn thing!"

He leaned his head over. "Frankie."

"What!"

"You're stepping on the gas."

"I know the difference between—oh. You're right." On my next try, the car started. While I steered us up the ramp and out, Bowers fiddled with the radio knobs.

"Focus. I need directions."

He pressed the final button, and a woman's voice told me in dulcet tones to turn right.

My husband leaned back and closed his eyes. "Just do what she says, and we'll get there in one piece."

The backed-up traffic on the bridge out of Coronado had me seething.

"Calm down. We know where she's going."

He had a point. It wasn't as if Edna could jump off the bus before her destination.

Following the computerized voice, I got off the freeway and onto Taylor Street, backtracked to Presidio Drive, and entered the park.

A gigantic cross made of brick rose from the ground.

"That's the Juniper Serra Cross," Bowers said, acting as tour guide. "It's made out of the materials from the old fort."

Because I was admiring the cross, I almost missed the turn into the parking lot.

I thought of Presidio Park as just that. An open park with picnic benches and a few trees. It was that and more.

A white building that looked like a church peered out from behind a woodsy area. The closer we got, the more tourists appeared, walking the grounds, sitting on benches, and relaxing.

I was not relaxed.

"Where is she?"

"She could be anywhere, but my guess is inside the museum."

The Juniper Serra Museum wasn't the original structure. The building marked the site of the first European settlement in California. There was a fort here before that. As far as who controlled the fort, it made the rounds through the Spanish, the Mexicans, and the Mormons. That's the unofficial history in a nutshell.

The building had covered arched walkways alongside it, and Bowers and I made it that far before a Hispanic man in a gray, pinstriped suit stopped us. A white carnation perched jauntily from the buttonhole on his lapel.

"There is a wedding and reception taking place inside, but you are welcome to walk the grounds. If you could try to stay out of the outdoor pictures, the bride would appreciate it."

A wedding? We exchanged a glance. "Is an elderly woman in a sweater and floral dress—an old dress, not a dress-up dress—one of the guests?"

"Is she Mexican?"

"No."

"Highly unlikely, then." He shrugged. "She would have stood out."

"Did you say there were trails around here?"

"A few miles worth. Not difficult to walk, from what I hear."

We thanked the man, and he wandered back to his

post. Just as I opened my mouth to suggest a walk, Bowers leaned against the wall with his eyes closed. His mouth and eyes had creases around them. Creases of pain.

I was a selfish, selfish woman. My enthusiasm had led me to neglect my husband's welfare.

"Let's get you back to the hotel."

He opened his eyes and stood. "I'm not a cripple."

"I don't think you can say cripple. Invalid?"

"I'm not an invalid, either," he said, failing to hide the wince when he put weight on his injured leg.

"No. But if you re-injure your leg, you'll be on a nookie fast."

"Back to the hotel it is."

Just as I placed my foot on the path back to the parking lot, I heard a noise from Bowers. Concerned, I turned and asked if he was all right.

"That woman. The one who came out of that grove of trees. It's Dr. Sylvia Yang, the vet from the zoo." He then explained her phone call confirming the chimp's pregnancy.

"Is it me, or is it suspicious that she's here the same time as Edna?"

"Very."

He called after me as I jogged over the lawn to cut her off, but he wasn't in any shape to follow. She jumped when I called her name.

"Hi. You worked with Harry Reed, right?"

She glanced over her shoulder toward the wooded area. "Go away."

"You know my husband." I waved a hand in his direction. "Detective Bowers. He met you in Antonio Sabata's office."

When I turned back, she was running to the parking lot.

Bowers caught up to me. "What did you say to her?"

"Hello."

"That's it? Odd reaction."

"My thoughts exactly."

Chapter Thirty-Four

Frankie: A Meeting with Jimmy

Once back at our cottage, I handed my husband two aspirins and sent him to bed with orders to nap for no less than one hour.

I gave myself a mental smack for running him off his feet. Literally. I should have looked out for him. Then I decided it wasn't my fault. It was the murderer's fault.

Over-thinking is a specialty of mine, and I went into high gear.

Number One. My husband's leg was acting up, causing him pain. This was a direct result of chasing suspects and clues.

Was Bowers enjoying his jaunt into vacation crime? If not, why did he keep disappearing with Edward Harlow and Detective Sykes? Bowers was as stubborn as I was. More so. If he hadn't wanted to play detective with those men, he would have found a polite way to decline.

Number Two. I'd been left behind more than once. Yet, I hadn't been bored. I'd done my own digging into Harry Reed's past with Nicholas Harlow. I instigated the chase that led us to The Presidio.

So, either I was making the best of a tough situation—I scoffed. It wasn't in me to be a martyr. Or patient. Or giving and kind, except to those who deserved it.

Number Three. All this excitement needed to go away so my husband and I could go back to normal. Or what would be normal once we put enough time into our marriage.

Detective Sykes had given me a way to gather information that might help bring the case to a close.

It made sense that professional killers were behind the deaths. The more I thought about Stanley's comment, the more certain I became. Jimmy liked exotic animals. If there were a white tiger cub floating around, and I was sure there was, Jimmy would be all over it.

And the bodyguard—I assumed that was Stanley's job—had said a love of exotic animals ran in the family. Were the men in the Coronet Room family? Like the Corleone family? Was the guy with the white hair their godfather? Or their real father.

When I thought of family, it brought memories of games of horseshoes and lots of Aunt Gertrude's Jello salad. I couldn't see Stanley and Jimmy tossing horseshoes, so they must be the other kind of family. Mobsters. Real ones. Stanley must have meant "family" in a figurative way.

Detective Sykes had called Jimmy a killer. The way I saw it, Harry had brought the cub to him, and Jimmy, a tad overexcited, had murdered the vet before he got the location of the animal. Either that, or he had the animal squirreled away at the hotel. But what about Edna's niece, Cynthia?

Could her death be an accident? I've heard of people swimming naked in icy water for fun. Maybe that's how

Edna's niece got her kicks, and she lost her footing and drowned. Except she wore clothes when she died.

She must have seen something and came to our cottage to tell Bowers. But how did she know he was a policeman? Why wouldn't she tell the sergeant?

She wanted to mew her troubles to my husband in hopes of some sympathy. Witch.

While Bowers slept, I tip-toed out of our cottage and crossed the beach. If I were going to help Detective Sykes, I would have to find Jimmy without my husband at my side.

In the Crown Room, convention goers were engaged in a debate about the best costume. More of an argument, really.

One lady in a burgundy, fur-lined, velvet jacket and cloche hat shook her finger at another woman in a long, silver, shimmering dress that only lacked a microphone and a piano.

"Just because it's long enough to trip over doesn't mean it's from the right time period."

"You think you're better just because your grandmother willed you her entire wardrobe?" She pinched the woman's jacket sleeve. "It's got moth holes."

"Ladies," Susan said, wrenching them apart. "You both look fabulous. Very authentic."

"Why don't we have a real best costume competition? Only for those wearing authentic outfits." Moth Holes preened.

"Because it wouldn't be fair. Many people rented their costumes for the weekend at our suggestion."

"Exclude them."

"Now, now. That wouldn't be much fun for those fans."

"Too bad. If they're gonna cheat, they deserve to sit it out."

Rhonda and Willie stood away from the chatter. They'd lost some of their enthusiasm. Who wouldn't with all the pettiness weighing down the atmosphere? But I wasn't here to commiserate. I was here to find Jimmy.

Since the last few times I'd run into the bad man, it had been in the lobby outside the Coronet Room. I positioned myself on the round, green couch and waited.

For once, Jimmy decided to stay put. As guests crossed through the room—some headed for the elevator and others the front door—my eyelids grew heavy. I was short on sleep, and this couch was comfy. If only I could stretch out . . .

"I understand I owe you."

My eyes snapped open. Had I been snoring? I rubbed my face to check for drool, and when I looked up, Jimmy stood in front of me, flipping his quarter.

"You owe me?"

"For what you did for my men. They wouldn't be here without your interference."

Stanley, at Jimmy's side as always, nodded for emphasis.

"It was nothing." I smothered a yawn. "Happy to interfere."

"I've been wanting to talk to you." He gestured not to the Coronet Room but to the hall leading to The Garden. "You coming?"

If we stayed outdoors, we'd be in sight of other guests. However, The Garden provided access to private rooms. No one would think of looking for me in a private room. "Are you sure you wouldn't rather go the bar?"

"Nah. Too many people."

Which was exactly my point.

He led me to a suite. As we walked the outdoor path, I caught the eye of every passerby. Most of them looked away, embarrassed by my scrutiny, but that was okay. When Bowers searched for my body, I wanted someone to pipe up and say, 'I saw a woman just like that outside with three men. She kept staring at me.'

When we got to Jimmy's room, Stanley knocked three times. A large man opened the door, and my escorts waited for me to enter first.

The interior decor was tasteful . . . and overcrowded. Men in suits stood in every corner.

I opened my mind to receive any communications from animals. If Jimmy had the cub, I would feel it. Nothing.

"You can ignore them," Jimmy said with a dismissive gesture toward his guards. "They aren't paid to listen."

When the men saw me, several broke their statue-like stances to grin at me. I recognized them as the men lined against the wall in the garage.

Returning to Jimmy's opening line in the lobby, I said, "I really don't need any thanks."

"We're done with thanks." He gestured to the couch, and I sat. He remained standing, which he did to intimidate me. "I want to talk to you about the dead body."

I'm not sure why, but I raised my hand. "Which one?"

He nodded. "Good question. You've been around quite a few bodies lately."

"Only two."

"Let's start with the first guy."

He made a rolling motion with one hand, and Stanley stepped forward. "Harry Reed."

"That's the guy. The vet from the zoo. What do you know about him?"

"Honestly?"

"I suggest you don't lie."

"Bad choice of words. Nothing. I know nothing. I met him for the first time at the zoo on Thursday afternoon outside the white tiger enclosure. Except I didn't know it was him." My fingers twisted together. "I saw a toy, a pink bunny, and I thought it was the tiger's, and since kitty's have favorite toys, I thought she'd want it back. So, I returned it."

"Returned it?"

"Threw it over the fence. Well, my husband did. And then these guys escorted us to an office. I got a lecture that included a request to not visit the zoo again. Harry was one of the guys lecturing me."

"Did you kill him?"

I blinked. "Kill him?" If anyone killed him, it was someone with Jimmy's reputation, but I couldn't say that. "He was stabbed with a gardening tool and dragged to our patio."

His eyes traveled over me in an impersonal way. "You haven't got the muscle for that. But your husband does."

The thought of Bowers committing murder at my request made me laugh. Jimmy didn't join in, so I made sure he knew I wasn't laughing at him.

"My husband is very straitlaced. Killing someone wouldn't enter his mind. He wouldn't do it, not even for me."

"They're on their honeymoon," Stanley offered.

Jimmy grunted. "Did Harry have anything with him when you found him?"

"With him? Just the clothes on his back. Honestly—

scratch that. Truthfully, I was preoccupied. You know. Freaking out. If there were, I didn't notice, and the police haven't said anything."

A dangerous gleam entered his eyes. "Why would the police tell you anything?"

"Not tell. Ask. They didn't ask me about anything on the patio, as in, 'Is this yours?' Frankly, I was hoping *you* could tell me something about him."

"Like what?"

"I don't know. You seem interested in him, so I thought you knew him. Or met him."

Something flickered in his eyes. "I never met him, but I'd heard of him and hoped to make his acquaintance."

"Because of your animals?" I quailed before his glare. "You know. The animals on your list. The rare and endangered animals."

"Yeah. I wanted to consult with him. Then somebody bumped him off, which makes me angry."

His face went red and he ground his fist into the palm of his hand. "Very angry."

"I can see how it would. I'm a little miffed myself. Someone left his body on our patio. Can you imagine finding a body on your patio in the middle of your honeymoon? I can tell you. It's not nice."

While I had their sympathy, at least the sympathetic gazes of the men lining the room, I went for it. "Do any of your friends from the Coronation Room have any ideas about what happened to Harry?"

He stepped closer. "They don't know about Harry, and it stays that way. Capisce?"

"Um, sure. It's not like I'm going to run into any of them, right? And they don't know me from Adam. Or Eve. Is it a business meeting?"

"You could say that."

Stanley laughed. "It's a board of directors meeting, and they're electing a new president."

Jimmy tugged on his lapels, pleased. But then he remembered why I was here.

"How long had he been dead when you found him?"

His assumption that I would know the gory details had an odd effect. I sat up straighter and moved my thoughts from escaping the room to considering his question. At least until he added, "The police are keeping their lips tight."

Would Bautista want me to keep the information a secret? I couldn't see where time of death mattered, so I gave him my best guess.

"He was, um, cold. Of course it was cold outside, so that might not mean anything. Oh! The blood I got on my arms hugging him was tacky. That takes a while, doesn't it?"

Sympathy left the room, replaced by shock and disgust.

Stanley gaped. "You hugged him?"

"From behind. Before I knew it was a dead body and not my husband. He had on a hat, and I thought—Oh, my gosh. You don't think I would intentionally hug a dead man, do you? Ugh. Yuck. It was a traumatic moment. One I might never get over."

My new friends looked relieved. Sympathy returned.

"Stanley tells me the other dead body was a woman. Do you know anything about her?"

"Just her name. Cynthia Ferrara."

He and Stanley exchanged a glance heavy with meaning. One that made me nervous.

"She's escorting her Aunt Edna."

Another glance.

"What does Aunt Edna look like? I want to offer my sympathy."

"Old. You can't miss her. She carries around a nasty little dog. Tanner."

The skin under Jimmy's eye twitched. "What was your connection to this Cynthia person?"

"None. She was just another guest at the convention." A woman who liked to flirt with my husband.

He raised his voice. "You're lying. Stanley tells me she died in a private pool near your cottage."

I choked. Jimmy knew where I slept at night.

"It doesn't make sense." He rubbed the sides of his face with both hands, a move that seemed unstable.

"Jimmy," the bodyguard said. "It's murder. It don't have to make sense. Take a deep breath."

Jimmy took three and let his hands drop.

"I apologize. It's strange, and I don't like strange thing."

"Maybe Cynthia wanted some alone time and decided to explore," I offered. "She fell in the pool and drowned. Lucky for her I was in the area, or her body might not have been discovered for months." I made a face at the thought of Cynthia's body after a few months.

"What were you doing in the parking garage?"

He switched subjects so fast, I had to think. "Getting my car."

"For what?"

It was time to stop sharing with Jimmy, especially as he wasn't reciprocating. "I'm on my honeymoon. We were going to see the sites. In this case, Presidio Park."

He stepped into my personal space and bent down.

"Now, why don't you tell me where the tiger cub is like a good girl?"

I flattened myself against the back of the couch. "I—I did. At the zoo. The San Diego Zoo. On Tiger Trail."

He studied me through dark eyes. I held my body still to keep from squirming.

Under his breath, he mumbled words that sounded like, "She beat me to it."

Finally, he motioned to Stanley, and the big man lumbered over and waited for me to stand. Which I did since standing was the first step to getting out of that room.

"Have a nice honeymoon."

The interview was over. Funny, but from the questions he asked, I got the impression Jimmy didn't know any more than I did about the murders. Or the tiger. Except he also believed there was another cub.

And that's exactly what I told Bowers when I tracked him down.

"I don't believe it." He ran a hand through his hair. "After I explicitly asked you to stay away from the man, you sought him out."

"I . . ." He was right. I did look for Jimmy. Waited for him, to be exact. "I'm sorry."

"You're always sorry, but not until you've blown off my request and done what you've damn well pleased. Do I count at all?" He pulled down his mask. His cop face. The one that showed no emotion. "When you're planning dangerous stunts, do I figure into your plans at all? Or am I an afterthought?"

Stunned, words escaped me. Because he was right. He had asked me to stay away from Jimmy. He'd even used the "P" word. Please. But that hadn't factored into my decision to seek the bad man out. I couldn't even say I'd considered and rejected his request. I hadn't thought about Bowers and what he wanted. And yet . . . every time he'd gone off with Detective Sykes or the sergeants, he'd first asked if I'd mind.

I was a selfish, selfish woman.

Dropping to the couch, I rubbed my stomach and fought off the urge to be sick. I didn't realize I was crying until he sat next to me and wiped the tears away with the back of his hand.

"You're right. I'm a terrible person. Self-centered. Only thinking about what *I* want. I'll never be as good to you as you are to me, and that's not fair to you."

He nodded. "As long as you admit it." When I sputtered, he touched his fingers to my lips. "You were about to tell me what Jimmy said."

It came out in stuttered dribbles between my hiccups and sniffs.

"You're right. It sounds as if he's seeking the same answers we are. It also sounds as if he's in the market for a tiger cub."

After a minute of silence, I glanced up to find him studying me.

"Are you weighing the costs of divorce against the pain of putting up with me?"

"I'm deciding whether it would be better to bring you with me or not. It might be better to have a woman present."

"You must bring me now that you brought it up. Those are the rules. Where are we headed?"

His answer was unexpected. "*All love begins and ends there.*"

"Robert Browning, according to Edward Harlow."

My shoulders tightened. "You're going to punish me by making me sit through a poetry slam."

His lips twitched. I couldn't resist and kissed him. "The full quote is: *Motherhood: All love begins and ends there.*"

While he waited for me to think it through, he got up and turned on the electric kettle and prepared instant coffee in two mugs.

"Dot . . . no, that can't be right. She looks nothing like Harry."

He handed me a cup, took a sip of the instant brew, and made a face. "Let's get real coffee from the convention and separate Dot from her sister."

Chapter Thirty-Five

Nicholas: Edward Gives a Hint

We settled on the Taco Shack and ate our lunch on two of the stools lining the wooden patio.

"I ran out of signed books," I said between bites. "I'll make a trip home when we're through. Do you need anything else? Besides a clean shirt?"

Edward looked down at the taco filling dribbling down the front of his white dress shirt. "Thanks."

After my last bite, I scrunched the wrapper and lobbed it overhand into the waste bin. My brother continued chomping, but I don't think he tasted his food.

"Tell your baby brother what's on your mind."

My joke didn't elicit even the smallest of smiles. He wiped the corner of his mouth with his napkin. "Are these murders crimes of passion? Or were they carefully planned."

"Dumping a body on a hotel room patio doesn't sound like a good plan. Cynthia's murder makes more sense. If the workmen didn't happen to pass the pool, she would have floated there until the hotel reopened the cottages to the public."

"True." He slipped me a glance. "Sorry. I didn't realize you were so affected by your experience in the pool."

"My stomach's stronger than Mrs. Bowers thinks. I was more devastated by the loss of Mrs. A's cookies." I swiped some crumbs from the table. "Do you think she's telling the truth?"

My brother finished chewing before he answered. Rule number twelve. Never talk with your mouth full.

"Mrs. Bowers? Why would she lie?"

"It's a humongous coincidence that Cynthia wants to talk to her and dies in the pool twenty yards from Frankie Chandler-Bowers' new accommodations. The dead bodies show up wherever she's staying. First, their patio at The Cabanas. Then, the pool at The Beach Village. So, either someone wants to frame her, or she's responsible for making those people dead."

"Or it's a coincidence. The Bowers' patio was at the far end of the beach. More secluded than leaving Harry Reed in the sand for anyone to find. And perhaps Cynthia Ferrara really did intend to speak to Mrs. Bowers and was followed by the person who killed her."

We exited the patio and stepped onto the walkway for an after-lunch stroll.

"I wonder . . ." Edward stroked his chin.

My brother wanted me to prod him so he could modestly reveal his brilliance. Let him keep it to himself. I wasn't in the mood.

"You were with Mrs. Bowers—or Miss Chandler, depending on if she intends to keep her professional name for business. Which animals caught her interest?"

"At the zoo? The route we took passed the primates. She also stopped by the tapirs, but her target was the white tiger."

"And the animals responded to her how? The ones she stopped in front of and, er, made faces at."

"A shower of poop, screaming, and a lot of bared teeth."

"Then she may well be telling the truth. She asked them about Harry Reed, and the animals didn't like him."

I threw back my head. "Aw, come on." That gave me a crick, and I decided against future dramatic gestures. "You can't believe in that stuff."

"I'm analyzing the facts. When you reached the tiger, what happened?"

"I was busy talking to Jose, the keeper. Incidentally, Jose thinks Harry was a stinker. Said he practically had to force animal updates on him, which is odd behavior from a vet. While I pumped Jose for information, the animal roared a few times, but I think that's typical tiger behavior. At least no one tried to scale the fence."

"Odd that the woman would lick your hand afterward."

I grimaced. "Let's say unexpected. I *am* attractive to women. Maybe she missed her husband and took it out on me."

Edward cocked his head. "Really? By licking your hand? What was the tiger doing when you left her."

"Li—" Licking her cub. "I don't remember."

"And then there was that incident with the seagulls. Perhaps they were telling her something."

"Or maybe she annoyed them and, being animals, they attacked her. Are you out of your mind, Edward? Are you suggesting she's skipping around talking to the birds and the bees? If so, why haven't they named the murderer? Oh. I know. They're dumb beasts. Beasts that can't talk."

My brother ignored me. "The only other animal I can think of is the dog. What's its name?"

"Tanner."

He chuckled. "I'd wager that little one could tell us a lot." He frowned. "Where did you find him?"

"Forget it. I already checked the area. So did the cops. He was cowering in the first safe corner he found. End of story." I shot him a glance. "So. Two murders in as many days. Not a safe place. Are we leaving?"

"The reservations are through Sunday. The hotel would be unlikely to refund me, so we shall stay."

"You might as well tell me," I said. "I'll find out anyway."

"Tell you what?" Edward said with feigned innocence.

"You know something. Or you've guessed." I held up a hand to stay his protest. "I know you as well as you think you know me. The only reason you would stick around is if there were a chance you could show up the police. And Detective Bowers," I added.

His lips twitched, giving me confirmation.

"Okay. Spill."

"Would you say we look alike? I don't mean that we're twins, thank Heaven."

Edward rarely took a straight path to answer my questions, but that was so far off track, I shook my head in disgust. "Fine. Don't tell me."

"I'm serious."

His expression said he was. "Okay. The answer is yes. We both take after Dad."

I waited, but Edward was finished.

"That's it? That's all you're going to say?"

"Nicholas, Nicholas, Nicholas. I'm not going to hand you the solution on a plate. Use that brain of yours."

Did he mean that Harry Reed had a brother? Or that Cynthia and Harry were siblings? I pulled up my only meeting with Harry Reed.

Harry was blond. Cynthia might have dyed her hair chestnut brown, but women usually went the other direction. The niece was my height in heels. Harry stood a few inches shorter.

Or did he mean the killer was related to Harry? Could he mean Cynthia's Aunt Edna had killed her? If so, he was crazy. Those women looked nothing alike, even with the age difference factored in.

Or he meant nothing at all and only said it to irritate me.

"What now? Are you going to follow up on the Robert Browning quote?"

"I left that to Martin Bowers."

"Oh. We're sharing, are we?"

"I don't expect Mrs. Reed to have anything to offer. I need to think. Perhaps if I relaxed, my thoughts would come easier."

"You're longing to mingle with your fans." I snorted with disgust. "Your ego is starved, and it needs a feeding."

"It would make this weekend a tax write-off."

Since I handled the accounting, I gave him my blessing. "Lead the way."

Chapter Thirty-Six

Frankie: Bowers is Hiding Something

"You know what tonight is," I said, snuggling closer to Bowers. We'd lit the gas fireplace and sat next to each other on the couch, with me resting my head on his chest and he stroking my hair. Both of us pretended the earlier outburst had never happened.

"The last time we'll have to eat dinner with the Harlow brothers?" he murmured.

"That is true. But afterward is the dance." I poked his side. "Dress up time."

He turned his head and kissed the tip of my nose. "Does that mean I get to see you in that white dress again?" He growled and chewed on my neck. I shrieked and smacked his shoulder.

He pulled back his head and pretended I'd offended him. "With screams like that, it's a good thing we don't have neighbors."

That made my giggles go away. "It's spooky. No one to hear my screams. Not that I'm planning on screaming a lot."

Bowers took offense and chewed on my neck again. With a contented sigh, he leaned back and stared into the fire. "It's been an extremely unique honeymoon, don't you think?"

"I wouldn't advertise it in a travel brochure." He laughed. "But I'm sorry we didn't get to see more of San Diego."

Mr. Fix-it was halfway off the couch before I grabbed his arm. "No. I'm not up to cramming it in this afternoon."

He returned to his position next to me. "We'll have to come back. But next time, we'll stay somewhere safe. Like a Marriott."

"I'd like that."

We shared a comfortable silence for a few minutes, but then my insatiable curiosity kicked in and spoiled the moment.

"Who do you think killed those people?"

"We'll let Bautista worry about that."

He shouldn't have said it so casually, as if the sergeant were tasked with picking up a pizza. I took his face in my hands and attempted to catch his averted gaze.

"You know."

"I don't know. I suspect."

"Who?"

"I'm not sure who. Not exactly. More of a what."

Using his favorite phrase, I crossed my arms over my chest and said, "Explain."

"It's more instinct."

"Bull bollocks. You shape that instinct with facts. With clues you've spotted. Deductions you've made."

"Okay. Tell me who has been interested in tigers all weekend."

"Jimmy. Jimmy did it? It was a hit?"

"I didn't say that. From what Sykes says, Jimmy has been occupied all weekend."

"What about the men he always has with him? They could have, um, carried out his orders. Except Stanley. I don't believe Stanley would do something horrible like kill a person."

The look of pity he gave me raised my hackles.

"You haven't been exposed to the worst side of people as I have, thank God. Some of the most dangerous people out there are charming."

"You think Stanley, or someone who worked for Jimmy killed Harry and Cynthia?"

He held my gaze. "Possibly."

I squeezed his hand with both of mine. "Bowers, I love that you want to protect me. But this time, we're both involved. I found Harry's body on our patio. I found Cynthia in our pool. Well, not our pool, but we are the only people in the vicinity who might have used it. Gee. I should stop walking the grounds. Anyway, isn't it better for me to know what's happening? Wouldn't I be safer that way?"

"Maybe." He looked me over as if he were pondering the purchase of a roast closing in on its expiration date. "I don't want you getting further involved. I'm afraid if I share my thoughts with you, you'll do something, um, inadvisable."

About to retort, I realized he was right. That didn't make me like it.

"If you can figure it out, so can I."

"Frankie." He said my name as a warning. "I mean it. Even if Jimmy and Stanley aren't involved in the killings, they are dangerous men."

"Then I won't bother with them."

"Instead, you'll bother the killer. That's no better." He scooted off the couch. "Looks like I'll have to stick to my promise and not let you out of my site."

In normal circumstances, those words made my tummy flip. This time, they were an irritant.

Chapter Thirty-Seven

Frankie: Confessions

Bowers wore a deep brown suit and peach tie to dinner that night, courtesy of Mrs. Abernathy. Nicholas hadn't yet returned the shoes, which was just as well. My husband's black tennis shoes could almost pass as dress shoes.

For once, we beat Nicholas and Edward to the table.

"Maybe they won't show up," Bowers said, opening his menu with enthusiasm. At least he didn't grumble when they walked into the restaurant a few minutes later.

Edward attempted to set the tone with a question. "Will you be participating in the talent contest tonight?"

Bowers made a gacking noise. I smothered my laugh with my napkin.

"I suppose talent nights have lost their attraction. Before television and the Internet invaded the populace, leaving them senseless drones, hearing the niece play the piano or auntie read a poem were considered enjoyable entertainment."

The elder Harlow brother sighed over a genteel era subject to a frontal attack by modern conveniences.

Movies available at the push of a button. Books, too, though I wasn't sure how many people read these days. Part of me sympathized with him. But the part of me that dreaded the thought of a crowded movie theater loved that I could watch my movies at home.

Also, I couldn't sing, and I disliked poetry unless it rhymed, so I'd be stuck listening to those who thought they had talent. A nightmare.

"What about you?" I asked. "Are you entered in the contest?"

"I'm afraid it wouldn't do. Auntie's fans might not approve of me turning myself into a spectacle with a juggling act."

"You juggle?" That, I would watch.

"Among other things."

I couldn't resist. "What's your talent, Nicholas?"

He gave me that wise-mouthed grin. "Are you asking for a demonstration?"

"Spare us," Edward said. As he unfolded his napkin, he slipped a glance at my husband. "This is our last night here. I admit to feeling unsettled by this, er, unfinished business."

Bowers looked up. "As long as we're making confessions, I wouldn't mind being here for the conclusion."

They were speaking in code. Dancing around the edge of the subject. And then I realized. They *both* knew the identity of the killer.

I turned to Nicholas. "Do you know who the killer is?"

He glared at his brother. "I'm keeping my own counsel."

Which meant no. As we placed our orders, I considered the younger Harlow. He'd come in handy when I'd needed an accomplice at the zoo. And he had tried to save Cynthia, ignoring the dangers—or at least discomforts—of jumping into an unheated pool. And he hadn't questioned me when I told him to move away from the chimps. In looking for a sidekick, I could do worse.

Bowers and Edward continued to exchange ideas in low rumbly voices meant to keep the conversation private. When Edward said, "Are we agreed on the principal?" I interjected, "What principal?"

My husband was so deep in thought he didn't hear me. "Yes." He nodded. "Definitely."

I turned to Nicholas. "Do you have a principal?"

"According to Edward, I have no principals."

"If only we had a way to confirm our theory." Edward toyed with his fork, lining it up with the butter knife. "I'd like to be certain."

"Confirmation isn't possible. At least, not until we move."

Nicholas decided to join in the fun. "We're moving?"

Only the pulse in Edward's jaw showed he'd heard his younger brother.

"Have you run your idea past Bautista?" Bowers murmured. As a cop, he would be super sensitive to the sergeant's feelings.

I rested my chin on my palm. "What exactly is your idea, Mr. Harlow?"

I'm certain he didn't hear me, because to ignore me would have been rude. By now, the two men had slipped into one simpatico mind and the world, including Nicholas and me, didn't exist. This irritated me a great deal.

I slapped my hand on the table and leaned toward Nicholas. "I'm on my honeymoon, you know."

"I've heard."

"Except my husband is more interested in talking to this author he just met."

"Too bad."

No response from the self-appointed captains of the case.

"Would you like to have sex with me?"

Nicholas grinned. "Right now? On the table? We'll have to rearrange the centerpiece. And I recommend moving the cutlery."

"I can hear you," Bowers said without looking at us.

Clasping my hands in front of my chest, I hooted. "Little ol' me? Can you really?"

He sighed. "We're discussing a scenario that takes concentration and thought."

"You hear that, Nicholas? They're thinking."

"Sounds rough."

"The two of us just happen to have brain cells to spare. What say we offer to help these big, important men with their thinking."

"Frankie," Bowers warned. "You're pushing it with the humor. It's a serious situation."

I stuck out my lower lip. "You're right. I'm sorry. I'll leave you in peace." I stood and dropped my napkin on the table. "Are you coming, Nicholas?"

Edward shot his brother a quick glance and a slight nod.

"Sure."

As we exited the restaurant, I told the younger Harlow he'd insulted me. "Why did you have to get the okay from your brother to come with me?"

"He signs my paychecks. Officially, I'm on duty."

Though I wouldn't say it out loud, having a large,

muscular man at my side gave me some comfort. Now I could move ahead with my own plan without worrying something ugly might jump out of the shadows.

"Where are we headed?" he asked.

"Back to the cottages."

"Last time I escorted you there, we found a body. Any surprises awaiting that I should know about?"

"I hope so," I mumbled because I wasn't sure I was on the right track. If memory served me, the cries that woke me last night were more intense than the ones I heard before. It was possible the tiger cub was merely hungrier, or more scared, but I based my next steps on increased intensity meaning closer proximity. What better place to hide a cub than in unused buildings?

"If I'm right, you can rub your brother's face in it after I finish with Bowers."

"I'm for that. Lead the way."

"They both think they know the identity of the murderer."

"What gave it away? Their insufferable murmuring? The way they excluded us as if we were window dressing?"

"They might have information we don't, but I still think we can beat them to it. We know Harry was meeting someone here. I think it was Jimmy."

Nicholas turned his head to look down at me. "Do tell."

"I really should save it for Bowers."

"He's busy whispering with my brother."

"True. Jimmy was mad about Harry's death."

"Mad that he killed him?"

"That's exactly why I don't think he did."

"And when did the gangster share this secret with you?"

"He might have, um, invited me to his room. But there were at least seven other guys there, so we weren't alone."

He stopped walking. "Tell me you're joking."

"The thing is, Jimmy didn't seem to know anything about the murders. He actually wanted to meet with Harry."

"Huh. There goes my best suspect."

Nicholas took his job as my bodyguard seriously, hovering over me as I unlocked the gate.

"I'm just going inside to find a flashlight."

He pulled out his cell phone and hit an app. "Already have one. Where to?"

I paused, closed my eyes, and cleared my mind. One eye popped open. "No comment about the faces, please."

With both eyes shut, I inhaled slow and deep. I spread a lighted highway that reached over the Cottages and Villas in Beach Village.

It took a minute before a startled yowl responded. My eyes opened, and I headed down the same path we walked last time.

Ground-level security lights lit the walkways, which made the abandoned buildings less intimidating. Still, all the interior lights were off, including those in our cottage, which meant plenty of places for unfriendly folks to hide.

I paused, sent out a mental, chipper, "Here, kitty, kitty," and listened. The cry, more hopeful and insistent this time, came from our left.

As I passed between cottages, a large form stepped out of the shadows, followed by several more. Jimmy.

"You've given us a head start. Now take us the rest of the way."

There were four men with Jimmy, including Stanley. I leaned toward Nicholas and lowered my voice. "How many can you take?"

"Two. Possibly three. Can you handle one?"

"No. Sorry." Back to Jimmy. "I'm not sure I understand what you're asking."

"Sure, you do. You're out here looking for the cub right now."

This came as a surprise to Nicholas. "We are? You mean there actually is a tiger cub?"

When Jimmy moved his hand to point at me, moonlight reflected off the gun. "Don't you know who this is? That's all right. She had me fooled, too. I looked her up on the Internet."

Darn those search engines.

"She's a pet psychic. And she's going to find that tiger cub for me, right lady?"

Nicholas turned off his flashlight and stuck his phone in his pocket. When the men stepped forward, he held up his empty hands.

"Frisk him."

"Come on," Nicholas complained. "You'll mess up my suit. Do I look like a guy who carries weapons?"

He had to submit to the search anyway. At Jimmy's instructions, the men searched me, too. One guy, the one with the nice tenor voice, gave me an apologetic glance. He performed the search in the most gentlemanly way possible. Not that I base that on experience, but he didn't touch anything he shouldn't.

Jimmy waved the gun. "Let's go."

"You have to give me a minute."

"Are you stalling?"

"I don't know where the cub is. Not exactly. Just that it's, um, around."

"Give her a minute," Nicholas said. "There are a lot of cottages to go through, not to mention the condos behind us. How big is this tiger cub? Not big? So, it's a small target in a large field. It's going to take her some time."

"You're a big target in a small field. I'll show you if you don't shut up."

"Wait!" I held up my hands and cocked my head as if picking up on a signal. Except there wasn't any signal. The tiger had stopped crying.

About to explain, my eyes met Jimmy's, and I saw no understanding in his dark, soulless gaze. My only option was to revert to my pre-psychic days before the ability to communicate with animals became an everyday occurrence. Back when I made things up.

It was time to perform, and I only hoped I could do it well enough to keep Nicholas and me alive and healthy until help arrived.

Chapter Thirty-Eight

Nicholas: An Unwelcome Party

My only objective right now was to keep Bowers' wife and me alive until help arrived. More so me, since she seemed to have something Jimmy Bianchi wanted.

If push came to shove, literally, could I take on four men? Each one stood over six feet tall. One was well over two hundred pounds. Maybe two-fifty. The way they handled themselves told me this wouldn't be their first fight. I'd probably live through it, but the guns were a problem.

I appreciated Frankie's honesty. Lots of women would have slipped into fantasyland and bragged about their ability to fight, only to take a step back as I leaped into the fray. It helped with my decision to stay put.

As I got accustomed to the idea that I was outnumbered and outgunned—as in I didn't have one—I realized I still held my phone in my hand. Casually, as if it were no big deal and the only thing a sane person would do, I turned off the flashlight app and stuck my phone in my pocket, muting the volume and hitting Edward on speed dial as I did so. I could only hope the lug head hadn't left his phone in the room. I'd hate to die because he did the polite thing.

"Take his phone," Jimmy ordered.

The thug named Stanley came over to claim it, and I had no choice but to hand it over. The screen had Edward's big face on it, meaning the call had connected, so I said louder than necessary, as if I were panicking, "You've got us where you want us. Which cottage do we search first? The Bowers? It's just behind us."

When I placed my lifeline in Stanley's oversize paw, I prayed he'd think Edward's face was my screen saver. He didn't even look at it before he dropped my phone into his overcoat pocket.

"Well?" Jimmy waited for the woman of the hour to respond.

Frankie stood still and made a move that reminded me of a dog sniffing the air.

"It's not here."

"Sure, it is," Jimmy purred. "That's why you came here, isn't it? To grab the cub for yourself?"

"Well, yes. But it isn't here now. Someone must have moved it."

Jimmy exploded. "Damn her!"

Frankie jumped. I might have, too. But he wasn't talking about us.

"You better figure out where she took it and fast." He jabbed a thick finger at one of the guys. "You. Get over to the hotel and make sure she and her friend haven't checked out."

She and her friend. I scanned my memory banks for women with friends. Polka and Dot were sisters. Maybe he didn't know they were related.

Rhonda and Willie were married, but I suppose they could still be friends. What if they weren't really married? With the age range of attendees, they might not have wanted to hear lectures on living in sin, which would make them friends rather than spouses.

Edna's friend, if a niece qualified as a friend, was dead. Or he referred to someone who wasn't part of the convention and none of those people were it.

The alleged pet psychic held up one hand. "I need silence." Damned if they didn't freeze in the act of leaving. Stanley shushed the guy next to him.

She put her hand to her forehead in concentration and did some deep breathing. Then she held up both hands and wiggled her fingers as if trying to touch a spirit as it floated past.

Something wasn't right. This was not what she looked like when we were at the zoo, and she was allegedly reading the tiger's mind.

When she turned in a slow circle and lifted her arms above her head, humming as she did so, it hit me. God help us, she was faking it.

Suddenly, her eyes opened, and she pointed to her right. "That way."

With Frankie in the lead and me following with a gun in my back, we proceeded to the sidewalk that ran between the resort and the beach. Every few minutes, she'd stop, cock her head, and mumble something.

The thing about knowing your life is about to end, it sharpens the senses. The briny salt air smelled saltier. Shadows I'd usually ignore had defined edges. I could almost see in the dark. And as for my hearing? Each disgruntled cluck from the seagulls near the shore rang out like a yell.

When we reached the point where their cackling sounded like they were close enough to step on my feet, Frankie stopped again. The ocean waves, slapping against the shore, brought up a saying I associated with mobsters. Sleeping with the fishes. That usually meant lakes, didn't it? Otherwise, bodies would inconveniently wash up for public viewing. I hoped this meant they preferred fresh water.

This time, when Frankie closed her eyes, she wiggled her nose and mouth and scrunched her cheeks, just like she had at the zoo.

"What's the holdup?"

She didn't answer, and Jimmy strode to her and grabbed her arm. Mistake. The sky pounded with fluttering wings and loud cries. I ducked, a natural response, but when nothing hit me, not even poop, I looked up. The birds concentrated their attack on our captors.

The gangsters covered their heads and waved their arms, and when that didn't work, they unsheathed their weapons and took potshots and the dark sky.

Frankie grabbed my hand. "Run!"

She didn't have to ask twice. With her hanging onto me, I couldn't break into a full sprint, but at times, I think her feet left the ground and she trailed me like a victory flag.

I didn't stop moving until we reached the hotel lobby. A few heads turned as we stood there panting, but they assumed we'd been frolicking in the sand.

The Crown Room would be the first place those goons would search. Frankie took an unsteady step forward and said, "Look."

The Coronet Room crowd must have been on a break.

The door stood open. A quick scan showed the room was empty. We stepped inside.

Almost empty. One of the guards by the window turned. I put my hand on Frankie's head and shoved her to her knees, joining her before she could protest. Crawling like two-year-olds, we disappeared under the draping tablecloth moments before movement announced the occupants' return.

After some jostling to avoid feet, the two of us held our breath.

"I've come to a decision," said a strong voice with the gravel of age.

The men went silent.

"Jimmy."

A pair of feet by my left hand pulled back as he scooted out his chair and, I assumed, stood.

"You've always been a good worker. I know you're loyal, and loyalty is very important."

A few voices murmured, mostly from our side of the room.

Someone cleared his throat. "Thank you, Enzo. It's an honor. And I'd like to say—"

"But!"

Enzo wasn't finished.

"You get distracted. Ever since you were little, something shiny passed by and you were off like a shot. Take this weekend. You were chasing that redhead around the hotel."

Frankie's eyes widened.

"It wasn't like that. It was business."

"Business?" Enzo asked the question in a deadly voice that said Jimmy better come clean, or else.

"Private business."

Someone, I assume Enzo, pounded on the head table. "There is no business this weekend except what goes on in this room. No, Jimmy. You're a good soldier, but I can't depend on you to stay focused. It's that thing, they got a name for it."

A voice called out, "ADD."

"That's it. ADD. Myself, I think it's a lack of self-control, which is also evident in your temper. Every time you have a tantrum, you look weak."

"Once I get this side issue taken care of, I'll be one hundred percent."

I almost didn't recognize Jimmy's voice, filled as it was with desperation.

"You gotta listen to me!"

We waited for the bullets to fly, but nothing happened except more shocked silence.

"My mind is made up. You can sit down."

When Jimmy complied, his foot kicked out, and he only missed Frankie because I jerked her back. The movement jarred the table, and we froze. Everyone topside must have assumed Jimmy did the bumping, because no one dragged us from our hiding place.

"I've given this a lot of thought. There is one man who never questions orders. Always carries them through, without complaining, I might add. He's someone I feel confident passing my authority to." After a strained, silent beat, he put us out of our misery. "Stanley."

Jimmy's feet shot to standing. "You can't put Stanley in charge. He's nobody!"

"I can't?" Enzo purred.

Jimmy wisely kept quiet.

"Stanley is your half-brother. And my word is final. Unless anyone else objects?"

It started with one clap, and soon thunderous applause filled the room. When it petered out, Enzo spoke again.

"And now, we will drink a toast to Stanley. All of us."

Champaign corks popped. From my point of view under the table, several sets of black shoes, probably waiters, made the rounds.

"To Stanley," the men said, responding to a silent signal.

Seconds later, a glass crashed on the floor to my right.

"Ack, ugh, ptui. Aaaaaargh!"

At least that's what I thought I heard before a loud thump, also to my right. When I looked, Jimmy Bianchi stared back at me from his position on the floor. He didn't blink. He didn't move. Jimmy was gone.

Frankie gasped before I got my hand over her mouth, but everyone was too busy dealing with the dead gangster to hear her. When she scrambled forward, I wrapped an arm around her middle and held her tight. Fear turned her into a writhing wild thing, and I caught a fist to the groin and had to cover a yell. As soon as I let go, she was off.

Chapter Thirty-Nine

Frankie: The Great Escape

Holding my breath while under a table full of mobsters goes high on my list of achievements. To keep calm, I tried to imagine I was a deer hiding from a hunter. Still. Quiet. Blending into the landscape.

And then the body hit the floor.

As soon as I looked into Jimmy's dead, dull eyes, all the noises I'd been holding back careened up my throat, preparing to deliver the loudest scream ever. Nicholas Harlow sensed what was happening and clamped a big paw over my mouth. It worked for a second.

Then Negative Frankie went to work on my imagination. Would the mobsters lift the tablecloth? Would they force me to drink poison like they did Jimmy? With two people breathing heavily in a confined space, how much carbon dioxide had replaced oxygen?

The one that got me moving was: *Do you know the last time Nicholas Harlow washed the hand that is now touching your mouth?*

All sense of reason left me. I wanted out, now.

Some prehistoric muscle memory kicked in. The same one my ancestors used when faced with a hungry T-Rex. My limbs took over. When Nicholas tried to stop me, I panicked, and they went into overtime. He grunted and let go, and my brain joined my body, repeating one message. Get out. Get out! GET OUT!

And so, I did.

Never have I moved so fast on my hands and knees.

"Son of a—"

Nicholas mumbled something. I assumed he was close behind, but it was everyone for themselves. Once I reached the end of the table, I stumbled to my feet and ran. Startled faces watched as I slammed into the exit door, jiggling the handle until it opened, and I was free.

Halfway through the lobby, I froze. Where to? The beach? Too exposed. The Crown Room? They'd expect it. At least, Stanley would.

Before I could make up my mind, Nicholas hooked an arm around me. As he ran, he carried me like a football until we made it to the corridor leading to the garden outside. He wasn't at his best, as he limped with every step.

Even though they were airborne, my feet kicked as if I were still moving under my own power. When someone grabbed my ankle, I yelled. Nicholas lost his hold on me, and I landed face down on the carpet.

The younger Harlow spun, and by the time he faced me, he'd assumed a fighting stance. Almost immediately, he relaxed.

"If you like your women living, we need to move it."

Bowers grabbed my shoulders and started to pull me up. He winced from the extra weight on his leg.

"Allow me."

Edward Harlow yanked me off the ground and tossed me over his shoulder, and we ran. At least, Edward ran. Bowers limped. So did Nicholas.

"What's the matter with you?" Edward demanded.

"Nothing I can't shake off," his brother snapped.

When we passed the costume room, I grabbed Edward's left ear and pulled, guiding him like a horse. "In there!"

As soon as we crossed the threshold, Edward set me down, made a slight bow, and apologized for taking liberties.

Bowers and Nicholas stumbled into the room, each with an arm slung over the other's shoulder for support.

I closed the door and listened for footsteps, but the only noise was the heavy breathing of the room's occupants.

My husband pulled me away from the door. "What happened. Is it Jimmy?"

The image of those staring eyes returned, and I scrunched my face to hold back the tears.

"They poisoned him, Bowers. Right in front of us."

He swore.

To assure him, I explained we were under the table, out of sight. At least until we ran for our lives.

He swore again.

"We're trapped like rats." Nicholas made me sound like Little Miss Mary Sunshine.

After a few deep breaths, I turned to check out the room.

"The talent show," Edward hissed. "The convention attendees have descended like locusts and cleared out the room."

Bowers grabbed the closest dress and shoved it at me. "We need to change our appearance."

He'd handed me that beautiful lavender gown. I held it up and pressed it against me.

"Do you like this color on me?"

He stopped rifling the remaining costumes long enough to admire the dress.

"But I can't wear it. It's a twenty-four. I'll trip over it."

"Frankie, honey, this isn't a fashion show. Wait a minute. A twenty-four?" He grabbed the dress and slipped it over his clothes. It wasn't bad, though the shoulders were stretched to the limit.

"I'm not wearing a dress." Nicholas crossed his arms and refused to budge.

"For Heaven's sake, no one is asking you to put on rouge. Either change your clothes or die," his brother said. "Ah. The costume from my talk. It was a tad tight, but . . . there."

He removed his shirt but not his undershirt and struggled into the sheath, leaving it unzipped. Then he dropped his drawers.

Nicholas, fussing with a large, gold, sparkling ballgown, announced he refused to take off his pants.

"Do as you please," his brother said, "but you'll be spotted in minutes. No man wearing a dress to the convention would leave on his pants."

I hadn't found a dress, but Bowers threw Edward's suit coat over my shoulders. He pulled a fedora from the rack and rested it on my head. Because it went down to my nose, he tipped it to the back of my head.

"That's fine. It hides your face."

We were a motley crew, but no one would think we

were the same people who entered the room. At least, not at a glance. From behind.

Edward put his hand on the doorknob. "Where to?"

"Back to the cottages," I said. "One in particular."

Chapter Forty

Nicholas: The Search

I felt like a damned fool.

Edward insisted we stay away from the lighting, so we trudged across the sand toward the Beach Front Village looking like a parade of imbeciles.

I swore.

"Language, Nicholas," came from the large shadow to my left.

"I'm getting sand down my socks, and I could build a castle with what's made it into my shoe."

"Wah-wah-wah."

If Edward wanted to mock me, I thought he should have saved it for when we were alone. To turn around and leave would have consequences, so I ignored him and kept moving.

When we got to the cottages and through the gate, Frankie started pulling on her husband's arm like a dog on a lead.

"This way."

We were now trotting. By the time we made it to the last cottage in the row, I'd gotten the creeps again.

Standing in the security lights while we considered the front door made me feel exposed. I had to resist the urge to crouch.

Edward and Bowers took care of the door. Under roughly four hundred pounds of muscle, it gave way.

"Didn't they teach you to pick a lock at detective school?" I asked as I stepped over a couple of thousand dollars in damage.

Everyone turned on their cell phone flashlights. Everyone except me and Frankie. She wasn't expecting a call and didn't have hers. Mine was in the pocket of a gigantic creature named Stanley.

We could have turned on every light in the place, had there been power, and we would have had the same result. No tiger cub.

"Could the animal have confused you? Sent the wrong directions?" Edward asked the questions kindly, with no intention of insulting the lady. I would have shaken her until her teeth rattled.

Frankie rubbed her nose. "The last time I heard—or felt—the cub, it was coming from here."

That was too much. "Then why didn't you come get it?"

"I didn't know it was here. I had to work it out. It's not an exact science. The little girl is frightened. And she's only a month old. What does she know about directions? Or communicating? It's only luck I picked up her signal."

Her condescending tone gave me flashbacks of fourth grade math class, when Mrs. Higgins loomed over my desk and told me I was being obtuse by refusing to state the difference between an isosceles triangle and an obtuse triangle. That got her a laugh, but I still say they were the same thing, and the name was a matter of preference.

"Can you pick up, er, anything right now?" Bowers asked.

She concentrated, then shook her head. "Every time I've heard it, she's been lonely and scared. Maybe she's happy right now."

"Why she?" I asked.

Frankie's eyes opened wide. "I don't know. An impression, I guess."

Bowers and Edward continued their second search of the cottage, while I sat on the couch and removed my sock and shoe. My big toe was bleeding from a sharp stone. I'm not a sissy, but the idea of contracting a weird disease from ocean life urine and carcasses didn't appeal to me.

When Edward made an exclamation, we all gathered around the beam of his cell phone flashlight. Against the wall behind the couch, at a spot where there were no windows, four scratches marked the walls. Evenly spaced scratches.

"Tiger claws," Edward breathed. "Like maybe it was stretching." He looked to Frankie for confirmation.

"Kittens can't retract their claws until they're about four weeks old. I don't know about tiger cubs."

"Or maybe the workmen bumped the wall when they were working in here."

No one answered, so I brought up something I considered more important. "Do you have any iodine at your place?"

"I always pack a first aid kit," Bowers said.

After one last search of the area, we left and headed for the Bowers' cottage. We weren't too concerned about discovery, as we walked like men—and one woman—and didn't keep our voices down.

"Do you think she's gone?" Edward asked Bowers.

"No. The hotel is under observation. Of course, disguises make the process a joke."

"Are you talking about Rhonda?" I said, taking a stab at the identity of the killer. She was the only character I'd met this weekend who seemed completely false. Nobody loves a movie that much, not even one starring Marilyn Monroe.

"Edna," Frankie said. "They're talking about Edna."

Bowers turned his head. "How did you get there?"

"Tanner."

Great. Every talking lion cub needs a talking dog for company.

"When I first connected with him, he pretended to be ferocious. He showed me the most fearsome animals quaking in his presence. Lions. Bears. I wondered—"

"Where would the companion animal of an old woman ever see a lion or a bear?" Bowers nodded.

"Exactly."

Other than that completely wild guess, I couldn't see where the others had narrowed it down to the old woman.

What reason would she have to kill her own niece? Or Harry Reed?

Of course, lots of old women had cats. She might prefer hers on the larger side. That explained Harry, but not the niece.

"I don't get it."

Bowers unlocked the front door of their cottage and held it open for us. I got two steps inside before my feet skidded to a halt.

"Of course, I could always ask her."

Chapter Forty-One

Frankie: Finding the Cub

Edna Tartwell sat on the couch in front of the television. In her lap, the tiger cub rested on its back, its thick legs wrapped around the bottle it sucked on.

I pulled in a gasp of air. Its solid white fur was flawless, making her—I still thought it was a her—resemble a cotton ball. Her nails dug into the bottle as she drank, and her only reaction to our entrance was the movement of her crystal-blue eyes. Just like her mommy's eyes.

"She's beautiful," I whispered.

My gaze landed on a tattered, dirty, pink bunny tucked into the corner of the couch.

"Did you attack me?" I demanded.

The old woman set the cub aside, stood, and aimed a handgun at us.

"Now don't you all look pretty," Edna said, taking in the fancy dresses worn by the men. She turned her head. "This complicates things."

For a moment, I thought she was talking to the tiger, but then a muffled yell came from the side of the couch.

Leaning forward, I could just make out steel-gray curls sticking from the top of a blanket wrapped in silver electrical tape.

"You kidnapped Polka?"

"Polka?" She nudged her victim with the toe of her orthopedic shoe. "That's not what it says on his driver's license."

Nicholas gaped. "His?"

"Barnaby Putluck," Bowers and Edward said at the same time.

"Very good. I just think of him as the witness Cynthia let get away. Sloppy work. It's the shoddy work ethic of today's youth."

Just as I wondered how we were going to talk our way out of our own cottage, someone knocked. We turned as one, feeling, I'm sure, as if hope hovered on the other side of the solid door.

"Answer it."

Detective Sykes walked in, took one look at Edna, and buttoned his suit jacket as if on an official call.

"Here you are. I regret to inform you your brother is in the hospital."

"Brother?" Nicholas asked.

"Jimmy Bianchi."

After Detective Sykes delivered the news, Edna removed her glasses and tucked them into the pocket of her button-down sweater. I assume this was to allow the tears to flow more easily. Without her glasses, Edna couldn't hide her ski-slope nose.

"What a relief. I couldn't see through those lenses. They were my mother's. The woman was half-blind. It explains why she never got our names right." She glared at the detective. "You came all this way to tell me about Jimmy?"

"It seemed appropriate to notify the next of kin."

"He's not dead?" I shook my head, amazed. "How could he survive poison?"

"They poisoned him?" For the first time, Edna looked scared.

"Who said anything about poison?" Sykes frowned. "He had a stroke."

Edna relaxed. "Serves him right. All of this is Jimmy's fault. Even Cynthia's death."

"He killed your niece?" I'd heard of family feuds, but murder was taking hostilities too far.

Edna waved her gun at the credenza. "Put your weapons there, handsome. Slowly."

Detective Sykes, the only one armed, complied.

"I said *weapons*."

"That's all I'm carrying."

"If I frisk you and you're lying, I get to shoot you."

He bent down and removed a second, smaller handgun from an ankle holster and placed it with the other, bigger gun.

As the danger intensified, thoughts flitted through my mind. Bowers and me on the first night of our honeymoon. My discovery of Harry's corpse. Cynthia's flirting eyes. And Suri.

I unintentionally flashed the cub an image of her mother. She dropped the bottle and gave a tiny roar that, though higher pitched and lacking volume, was a fair imitation of her mother.

Edna shot a glance at the infant predator. "There, there. Not much longer and you'll be nice and comfy in your new home."

"But her home won't include her mother," I protested.

The woman had the nerve to look affronted. "I'll take care of her."

"But you're not her *mother*. She *needs* her mother."

"Mothers are overrated." She scratched the tip of her long nose with the back of the hand that held the gun. "Look at mine. All she cared about was the men in the family. They always came first and got the best of everything. New clothes instead of hand-me-downs. The shotgun seat, even when I called it first. The last meatball on the platter. Why? They had the business. I had to make my own way."

"They left you without an income?" Just as I was about to feel sorry for her, she squashed that idea, right after she yanked her gray wig off, stretched, and cracked her back. Gosh. She was taller than I thought, and long, brown hair cascaded over her shoulders. Only the Bianchi nose and plentiful wrinkles kept her from being a knockout.

"I have plenty of money. More than I know what to do with. But there's only so much shopping and lounging around you can do before a person loses her mind to boredom. And then she does unpleasant things to amuse herself. Things even Father disapproved of." She gazed at the tiger with adoration. "And then I discovered my true love. Wild animals. When I started my private zoo, life finally seemed worthwhile."

"You mean you've stolen from other zoos?"

"I never stole anything in my life. I purchased all my pets. With cash." The crease between her eyebrows emphasized her age. "But then my brother decided he had to have a private zoo as well. Always copying me. That man wouldn't know an original idea if it walked up and bit him."

"So, you lured Harry Reed to the beach and killed him for possession of the tiger cub," Edward said.

She waved her gun at him. To his credit, he didn't flinch. "I'm no welcher. But Harry was. He showed up and said he wanted more money because the tiger was white. He said he had another buyer ready if I didn't pony up. I'll give you three chances to name the buyer."

"Jimmy."

"Let me guess," Bowers said. "He wanted seventy-five thousand dollars."

She nodded. "That's a heap of money."

"So, you killed him," Sykes said.

"Nope. Cynthia did. If he had played fair, he'd be alive and spending his prize."

"Why did you kill your own niece?"

She threw back her head and laughed, keeping her eyes on us as she did so, which made her look like a maniacal killer, no matter that she hadn't killed Harry. "Cynthia wasn't my niece. She was my bodyguard. And some bodyguard she turned out to be. First, she got sloppy and allowed a witness to get away. Then, she left the bunny on the beach. If that weren't bad enough, I caught her searching for my hiding place. Do you know she had the nerve to pull a gun on me? Said Jimmy was paying her more to get the cub. No hard feelings."

Nicholas raised a finger. "Cynthia wasn't shot. At least, not that I saw."

"They don't call me Enterprising Edna for nothing. I'm handy in a fight, cause I don't fight fair. It didn't take much to distract her, get her in the water, and hold her head under."

"But you weren't wet when we found you."

"She used the pool net," Nicholas said. "And she dropped some kibble in the pool during the struggle."

"Did I? Don't think I polluted the pool. Tanner's food is organic." She sighed. "Cold water is invigorating. Or the killing made me feel alive. I enjoyed it. Even though I held her under with the pool net, I got wet. All that inconsiderate thrashing. So, I ran back to our room and changed. Killing made me thirsty, so I headed for the bar. That's where you found me."

"Cynthia never wanted to talk to me?" I wanted clarification.

"About what? The only thing you two had in common was an attraction to your husband."

Bowers blushed.

She gathered the cub and its bottle her arms. "I don't want to hurt anyone. Too messy. Except the witness. He's gotta go."

Sykes sent a curious glance to the bundled heap on the floor.

Edward spread his hands. "My dear woman, the only thing he witnessed was your bodyguard killing someone. How is that a danger to you?"

"You're right." She nudged Barnaby with her toe. "But he might hold a grudge over the kidnapping."

Muffled protests came from the floor.

"That's what you say now. I can't afford for you to change your mind. This tiger is mine, and I'm taking her back home with me."

"She's not yours," I insisted, stepping into Edna's path. "She belongs to her mother. And the zoo."

Her responding glare held a glint of the crazies. This woman would never listen to reason.

The cub fixed her crystal-blue eyes on me. I built a mental highway between her mind and mine—more of a non-threatening, meandering dirt road—and replayed my visit with Suri.

The cub jerked, especially when she "saw" her mother licking her sibling. A pang of longing for maternal affection mixed with sibling jealousy twisted in my chest. The cub cried out. The longing grew.

When it reached a consuming peak, I showed Edna sneaking up on Suri and bopping her on the head, just like a Punch and Judy puppet show.

The reaction came fast. Her claws sunk into Edna's arm, and the cub's teeth found a soft spot near her armpit.

Edna yowled and dropped the gun. Edward took care of tackling her, while Bowers wrapped me in his arms and turned so I was protected from the fray.

When it was over, Sykes was snapping on the cuffs. He gathered his weapons and put them where they belonged and, as calm as could be, made a call on his cell phone.

"Got her. We're at the Bowers' cottage."

The commotion had scared the cat. Dogs run. Cats hide. I pulled a beef stick from the welcome basket and ran to our sleeping quarters. Bowers found me half under our bed with my butt sticking in the air.

"Gotcha." I scooted back with a white ball of fur snuggled in my arms. Of course I didn't give her the beef stick. It wouldn't be good for her.

By the time we returned to the living room, one of the men had released Barnaby Putluck from his blanket prison. His eyes carried a dazed expression, and his gray wig sat askew on one side of his head, revealing the dark hair underneath.

"Bautista's on his way." Sykes motioned Edna to lead the way out the front door.

As Barnaby walked past, the detective informed him his sister was worried about him.

"Jenny! I forgot about her, what with hiding for my life."

As soon as we were all outside, Rhonda and Willie stepped out from either side of the cottage with their own weapons drawn.

"Freeze."

"Rhonda?" I said, dazed.

Sykes directed them to his inside jacket pocket, and once Rhonda checked his credentials, they both lowered their weapons.

"Feds," Edna said with disgust.

Willie corrected her. "US Fish and Wildlife Service. At your service."

Rhonda giggled. "You're bad."

"This is Edna Bianchi—" Detective Sykes began, but Rhonda cut him off.

"We know. Is that the cub from the zoo?"

I nodded. "Suri's baby."

Before I could hand her over, the first shot came, blasting sand into the air. The baby cat jerked in surprise, so I pulled her close and tightened my hold on her.

Nicholas spun toward the source of the shot. "What the—"

Bowers pushed me to the ground. As I went down, Detective Sykes launched himself in front of Nicholas Harlow in time for the second shot.

There wasn't a third.

Nicholas moved to where Edward hovered over Sykes. By that time, I was on my feet. I turned and buried my face in Bowers' chest. He held me and made soothing noises. All the while, I could feel how tense his muscles were. At least until they relaxed.

He turned me around.

I covered my face with the hand that wasn't holding the cub. "I don't want to look."

But then I did.

Edward held out a hand and pulled Detective Sykes to his feet. The detective met my gaping expression and rubbed his chest.

"Kevlar."

"Did you just save my life?" Nicholas demanded. He didn't sound happy for someone who'd been plucked from death's clutches.

Detective Sykes smirked. "I did."

Nicholas spread his arms and turned a full circle. "Somebody kill me now. I do not want to owe this man."

"But you *do* owe me," Sykes purred.

When Bautista marched the shooter out from behind the bushes, I gaped.

"Oswald? How could you!"

"His name isn't Oswald," Rhonda said. "He's wanted by the FBI for interstate flight, among other things. His name is Clancy McArdle. A killer for hire."

Since there were other people with guns to keep Oswald from bolting, Bautista holstered his weapon and put the handcuffs on the killer.

Nicholas waved a finger between his brother and the detective. "You knew! You knew he was here." He raked his fingers through his hair. "For the love of Mike, he tried to partner up with me for the treasure hunt."

"But we didn't let him," Rhonda said.

The younger Harlow looked sick.

"It's nothing personal," Oswald/Clancy said. "We all gotta make a living. And I bet we would have made a good team. Maybe even won."

Edward studied his friend with pursed lips. "Were you assigned to look out for him after the threats?"

Detective Sykes kicked at the sand. "I took a few days off. Shauna thought it was a good idea, too, as long as I didn't have fun." The smile returned. "And now you're in my debt. Don't worry, Nicky. I'll think of a way you can repay me."

"Nuts."

While the officers sorted out which criminal belonged to whom, Bowers took my hand. "Since you seem to have everything under control here, I'm going to take Frankie back to our cottage."

All those holding badges shook their heads.

Sykes gestured toward our temporary home. "We'll need to search it just to make sure Ms. Bianchi didn't hide anything. Until the local police finish with it . . ." He shrugged apologetically.

It looked as if we were homeless again.

Chapter Forty-Two

Frankie: It's a Wrap

In our new suite on the first floor of The Victorian—someone had conveniently checked out this morning—I curled on the spacious couch next to my husband with Tanner in my lap. I was giving him a full-face massage because it was the only way to keep a grip on those jaws to keep him from biting anyone. Including me.

We'd retrieved him from Edna's room, and, so far, he was behaving himself. Of course, the tiger cub asleep in Bowers' lap may have subdued his bullying tendencies. He might be in love with her. Or he might be terrified. I hadn't asked. Everyone deserves their privacy. And their dignity.

"She's kind of cute," Bowers said, rubbing the baby cat's belly. "We should think about getting one for Emily."

"She's cute now, but when she grows big enough to *eat* Emily . . . not so cute."

When someone rapped on our door, Bowers glanced

down at the sleeping kitty and shrugged, so I climbed off the couch and carried Tanner to the door.

"What a cute doggie!"

I hadn't expected a girlish squeal from the woman who'd snubbed me in Presidio Park. Dr. Sylvia Yang peered over my shoulder and gasped. I forgot she hadn't yet seen the snowy white, stripeless cub.

She crossed the room in short, quick steps and bent over the sleeping tiger, her hands hovering over it as if she were afraid to touch it.

About to close the door, I jumped back as a man with a cage followed the vet into our room.

Dr. Yang carefully scooped up the cub, waking her. She blinked those dazzling blue eyes at the vet, who was running her fingers over the animal in an expert manner.

"Darling, darling girl. We need to get you to your mommy."

She placed her on a blanket in the cage and locked the doors.

I sent my husband a nervous glance. This woman had met with Edna Tartwell on the sly. Was she really intending to return the cub to its mother?

"Just a minute," I said, just as newcomers knocked. I hadn't closed the door properly. Rhonda and Willie entered the room.

"Dr. Yang," Rhonda said, shaking the vet's hand. "I'm so glad to see you."

"Yes. Everything turned out satisfactory."

"Hold on." I raised my hand. "I need to tell you that my husband and I saw Dr. Yang—"

"With Edna Tartwell." Willie smiled. "The good doctor agreed to help us. We've had our eyes on the Bianchi siblings for a while, and when we discovered they would both be here at the same time, so close to a major zoo, we looked into the recent births. When the white tiger only had one cub, and we heard about the unusual circumstances of the birth . . . "

"We had to check it out," Rhonda said. "The convention was a bonus." She shook her head. "We missed Harry Reed. But when he turned up dead, we knew our instincts were correct. And then when we heard that Carla the Chimp was expecting, it was the perfect opportunity to approach Edna."

"That was dangerous." I shivered at the memory of Edna's casual reference to a woman she had killed.

"No one messes with my animals." Dr. Yang said this in a matter-of-fact tone that was somehow scarier than a yell. "I let that woman know I was ready to step in where Harry left off. Then I said I had to get back to the zoo to check up on Carla. I made baby chimps sound so cute and desirable. Though neither of us said anything specific, she got the message, foolish woman. To think of Carla as a sweet pet. Ha! The chimpanzees are the most feared animals in the zoo."

"And you heard about the pregnant chimp through Detective Sykes," Bowers said. "He never mentioned knowing who you were."

"Detective who?" Rhonda said with all innocence. "We were in Dr. Yang's office when she called you."

"We guessed you weren't just a normal couple," I said, relieved to find all that happiness had been an act.

Rhonda frowned. "How? We're good at this."

"Nobody is that enthusiastic all the time. It wasn't normal. I mean, the handclapping and *this is the best movie ever . . .*"

My words trailed off at their blank expressions. They

didn't understand what could be suspicious about their actions. They *were* the happiest people on earth.

"Never mind."

Before Dr. Yang left with the tiger cub, I asked if she wanted a puppy. "I'm not sure what the procedures are when the owner is in jail, but I can't take him on a flight home with me. And my cat would never tolerate him."

"Are you homeless?" she said to the dog in baby talk. "Wet's go home, sweetness."

When Tanner licked her face, I almost passed out from shock.

The next arrivals made it a full house. Nicholas entered the room in front of his brother and took a seat on the couch. "Where's Sykes?"

"Detective Sykes went home to his wife," Bowers said.

Edward made the rounds with polite greetings before taking one of the kitchen chairs.

"I should have known a woman was behind the killings," Nicholas said through his yawn.

"What was your first hint?" He didn't catch my sarcasm.

"Take that flower you found on the patio. There weren't any daisies on Harry's hat. Only sunflowers. No man would stand for pink daisies on his hat."

"It was a purple carnation."

He dismissed me with a wave. "Whatever. Sunflowers are pushing it, but daisies—or carnations—cross the line."

The males in the room looked thoughtful.

"That's it? That's the reason you decided the killer wasn't a man. You do realize we are at a convention where men dress as women. Why couldn't it have been one of them?"

"Sure, there are, but I didn't see any of them flaunting it in public places, like on the beach."

"But it took muscle to move the body." I longed to break his logic. "Wouldn't that point you toward a man?"

"Cynthia did it alone. All right. At first, I questioned that," he admitted. "But Edward reminded me that there are female firefighters who can drag a person from a burning building."

I grinned, triumphant. "You just ruined your own theory. Someone had to wrestle Cynthia—a woman strong enough to drag a dead body—into a pool and drown her. Wouldn't that take an even stronger person?"

"Why are you arguing against your own sex?" my husband murmured in my ear.

"I'm not. I'm just trying to prove Nicholas wrong."

His expression changed to one of deep understanding.

"Edna did that all by herself, so obviously it could be done by a woman. It's all about leverage. Besides. Two women fighting in a pool is a classic scenario."

The men in the room got dreamy expressions. All except Bowers, who was too smart to condone the sexy catfight fantasy. At least in front of me.

I remembered Edna's nickname and her admission she had done horrible things in the name of boredom. "Will you admit both women were big girls with unusual skill sets?"

"Yes. Definitely."

Edward sighed. "Nicholas, admit it. You thought the killer was a man."

"No, he didn't." I suddenly remembered the overheard conversation and quoted him. "You thought *I* was a lady killer, as in a woman who kills. Not the male Lothario kind. You thought I killed Cynthia. Tanner got loose and I tracked him down and pretended to look for the non-niece. And thank you, Edward, for comparing me to a jedi. That's pretty cool."

As I repeated the conversation, Nicholas' eyes grew until they threatened to pop out of his skull.

Edward laughed. "Who was your spy?"

"The chipmunk?" Nicholas mumbled. Then he shook his head. "Not possible. I don't believe it. Our voices carried on the ocean breezes and you overheard us."

I decided to give him a break. "Maybe."

Bowers squeezed my shoulders in approval.

Nicholas turned his attention to the federal agents. "Are you two really married?"

Willie clasped Rhonda's hand. "Twenty years strong."

I slipped a glance at Bowers. "What's it like working with your spouse?"

Rhonda leaned her head back to assess her husband. "Pretty good. We anticipate each other's thoughts and actions, which is helpful."

"And we always get our man," Willie added. "Or woman."

Rhonda ran her long fingernails up her husband's arm. He shuddered. "Are you up for the dance?"

He wrapped his arm around her shoulder. "Now, would I miss an opportunity to hold you close?"

She grinned. "You're bad."

"No, you're bad."

They skipped the Eskimo kiss and went back to their room to change.

Edward seemed reluctant to leave, but at Nicholas' urging, they, too finally left.

Bowers stretched. "It's our last night. Did you want to put on our costumes and go to the dance?"

"I think I've had enough dress up to last me a lifetime."

He studied the carpet. "Well, you might want to try on that white number one last time."

"Why, Detective Bowers. Are you flirting with me?"

He pulled me to him. "Yes, Mrs. Bowers, I am."

I pushed against his chest. "I forgot to ask if Jimmy were going to recover."

"I don't care." He lowered his head and kissed me. We never got around to the dress.

Chapter Forty-Three

Nicholas: Heading Home

Everyone had decided to check out at the same time. Funny, but the convention attendees looked like average people out of costume, most of them grandmas and grandpas.

The reception desk clerk had golden eyes, mocha skin, full lips, and short hair that hugged her head. Call me a sucker for beautiful women, but I skipped the bits about my near-death experience, being forced into a dress, and my sore toe, and told her I'd loved every minute at the hotel, thank you.

She glanced down at her screen. "We've added a charge for a cot. Is that correct?"

"Unfortunately, yes."

I picked up our bags and headed to the valet out front, where Edward waited.

"The vacation is over. As soon as we get home, we must answer fan mail. And I have some notes that need typing."

"Did you actually say vacation?"

"We stayed at a historic hotel, enjoyed the company of new friends—"

"You mean your new fans."

"That, too." He slipped me a sideways glance. "Do you feel better?"

"If you are referring to the fact that the hired killer who wanted me dead is behind bars, yes and no. Yes, because he's not free. No, because someone thought it worth money to kill me. And they may have other resources."

"Detective Sykes told us they'd rounded up the last of the miscreants."

"They have phones in prison."

"Nicholas, Nicholas, Nicholas. You worry too much."

There it was again. The desire to kick my brother's rear.

He stretched. "Didn't you mention Mrs. Abernathy baked in our absence? I miss her cooking."

Finally. Something we could agree on.

* * *

Frankie

Before we left the hotel, Dot dragged over her sister. Or was Barnaby supposed to be her brother now?

"Barnaby told me all about last night. How exciting. And how brave you all were."

"It was a surprise to find out your sister was a man."

Pink took his hand. "Don't be mad at Barnaby. It was my idea. He came to me that first night. I've never seen someone so scared."

"I went outside to get some fresh air." He grinned.

"And to relive Sugar Cane's race to the boat that final night. Not that there's a pier, but the ocean is there. I saw two people talking. Suddenly, one shoved something at the man. When he fell, I realized he'd been stabbed. I knew the person saw me."

"Why didn't you tell someone?"

"It wasn't like I could identify the killer. Not for certain. I could tell it was a woman, but all I really saw was a long, dark jacket. But they looked right at me. And I thought I saw a flash of pink. I just ran."

"And dropped your glass," Bowers said.

"Did I? I don't remember. I ran for my life. I thought the killer was on my heels. I shot up the stairs, intending to go to my room, but that didn't sound safe. Felicity was the only person I'd met, so when I saw her headed down the hallway . . . I was afraid she'd think I was crazy."

She giggled. "I had to help him. So, Barnaby became my sister."

"I knew whoever saw me would recognize my captain's uniform. And my glasses. That was the hard part. Knowing the killer might be around and recognize me without being able to spot him first. At least I thought it was a him until I saw the women with the pink spats in the lobby. I was certain that's what I saw from my position on the beach."

He smiled at Felicity with affection. "This lady saved my life."

"Will you come next year if this becomes an annual event?"

The two of them giggled at each other. "Absolutely," they said.

* * *

We returned the car rental, checked in our luggage, and headed for our terminal.

"I'm sorry our honeymoon didn't go as expected," Bowers said. His limp seemed better this morning, but it was still there.

"What did you expect?"

"It's what I thought you would expect. Dining out. Romantic strolls. A lot of alone time."

"It certainly wasn't that. I couldn't have imagined the reality in my nightmares."

He stopped walking. "Was it that bad?"

I placed my hand on his chest. "This was supposed to be a time for you to relax. A stress-free environment before you return to work after your injuries. Instead, you spent half your time working with other cops on a murder. You re-injured your leg with all the running around. You didn't get a break."

"Did all the aforementioned ruin the weekend for you?"

"For me?" Had it? "Well . . . no. We never got to see San Diego, but it will still be here if we come back. I'm more concerned about you. A honeymoon is supposed to set the tone for the rest of the marriage. It's almost a preview of what life together will be. I'm afraid we had a bad start."

I knew that look. His conflicted look. He wanted to tell me something, but he wasn't sure how I'd take it.

"Spit it out."

"Are you sure?"

"Duh. Of course, I'm sure."

He chewed on his lower lip to hold back the smile. It broke free into a full grin. He picked me up and swung me in a circle before setting me on my feet.

Caught up in his enthusiasm, I laughed. "What is it?"

"That was the best vacation ever."

"Oh, my gosh. Are you serious?"

"I'm not serious. I'm a man." He waited for my response. "You're supposed to say, '*Nobody's perfect.*' You know. The famous last line of the film?"

I sucked air through my teeth. "I have a confession. I've never seen the movie."

He gaped. "You've never seen *Some Like It Hot*?" He swung an arm around my shoulder. "This is a serious problem. One that we'll rectify as soon as we get home."

Home. Our home. It still hadn't sunk in that Bowers would walk through the door with me and stay.

We'd just experienced a crime-riddled weekend with mobsters, murders, and missing persons. And we came through it fine.

I looked at my husband, his smile as he took my hand in his, and decided this week was the perfect beginning to our life together.

A Note from the Author

This was such a fun book to write. *Some Like it Hot* is a favorite movie of mine. The exteriors were shot at The Hotel del Coronado. The interiors were not.

Sometimes I had to change details, such as the construction dates and some minor details on the layout to make it work, but I think I remained true to The Del.

I stayed there long ago, and the luggage *did* roll because of the warped floor.

Jacqueline Vick

Acknowledgments

Mary Burkhardt, Senior Account Supervisor for J Public Relations, was kind enough to answer some (odd) questions about The Hotel del Coronado that I couldn't find answers to myself. Any liberties taken with that information were mine.

Kerry Cathers, your editing skills are much appreciated, as is your sense of humor.

To the *real* Rhonda and Jeff Fisher, whom I have never seen rub noses like Eskimos or heard say, "You're so bad." Thanks for letting me play with you. I hope you like the end result.

The Mystery Buffs, my readers' group, are a supportive group who keep me on my toes. You can sign up here.

Kim Taylor Blakemore and Foster Vick are always kind enough to read the final version. I can't thank you enough for your generosity and feedback.

And, finally, thanks to Al and Bev. Without them, I wouldn't be here.

Some Like Murder Hot Book Club Questions

1. *Some Like It Hot* takes place during a time of rigid social rules, including how men should behave with women: i.e. standing when women entered the room, opening doors for women . . . As these manners have retreated into the past, do you find respect for women has diminished?

2. Frankie has high expectations for what makes a good wife. What do you think makes a good wife?

3. Nicholas sometimes feel inferior to Edward. Do you have a sibling or family member you feel you need to compete with?

4. Julian Fabrizio is a mobster. Frankie thinks he's a nice guy. Can someone be involved in criminal activities and still be a nice guy or gal? Or is Frankie naive?

5. Many zoos work to provide a good atmosphere for their animals. Some believe seeing these impressive beasts up close helps with conservation efforts. Do you agree that zoos have a purpose?

6. Frankie is insecure and impulsive. Bowers is steady and methodical. What makes their relationship work?

7. Edward is brainy and sure of himself. Nicholas is emotional and operates on instinct. And yet they make a good team. How do they do it?

8. Nicholas is in hiding because he did his civic duty. Do you think he should have kept quiet and stayed safe? Have you ever had to give something up to do the right thing?

9. Detective Jonah Sykes was willing to risk his life to protect Nicholas. Do you think you could do the same if the situation arose? Or would you weigh the pros and cons first?

10. Rhonda and Willie Fisher are described as "the happiest couple on earth". They are so enthusiastic that Frankie thinks they are faking it. Is there a person or job that make you feel that joy?

Also by Jacqueline Vick

The Frankie Chandler Mysteries

Barking Mad at Murder

A Bird's Eye View of Murder

An Almost Purrfect Murder

What the Cluck? It's Murder

A Scaly Tail of Murder

A Scape Goat for Murder

Some Like Murder Hot

Harlow Brothers Mysteries

Civility Rules

Bad Behavior

Deadly Decorum

About the Author

Jacqueline Vick writes the Frankie Chandler Pet Psychic mystery series about a woman who, after faking her psychic abilities for years, discovers animals *can* communicate with her. Her second series, the Harlow Brothers Mysteries, features a former college linebacker turned etiquette author and his secretary brother. Her books are known for satirical humor and engaging characters who are desperate to keep their secrets. Visit her at www.-jacquelinevick.com

Made in the USA
Las Vegas, NV
12 August 2025

26215481R00204